A Voice Beyond Reason

Matthew Félix

A Voice Beyond Reason
by Matthew Félix

Published by solificatio

2016 Trade Paperback Edition

matthewfelix.com

Cover: Erica Heitman-Ford

ISBN-10: 0-9977619-5-4
ISBN-13: 978-0-9977619-5-5

1

Standing in his bedroom window, overhead he saw an entirely unexpected layer of clouds. Pablo wondered if it was going to rain. The olive and almond trees he saw in front of him, extending down the many ridges of the mountainside toward the valley far below, were in desperate need of it. Likewise, the small yellowish grapevines that clung in other places to the sheer, rocky slopes were withered and appeared sickly, desperate for water after a year in which scarcely a drop had fallen. It seemed funny to him that the sea, visible in the distance, could offer no help. It was only thanks to the springs farther up the mountain and the little water left in the reservoirs in the valley that an all-out disaster had been averted. No one even wanted to think about what would happen if the winter and following spring proved just as dry.

Turning to look at the clock, he discovered that if he didn't move quickly he was going to be late. The store wasn't going anywhere, but they were expecting a big produce shipment, and his parents weren't going to be happy if he didn't show up on time. He was lucky they hadn't dragged him along with them when they had left home an hour before.

A quick shower and a shot of espresso later, he stepped

out into a fresh new day. The walk to the village's main plaza was about a ten-minute one, regardless of which combination of whitewashed alleys he took to get there.

A few houses down, he came upon Señora Muñoz. A rotund octogenarian dressed in all black, her dark garb was in stark contrast to the silver roots highlighting the immaculately executed part of her hair. Water trickled out the bases of her plants, which were spread the entire length of the exterior of her house, as was typical in the village. In some places, the neighbors even seemed to be engaged in friendly competition, hanging all sorts of colorful, fragrant flowers outside of their homes—geraniums being a particular favorite—and placing lush potted plants on the ground below. Her house was no exception, and the alley was all the more beautiful for it.

Pablo ascended an incline that opened onto a small square where a house was being remodeled, before he again veered up some wide steps. He then made a sharp turn up another flight, at the top of which—his heart beating a little faster for his effort—he found himself on comparatively flat ground, at the end of another alley.

Taking in the familiar scent of jasmine, he was greeted by one of his favorite village characters. At first the stocky little dog did his best to bark menacingly, as though he didn't recognize the intruder. Upon realizing who it was, however, he ran forward, elated as though he hadn't seen his friend in years, though in reality they saw each other at least once almost every day. He wagged his tail ecstatically, and his entire cinnamon-colored body shook with delight. Pablo took a moment, as he always did, to say hello to his friend. He patted him on the head and obligingly scratched his belly, unmistakably what the little pooch loved most.

It was only when he stood to be on his way that Pablo noticed Señor González. Given the reception he'd received from his dog, Pablo had failed to see Señor González himself, hidden in the shadows of his doorway like an overlooked or forgotten detail. They greeted each other, and Pablo paused to admire the old man's latest project, a basket he was making with dwarf palm leaves he had prepared himself.

Señor González inevitably sat in the same simple wooden chair and wore the same gray cardigan. His back hunched from being in the same position day after day, his eyes strained through bottle-glass thick lenses as he concentrated on the task at hand. His plump fingers still nimble, apparently undaunted by their advanced age, he made quick and steady progress.

Leaving his old friend to his work, Pablo continued up the alley. After passing through the archway—one of only three left from when the village had been under Moorish control centuries earlier—he came to the street leading out of town in one direction and into its main square in the other.

As he entered the square, Pablo scarcely noticed the town hall. Despite being ten minutes behind for as long as anyone could remember, the clock on its tall tower dominated the village center, its long porch covered with intricate and elegant Islamic-inspired tilework. Neither did he notice the old men sitting on the benches, as though the plaza itself were a theater in which some great drama was unfolding.

Houses hovered above the tower, clumps of them jutting out at random angles and in irregular layers dictated by the underlying shape of the mountain. As though taken directly from one of Picasso's cubist works, each whitewashed, terra-cotta-roofed structure demanded to be beheld from its own, independent perspective. Ultimately, though, they all combined to form not only the backdrop of the plaza, but the cohesive whole that was the village itself.

Still higher up, mountaintops could be seen. The vertical faces of their imposing steel-gray peaks enlivened with hues of rust and copper, their bases were adorned with light-green pines and a variety of darker Mediterranean bushes and grasses. It was there that the nature reserve in which Pablo was so fond of spending time was found.

Being from the village, Pablo paid it all little mind. Instead, breezing through the plaza like a gust off one of the peaks, he continued toward the church, turning onto a narrow cobblestone alley lined with shops. On the lane itself or a stone's throw away, there was a bakery, a green grocer, two butchers, and two small markets, including his family's. Offering not only food and beverages, but health care products and some basic kitchen- and hardware, it competed with modest success against the larger chain supermarkets down in town, where most villagers did the bulk of their shopping.

Pablo arrived to find fruits and vegetables streaming through the back door. Never one to stand back and watch, his father, Antonio, had rolled up his sleeves and jumped right in. Just a few kilos differentiating his medium-sized, athletic frame from his son's, he was covered in sweat. A smudge besmirched his otherwise classically handsome face, almost seeming to complement his dark hair and deep-brown eyes, all traits Pablo had been fortunate enough to inherit.

Something Antonio had just said had sent the deliverymen into a raucous fit of laughter.

"What's so funny?" Pablo asked.

"*Ay hijo*, trust me, you don't want to know," said his mother with a roll of the eyes and a knowing smirk. Her own sleeves rolled up, she held a clipboard in one hand and pushed a wisp of hair out of her face with the other. Though raising two children and running a store had led to more practical choices over time, to shorter hair, to clothing more focused on function than fashion, she, too, was attractive. She had bright eyes and fine features, her expression shifting effortlessly from all business to a good laugh, her body kept fit by constant activity. "Boys will be boys."

The day was a typical one, events at the store rarely deviating much, if at all, from long-established routines. Alma hobbled in for her weekly supply of cheese and chorizo. Fede needed more wine, despite having stocked up the day before. Pablo's mom's friend María didn't need anything at all, stopping by just to talk about the weather, spread some gossip, and express her profound indignance about the latest scandal to hit the headlines.

Pablo's friend Rafa stopped by, too, the dungarees and steel-toed boots he wore on the construction site doing nothing to detract from his swagger, the solid contours of his muscular torso visible from beneath his nearly threadbare T-shirt. Between his brazen joie de vivre and his seductive charm, his love life never knew a dull moment. After updating Pablo on his latest conquest, he told him about a car that was even more seductive than the girl. He then bought some snacks for the workday and turned to head out.

Before Rafa could go anywhere, Pablo's girlfriend Rosa came in with Pepa. Inseparable best friends, they both worked at the day care center down the street. Pablo had always thought they looked so much alike and had such similar mannerisms they could be mistaken for sisters, no doubt largely a result of their spending so much time together.

"*¿Qué tal chicos?*"

Rosa's dark hair was pulled back, accentuating her prominent cheek bones, bright, almond-shaped eyes, and long lashes. The lipstick she wore rendered her lips a little fuller, her smile a touch more alluring. Her shirt and shorts were just as flattering, as if tailored to the feminine curves of her otherwise petite frame.

"Do you guys want to go up to the rock circle after work?" she asked, cutting to the chase, since everyone either had something else to be doing or somewhere else to be. On warm nights like the one in store that evening, they often made the hike with drinks and snacks in tow. Tonight seemed like a perfect night for such an outing.

"I can't because we've got rehearsal for the festival," said Pablo. "Maybe tomorrow?"

The village festival was next weekend, and, just like previous years, Pablo and his father would be singing in it. They had already been practicing for several weeks with a few musicians, and they'd do so a couple of more times before the day of the performance rolled around.

"I can't tomorrow, because I've got a test the day after," said Pepa.

"Tomorrow's not good for me either—I've got a date," added Rafa with a grin.

"You guys just go up without me," Pablo insisted. "It's no big deal. I'll head up next time."

"Can't you come up after practice?" Rosa suggested. "I feel bad leaving you behind."

"Maybe—it depends how late we go. You guys head up. If I can make it, I will."

2

Although things slowed down after the siesta, late afternoon still brought with it a predictable succession of familiar faces.

With one notable exception.

The man came in while Matilde and Josefina were still there. Both old ladies chatty as usual, lingering at the counter with their purchases, initially Pablo was distracted and paid the stranger little mind. But then it hit him. With the man's arrival, the entire atmosphere in the store had changed. Although he did nothing to call attention to himself, perusing the aisles like any other customer, Pablo couldn't take his eyes off him. This wasn't just another Brit or German from the coast. Although Pablo struggled to say exactly how or why, there was no doubt: the old man was different.

Of average height with curly white locks, a well-kempt matching beard, and almost unnaturally clear blue eyes that were all the more striking set against his olive complexion, he could have been from just about anywhere. And while the color of his hair suggested a certain age, as did deep yet charismatic crow's-feet, his movement was deliberate and fluid, his gaze youthfully alert. Though Pablo kept a close and curious watch on him, it was only when the man approached the counter that their eyes finally met.

"*Buenas.*"

"*Buenas,*" said the old man, with a smile. "If I were to place a large order, would it be possible for you to deliver it?"

Pablo thought he detected an accent.

"I'm not sure. I mean, yeah, probably. *¿Padre?*"

"Of course," Antonio replied. "We can have Ernesto deliver it, as long as it's large enough."

"That won't be an issue," the stranger assured them with a laugh, taking out a long list and laying it on the counter. "My cupboards are completely empty!"

"I guess so!" Pablo's father acknowledged, glancing at the list. "Your name and address?"

"On the bottom."

"Oh. Right."

Although probably imperceptible to the old man, Pablo didn't fail to notice his father's split-second hesitation. Something on the paper had caught him off guard.

"Wonderful. In that case, I'll just take these for now."

"Sure," said Pablo, as he started by ringing up a bottle of shampoo.

"*Fíjate,*" said Antonio, once the old man had paid for his things and left.

"What?"

"Carmen, you're not going to believe this," his father called to the back room.

"What'd you say?" Pablo's mother replied, appearing in the doorway, clipboard still in hand. The concentration that had furrowed her brow gave way to a look of curiosity.

"I said you're not going to believe who was just in here."

"Who?"

Pablo was even more curious than his mother.

Antonio showed her the bottom of the list.

"*No me digas.* You've got to be kidding me. After all this time! Victor Sarquino? I wish I'd seen him. What do you think he's doing here?"

"No idea, but looks like he's staying a while."

"*Qué extraño.* No one from that family has set foot in this village for what, twenty-five years? Since we were kids?"

"At least."

"I hope he's not up to something."

"Like what?" Pablo still had no idea what his parents were talking about.

"That man's family owns half the mountain," his father replied.

"What do you mean? I've never even heard of the Sarquinos."

"That's because they left a long time ago," his mother explained. "But they've had roots here longer than just about any of us."

"You actually believe those stories?" Antonio challenged.

"*¡Claro!* Why wouldn't I? They're true! My father actually knew Victor when they were kids—not for very long, before the family moved away. Back then everyone knew that the Sarquinos were the oldest family in the village, here before the Moors left and the whole town was repopulated with Christians. It was common knowledge. It's really not that farfetched to think that a few well-off families were able to stay. Even way back then, money talked—and conversion could get you even further!"

"And they own half the mountain?" Pablo asked, fixated on that revelatory detail.

"They left when your grandpa was a boy," explained his mother, "but they didn't give up their lands."

"At least you're right about that," agreed Antonio. "My cousin grazes his flock on one of their parcels. If any of the Sarquinos know, they don't seem to care. I don't think he's ever paid anyone a *céntimo*."

"Maybe not, but I do think María's family pays them something for the plots where they've got some olive trees. I just really hope he's not here to stir things up."

"Oh, Carmen, relax. He's probably here for the same reasons as anyone else. That family doesn't need the money."

"They didn't need the money before, but who knows now? It's not every day that a Sarquino shows up."

"Just on holiday," Antonio insisted, giving her a reassuring squeeze on the shoulder as he returned to the back room. "No one's going to lose their orchards."

3

When the old man's order was ready the next day, Pablo insisted he be the one to deliver it. It was a large one, but everything would easily fit into their van. Besides, they weren't that busy, and it wasn't that far. There was no need to call Ernesto.

What wasn't so easy was finding the old man's house. Pablo couldn't place it, and it didn't have a number marker. So, after speeding through the traffic circle on the edge of the village, he paid close attention for landmarks that met his father's description. A neighbor's house. A distinctive curve in the road. A huge olive tree with a hollow trunk.

After passing by a space in the guardrail that opened onto nothing but bright-blue sky, Pablo made a U-turn. As he approached the gap carefully, he saw that it did in fact conceal a steep gravel driveway descending through tiers of olive trees. That had to be it.

Making his way down the winding gravel road, he was as curious as anxious. What would the old man's house be like? What would the old man himself be like? Who was this stranger who had made such an impression on his parents and, even before that, on him?

As Pablo came to the end of the driveway, he was surprised

by what he found. Rather than some grandiose old manor that had been lost in time, an elaborate, sprawling ruin bearing testimony to countless stories of generations gone by, he discovered a simple home with a traditional whitewash exterior and terra-cotta shingle roof. A wooden door and two windows made up its simple façade, and on a stone porch in front was a set of table and chairs, partially shaded by a vine-covered trellis. Several potted plants were scattered about, and a large, bright-red bougainvillea draped over the entrance.

The house was located on a large plot abutting a small but very steep scrub-covered valley. On the other side, a huge mountain flank rose up into the sky, covered in patches with the yellowish-green leaves of the local grape variety. A small vegetable garden had been planted within sight of the porch, and carob, fig, and a couple of pomegranate trees dotted the property, in addition to the terraces of olive trees Pablo had seen on the way down the driveway.

What most struck Pablo about the place was that it was so private. Apart from a couple of distant houses atop the neighboring flank, it wasn't possible to see another dwelling. Other than far-off sounds rising up from the valley, as well as an occasional disturbance from the road—against which the olive trees served as effective buffer—the place felt like a self-contained haven from the outside world.

Turning his attention back to the house, Pablo saw that the windows were open, but the door was closed. Other than a few birds twittering in the bushes and a breeze stirring the needles of some nearby pines, there wasn't a sound.

Pablo called out. Nothing.

He knocked on the door. Silence.

Wasn't the man expecting the delivery? What was Pablo supposed to do with it? Should he wait? He had to get back to the store. Could he just leave it there? Some of the items were frozen. They couldn't stay out for long.

Maybe the man was napping. Or in the bathroom.

Pablo knocked again.

Nothing.

He would wait a few minutes. If the man didn't show up, Pablo would either leave the delivery on the porch or take it back to the store and try again later.

If the tabletop were any indication, the old man hadn't been gone long. There was a book whose title suggested it was related to Arab philosophy, several pages of which were dog-eared. Onto the smooth black cover of what appeared to be a journal, a fountain pen clung like a remora to a shark, perfectly at home there. A copy of *El País* eclipsed a recent edition of the *International Herald Tribune*, apparently folded to wherever the old man had left off prior to vanishing.

As sheep bells clanged in the distance, Pablo looked up to the clear blue sky. He could be waiting all day. Besides, if the old man wasn't home, it wasn't his fault. All the same, Pablo would feel bad if the frozen items thawed. And if they did, the man was sure to complain, and the store would have to replace them.

Still debating how long to wait, Pablo stumbled upon a possible solution.

A short distance from the patio was an old stone well, complete with rope, pulley, and bucket. What if?

Pablo walked over and pushed off the wooden lid. Cool air gusted up from the darkness.

Loading the bucket with frozen meat, chicken, and spinach, he lowered it to just above the water level. He then replaced the lid, and put the rest of the order conspicuously on top of it.

Problem solved and mission accomplished, he headed back to the store.

4

One of a few the village had each year, the three-day festival was in honor of the town's Virgin Mary. Like a prison inmate granted temporary leave from her cell, the statue would be paraded around town for her annual tour only to eventually end up right back where she started. It was little wonder that, on more than one occasion, a zealous member of the faithful had professed to see a tear or two falling from the wooden lady's eyes.

In preparation, the village had been decked out in its finest. Strands of lights in elegant patterns transformed the whitewashed walkways into a multicolored fantasy world where the celebrations would continue well into each night. Food and beverage booths had been set up on the main square, and a large stage on which entertainers would be performing all weekend had been erected in front of the town hall. The clock tower, whose command of the plaza was ordinarily undisputed, was almost dwarfed by the impressive setup. The soccer field had been transformed into a miniature arena in which exhibitions of Andalusian equestrianism would be featured, and a parking lot had been converted into a small-scale amusement park.

Every night for a month before the event, a large cannon

had been fired off, a ritual whose purpose historically had been to remind people in the countryside that the festival was fast approaching and they needed to start making preparations for the journey into town. Nowadays, the cannon was mostly symbolic, carrying on a tradition that in practical terms could have been more easily addressed by modern forms of communication.

Tradition being tradition—and no one interested in calling it into question—it was as if the sound of the cannon reverberated not only into the provincial countryside, but throughout Andalucía and even the rest of Spain. In the days leading up to the festival, friends and family from afar heeded its explosive call and made their ways home.

"Do you guys want another one?" asked Juan.

"After the performance," Pablo replied.

"I thought you were supposed to drink lots of fluids."

"Yeah, Pablo," prodded Rafa, "got to keep the cords lubed up!"

"Not with those kind of fluids," Rosa laughed. "You guys are going to get him drunk before he even goes onstage!"

"But maybe Juan's right—Pablo might sing even better drunk," joked Pepa.

The second day of festivities well under way, Pablo had already crossed paths with many of his own friends and family in town for the occasion, including his cousin Juan. A rugged free spirit, over a year prior Juan had left the village behind to see the world. First he'd taken Andalucía by storm—a string of jobs, a string of girls. Then he'd made his way to Madrid, where it had been more of the same. Recently he'd made yet another move.

"So how's Barcelona?" Pablo asked, when Juan returned carrying four cups of beer. His thick forearms and large hands almost made it look easy.

"Let me help you with one of those," Rafa volunteered.

"Awesome. Working in the shipping warehouse is brutal, but it keeps me in shape and the pay is good—and, besides, it's worth it to live in the city. There is so much going on.

Seriously, it's hard to keep up. And the women—don't even get me started about the women! *¡Coyons, tío!* It's too much! The clubs are great. The beaches are great. All the concerts come to town. I'm never coming back!"

"I guess we're lucky you made it down for the festival," Rosa quipped, as she carefully pried another one of the beers from Juan's grasp.

"Yeah, but I have to work Monday, so we won't be here long, right Pablo?"

"We?"

"Well, yeah," Juan insisted with feigned disbelief. "You're still coming back with me, right? You promised."

"Oh. Yeah, well . . ." Pablo hesitated, catching on and playing along. "I'm not sure she'd be up for it."

"What? Moving to Barcelona?" Rosa scoffed, lowering her cup before it even made it to her lips. "*¡No te lo creas!* I'm fine right here. What's wrong with our beaches and clubs, anyway?"

"So, is that a no?" Juan taunted, shooting Pablo a wry smile.

"Sometimes Rosa's really hard to read," Rafa interjected, before she jabbed him in the ribs.

"It's just that she has a plan," Pablo explained.

"Wait, don't tell me—you get married, you buy a house, and you have five kids?" chided Juan. "Oh yeah, and you take over the store, of course."

"You mean she told you, too? I guess the secret's out," said Pablo, as if conceding defeat.

"Five? No, I'd say three's more like it," Rosa retorted, unapologetic.

"What the hell!" Juan protested, unable to believe his ears. "You guys are barely even out of high school, and you've already got your whole lives planned out! Come on! Live a little! There's time for all that other crap later!"

"Yeah, well, speaking of time, you've got to get going, don't you?" Rosa said, turning to Pablo.

"You're right. I should get going," he agreed, looking up at the clock tower. "I don't want my dad to be wondering where I am."

"*¡Suerte!*" Juan called out, raising his cup. The others followed suit, Rosa adding a peck on the lips for good measure.

The sun beat down hard overhead. Fortunately, a slight breeze offered some relief to the performers. After all, the celebrations certainly would have been marred if, one by one, the musicians, singers, and dancers started dropping like flies midway through their performances. It had happened before. Just a couple of years earlier, in fact. No one wanted a repeat of that disaster, especially since the village's reputation had yet to fully recover.

Thankfully, none of the members of the dance troupe before him showed any signs of light-headedness, nor abruptly collapsed as they went through their perfectly synchronized, dizzying routine. Once they struck their final poses and took their collective bow, Pablo's turn at the mic came at last.

"Break a leg!" said his father, with a reassuring squeeze on his shoulders. He'd be joining later in the set. For now, it was all Pablo.

A flurry of butterflies battered Pablo's belly as he climbed the stairs, cracking through their chrysalises as he took to the stage. He knew from past experience the only way for them to take flight would be through the microphone.

The plywood floor gave slightly as he took each step, giving him the sensation of bouncing toward center stage. In reality, he approached it calmly and deliberately, feeling the weight of a thousand expectant sets of eyes as he did. When he got to the mic, like a buoy in rough seas, he grabbed hold of it with a firm grip. Letting out a heavy sigh, he looked up at the sun, shining on him like a giant spotlight in the sky.

Coming back down to earth, he looked around the plaza. It was dramatically different from his privileged perspective over it. As he skimmed the countless faces looking up at him, it felt as intimidating as empowering to be the focus of so much attention, to be both unspoken question and imminent answer.

Even more intimidating was an unexpected exchange with a single pair of eyes. Piercing. Foreign but familiar. It took him a second, but then he remembered. The stranger from the store, the old man who had stood him up when he made the delivery. There he was again, standing out in the audience just as he had at the store, the same faint, enigmatic smile on his lips. For a moment, Pablo was so mesmerized by the intensity of their interaction, he almost forgot what he was there to do. But then he snapped out of it.

Nodding to the musicians, he followed the course laid out by the unmistakable strum of flamenco guitar, as rhythmic as melodic, as unabashedly bold as delicately nuanced. He then channeled his nervous energy into a series of impassioned notes that came from someplace deep, deep inside himself.

Beverages came to a halt in midair. Food was set back down onto plates. Conversations were put on indefinite hold. All eyes were locked on the stage, on the young man belting out a heart-wrenching introduction to a song that promised to be infinitely more worthy of their attention than whatever it was they had been doing a moment before.

A promise on which Pablo delivered.

He didn't merely sing the song. As though channeling its anonymous protagonist, he gave the composition its voice. He lived and breathed its narrative, conveying its anguish and passion with the same finesse he hit each note and enunciated every phrase.

The sorrow and longing expressed in the melancholic melody became Pablo's sorrow and longing. It didn't matter that his youth prevented him from having the life experience to relate firsthand to what was recounted in the song. Then and there, it was as if he had personally lived every line—if not in this life, perhaps in a distant past one. Losing himself in each of them, he poured his heart and soul into the tragic story they so dramatically told.

His voice soared over the plaza at times, inviting the audience to take to the sky with it, a powerful raptor with wings widespread. At others, it timidly recoiled. As if self-conscious of the vulnerability to which the preceding moments of brazen defiance and brutal honesty had left it exposed, it almost seemed to ask for understanding, respect, and even forgiveness.

Except there was nothing to forgive. Instead, as Pablo's first number drew to a close, and he slowly came to—one minute in another time and place living the life of some troubled, love-sick soul, the next back in his own body in his own village—what the crowd did was applaud and cheer. And riotously demand more.

So it went for the rest of the songs, not least the duet with his father.

Singing with his dad was how Pablo had gotten his start. It had been on that very stage, no less, when he was just a little boy. Doing so now was one of the most natural things in the world. And the most fun. While the performer in him loved having the spotlight to himself, it was a joy and a thrill to share it with someone with whom he had such an effortless synergy—never mind someone to whom he was indebted for even being onstage at all.

In a way, it was also a relief. Like life itself, having someone to share it with made the performance that much easier, that much more fun. He and his father relied on each other. They challenged and played off each other. And the audience ate up every last note.

Before he knew it, Pablo found himself amidst the final words of his final number. Having made the most of his moment front and center, he gestured his thanks to the exuberant crowd and reluctantly made his way offstage. As he did, he discovered a cheering throng waiting for him at the foot of the stairs. Family, friends, and even some unfamiliar faces had gathered to congratulate him on a job well done.

"You were amazing!" chimed Rosa and Pepa in unison, showering him with hugs and kisses.

"Wonderful!" said a man who looked vaguely familiar but Pablo didn't have time to place.

"You've got such an incredible talent!" added an old

woman.

It was the last comment that meant the most, coming as it did from his father, who couldn't have been more proud.

"You sure are a tough act to follow, aren't you?"

5

Pablo's time to shine having coming and gone, the rest of the day and all the next he enjoyed the festival like any other attendee. He caught up with friends and family. He accompanied the *Virgen* on her pilgrimage, and he threw himself into the celebrations that followed. He played games, went to one of the equestrian exhibitions, and watched some of the other performances.

A lot of his time was spent with his friend Jorge. Smart to the point of bordering on socially awkward, Jorge was the one girls would go to when they needed help with their homework—not when they were looking for a date. Though he held his own on the soccer field, his small, thin frame lacked the athleticism and prowess of someone like Rafa. And, though he wasn't entirely unattractive, his glasses always seemed to make his eyes look bigger than they were, out of proportion with his narrow nose and thin lips.

None the more confident for his lack of experience, Jorge had never had much luck with girls. Consequently, for the past year and a half his primary focus had been his agronomy studies at the university in Málaga, where he commuted a few times a week.

When it happened, Pablo had nearly convinced Jorge to

approach a girl in the bar where they'd been having a drink. At the same time, Pablo's father was on the other side of the village, having some beers with his own friends.

All it took was a whiff. As soon as he smelled it, Antonio knew exactly where the smoke was coming from. It roused him like the acrid stench of his own burning flesh.

Throwing his beer to the ground, he left his friends behind, baffled. There was no time to explain. He didn't have a moment to lose.

He was the first to get there. Sunday night on a festival weekend, the alley was empty.

Empty, but aglow.

It had started as it always does, a spark giving way to a flame. One flame had given way to several, then burst into countless, in no time erupting into a raging conflagration.

As Antonio's friends appeared at one end of the alley, more people arrived at the other. Before anyone could stop him, Antonio dove into the store, one arm raised, his mouth covered with his shirt.

News of the fire spread almost as quickly as the fire itself, soon reaching the bar where Pablo was hanging out with Jorge. As the alarm sounded, mayhem ensued. A stampede set off for the store.

Once there, Pablo fought his way through the crowd. Some firemen who had already arrived prevented people from getting too close. Pablo saw his mom being comforted by his sister, who had come up for the festival.

"What's happening?" he cried out to them.

Speechless, all Carmen could do was motion to the store, to the flames coming out the windows, the blaze now shooting through a hole in the roof.

His sister, though also at a loss for words, mustered the only two Pablo needed to hear.

"He's inside."

"Inside? Who?"

"*Papá. He's inside.*"

His father was inside? At first Pablo wasn't sure he had

heard right.

But then reality hit.

"Why? Why did he go inside!"

Neither his mother nor his sister said a word.

Now completely beside himself, Pablo panicked. Despite the bright spectacle, a dark, ugly shadow overtook him, a profound sense of foreboding.

How long had his dad been inside the store? What was he doing there? What was he hoping to salvage? There was no safe. All the important documents were in the office at home. So was most of the stash of cash that never made it onto the books. Why would he take such an outlandish risk? What could possibly be so important?

Pablo longed to rush inside and drag his dad out. Instead all he could do was watch, mesmerized despite the horror, just another impotent spectator. Searing flames danced against an indifferent, opaque sky. Wood crackled like bones breaking, like a *falla* splintering into a thousand pieces during the *cremà*, the pyrotechnic climax to Valencia's festival of fire. The heat was stifling and the smoke suffocating, dust, ash, and debris sent airborne like demons enraged.

Where was his father? When was he coming back out?

It would have been impossible for Pablo to say how much time passed. But when Antonio did finally come out, it stopped altogether.

Pablo no longer saw the firefighters battling to contain the blaze. He no longer heard the voyeuristic onlookers shocked and enthralled by the flaming spectacle. The only thing that registered when they brought out his father's body was his mother's agonizing cry. His own body very nearly collapsed.

Either to make things easier for the family or because he genuinely believed it, Gonzalo—one of the firefighters, whom the family had known forever—insisted Antonio died instantly. The beam that had supported the roof for centuries fell back to Earth, and his life was over. It was that simple.

Except it made absolutely no sense.

Except it couldn't possibly be happening.

Stunned by the surreal horror, Pablo was utterly incapacitated. His mind, body, and spirit went numb, and he detached. From the scene. From everything and everyone in it. From friends, family, and strangers, their hysterical questions, concerns, and unsolicited advice. Like the store itself, a part of him going up in smoke.

6

Every time he went up to the soccer field, Pablo diverted his gaze away from the cemetery. He hated the notion that loved ones could be shelved like discarded possessions, their remains stashed into walls of cubby holes that always reminded him of pigeon roosts or swallow houses. He hated the weathered old photos of dead people smiling from the grave, there to reassure the living they had passed over to a better place. He hated the plastic flowers that, unlike the deceased they were tactlessly intended to honor, would never, ever die. And now that his father was being put into eternal storage there, he hated the cemetery and its ridiculous filing cabinets for the dead even more.

How could his father's body actually be in that jar? How did they dare do that to him? As if dying in the fire weren't enough, they had reduced him to ash? It was like seeing an unfinished crime all the way through to its heinous end.

The fact the funeral was taking place on a blue-sky day—a day that in its very essence was a celebration of life, one made for exaltation not lamentation—made the entire experience that much worse. That much less real. His father had existed, now he didn't. From one day to the next his body wiped clean from the face of the Earth, his ashes swept into a fancy jar about to be locked away forever.

His eyes trained by a lifetime on the trails in the nature reserve, every time a falcon soared across the sky, a songbird landed on a nearby tree limb, Pablo couldn't help but look. Before he could stop himself, reflexively, he had already identified them. So now he was bird-watching at his father's funeral.

What were they doing there? Why couldn't he shut them out, just like he had everything else? How could life continue joyful and uninterrupted all around him—the chirping birds, the fluttering butterflies, the colorful flowers ecstatically turned upward to the sun—oblivious to the devastating death being mourned in its midst? Unjust, unfathomable, irrevocable death.

A huge turnout of well-wishers had come to see his father off, all dressed in their Sunday best. It was an event. Everyone in town knew Antonio, after all. And anyone who knew him was bound to love him. His broad smile. His hearty laugh. The way he always made a point of looking you in the eyes.

The priest mechanically recited his dispassionate prayers, as though he'd said them one too many times. Pablo's mother and sister sobbed uncontrollably, each making futile attempts to console the other. His niece and nephew looked up at them with wide-eyed, helpless concern.

Pablo dreaded the condolences that would follow, his anxiety mounting with each word that brought the priest nearer to the end. Under ordinary circumstances, it would have been bad enough. This was infinitely worse.

Yet again his thoughts returned to the night of the fire, to the moment he first knew. His mother sobbing in his arms, he had wanted to say something.

When he went to, nothing.

Startled, he reassured himself. He was simply at a loss for words.

Except he had plenty of words to say.

Didn't he?

His mother turned and asked him a question—he couldn't remember now what it was. What he couldn't forget was what happened next.

Nothing.

His father. The store. Now his voice.

He couldn't believe any of it was happening.

7

It was impossible to say how long the store would be closed. Besides the damage, which was considerable, there were dealings with the insurance company, which were maddening.

Carmen quickly learned there were as many answers to any given question as there were people who picked up the phone. It was a bureaucratic quagmire, starting with the process for filing the claim. Assuming she could figure that out—which she would—there would be the logistics associated with making the repairs. Contractors. Estimates. Materials. Then there would be the project itself, bound to go over budget and over time, no matter how closely she managed it.

"I can't be here right now," she announced one morning at breakfast, the rich aroma of her coffee filling the air before Pablo even made it downstairs. "It's not good for either of us. The village is too small, too full of reminders. For now there's nothing we can do here anyway, so I think we should go stay with María in Málaga. We should all be together right now."

Pablo hadn't seen that coming.

Sitting across from his mother, sipping his own coffee but not bothering with breakfast, he held her gaze. Having just rolled out of bed, his hair was a mess. Dark bags hung from his eyes.

He wasn't going anywhere.

"*Hijo*," Carmen began again, steadying her voice, "I cannot be here right now. The village is too small. The smell of the cinders wafts over the roofs into the plaza, and all I can see is fire. All I can see is . . . I need to be with my family—all my family. My son, my daughter, my grandchildren. Pablo, I'm suffocating. I need some time away from here."

Pablo understood.

But he had different needs.

"You still won't say anything?" she beseeched, her hopes again slipping away like they already had so many times.

Pablo looked down at his coffee, frustrated.

She acted like it was a choice.

"I'm leaving tomorrow," she pronounced, regaining her composure. Getting up to wash her mug, she added, "I hope you'll come, too. So we can all be together."

8

Pablo didn't move.

He heard his mother in the kitchen. He heard her come back upstairs. A quick shower. Bags zipping. Thumping as they plodded down the stairs. He could have helped her. Ordinarily he would have helped her. But now he didn't move.

On the phone with his sister. Silence. The garage door going up. Muffled car chimes, doors opened while she loaded her things.

A vague pause during which he couldn't make out what was happening. Longer than he could explain. The garage door coming down, violently, a meteor crashing into the earth, shaking the entire house.

Silence.

She didn't have the strength to fight. She didn't have the heart to force him to do something he didn't want to do. Málaga wasn't that far, and the village was full of eyes who would keep watch over him for her.

He could stay.

9

Pablo hadn't moved. At least not much.

He hadn't showered. He had hardly eaten. He was still wearing the same clothes as when his mother left. Nightclothes.

For three days he had drifted in and out of slumber, in and out of dreams and nightmares and places in-between. The worst nightmare seizing him when he woke up, dark, ugly, violent, over and over he had chosen sleep.

Late on the third night, his bedroom was pitch black. The air was heavy and stale and sour from cycling endlessly in and out of his dormant body, nowhere else to go. A window never cracked, the door never left open, even though he was alone.

As Pablo floated in that liminal state somewhere between sleep and wakefulness, he was jarred to consciousness.

Someone was there. At the foot of the bed.

Despite the initial jolt, he kept calm.

Someone was there to see him. That was all. There was nothing to fear.

Propping himself up on one arm, he turned to look.

His father smiled, without saying a word.

"*Papá.*"

As tears welled up in his eyes, Pablo found himself awash in an all-pervasive, unconditional love. A love that emanated from the inside out, one he felt from head to toe, resonating in each and every cell. A love unlike anything he had ever experienced.

It was OK. Everything was OK.

His father lingered another moment, his peaceful, reassuring smile never wavering.

And then it was over.

Still propped up as though looking his father in the eyes, for the first time since losing him, Pablo broke down.

He convulsed with uncontrollable sobs, sobs hurled from someplace foreign to him, deep emotional recesses into whose depths he'd never had cause to venture.

Sobs of grief. Sobs of relief. Sobs of wonder and gratitude.

Like a battering ram on a castle gate, they burst his heart wide open.

10

It wasn't until he put it out of commission that the phone finally stopped ringing. Before it had, countless messages. Messages he had no intention of listening to, never mind returning. He didn't even bother to check who called. People who meant well, but didn't get it.

He just wanted to be left alone.

The outside world kept at bay, inside it was all music. A beer in hand, vinyl by vinyl he worked his way through his father's extensive collection, losing himself in song. Melodies, lyrics, and memories. Songs his father had sung to himself. Songs he had introduced to Pablo. Songs they had performed together. The great musicians for whom his father had instilled in Pablo his own starry-eyed appreciation: pioneers of flamenco, legends of Spanish guitar, even renowned American soul and blues artists. Antonio had always been adamant their roots were all the same.

Music filled the house, but like a bird blind to the dawn Pablo didn't sing a note. He didn't so much as hum. Whereas ordinarily he couldn't be stopped, for the first time in his life he wasn't even tempted. Abandoning his place center stage for a seat at the back of the theater, rather than throwing himself into each song, giving voice to the stories they told and the emotions they conveyed—joy, anguish, and hope, love unrequited, boundless, or impossible—all he could do was listen.

He still didn't understand it any better than anyone else. It frustrated no one more than it did him. It frightened him, too. What if it never came back? Everyone seemed to assume it would, but what if it didn't? Never mind talking, what if he could never sing again? It had always been such an integral part of who he was. He didn't even want to think about life without song, as if losing not only his father but the store as well hadn't been more than enough.

The store. Initially its demise had been upstaged by the loss of his father; but, a painful void had soon overtaken the special place it had always held in Pablo's heart. The store itself was a special place, after all. One his parents had built from the ground up. One that had become a village institution. One that was not only the sole source of the family's livelihood, but like a second home to them all, as well as many of their friends and so much of the community.

If the village was his world, the store was the heart of it. It was his anchor, the one constant he'd never thought to question. He was always there. Or headed there. Or coming back from there. Yet from one day to the next it was gone. Another loss. Another death, albeit one they hoped to resurrect from the ashes. Seeing it in shambles was hard. So hard, in fact, that he hadn't seen it. Not since that night.

Strategically inserted into the gap between one song's ending and another's beginning, Pablo thought he heard a knock at the door.

He turned down the music.

There it was again.

Just like phone calls, there had been a lot of knocks at the door. Sometimes they were tentative, as though they knew they were intruding. Sometimes they were demanding, already resenting what was sure to be rejection. This one, though, felt different. This one, he could tell, he needed to answer.

He opened the door. Making contact with the outside

world for the first time all day, he was struck by the feel of cool, fresh air on his face. The sun faded into evening, and swallows circled overhead. A car door slammed in the alley. Those impressions, however noteworthy in the moment, were fleeting. Instead, Pablo's attention was drawn to the enticing smells of tomato, onion, and garlic, his stomach brought to its knees.

Rosa looked up at him like someone unsure a bet is going to pay off. Her hair was down, falling below the shoulders, and she wore a simple, form-fitting shirt and jeans. She held a paper bag.

"I thought you might need some of this," she said, handing it to him. "My mom made it."

Pablo said nothing, fixated on the bag like a castaway presented with real food for the first time in months.

"Can I come in?" Rosa asked, when Pablo showed no signs of extending an invitation.

He looked up. He didn't want to see anyone, not even his girlfriend. But she was there. And she had brought him food. It was a kind and thoughtful gesture, and he certainly wasn't going to turn her away.

"It's OK. We don't have to talk. I just wanted to see you. I just wanted to make sure you were doing all right. Everyone's worried."

Turning from the door, he took the food to the kitchen. Rosa showed herself inside, as she had done countless times before.

Walking into the living room, she was met by a slow *cante hondo*, a brokenhearted lover impotently protesting the agonizing injustice that had rendered his secret love impossible. Album covers were scattered on the floor as though the phonograph had spit them out, sleeves and records in random, commingling piles that would have left Pablo's father heartbroken as well. Several empty bottles of beer. A few miscellaneous wrappers and some tissues on the floor. A blanket in a pile on the couch.

Rosa breathed a sigh of relief. It could have been much

worse.

Pablo came back from the kitchen, steaming plate in hand. Lingering in the doorway, he seemed reluctant to step into the room.

He looked at his plate, then at Rosa, inquisitively.

"No, thanks. I'm not hungry yet," she answered.

He didn't know what to make of her visit. Of course he had expected it. And if he wanted to see anyone, it would be her. But now that she was there, he wasn't sure how he felt. Glad to see her on one hand, suspicious on the other. She hadn't come alone, after all. Not only her mom but his own, too, was checking up on him.

"I saw Jorge today," Rosa offered. "He didn't say anything, but I think his parents are buying the *finca* next to theirs. It's been abandoned since old Señor Díaz died, and my mom said they've been talking with the sons and daughter for a while about buying it. None of them ever comes back anymore, and they'd rather it stay in the hands of locals, as long as they can get a fair price."

Pablo showed no reaction. He appreciated what Rosa was doing. But he just didn't care about goings-on in the village. It all seemed so remote, inconsequential.

"Anyway, Jorge says hi."

Pablo felt a pang of guilt. He hadn't seen Jorge since the funeral. Usually they saw each other several times a week, if not every day.

He sat down on the couch with Rosa, careful not to spill anything.

"Pepa says hi, too. She's thinking about quitting the day care center so she can focus on her studies. I keep begging her not to—she doesn't work that many hours to begin with, and we really need the help."

Pablo looked at Rosa, then back down at his food. None of what she was saying mattered. It just didn't. He couldn't pretend that it did, not after what had happened. He couldn't get over how quickly people could move on, how quickly they seemed to expect him to.

Rosa could sense Pablo wasn't engaging. She knew him well enough to know his detachment went beyond his inability to speak.

An awkward pause followed. She moved closer, taking his half-empty plate and setting it onto the coffee table. She then took his hands into hers and looked him deep in the eyes.

"Pablo, how long are you going to keep quiet? You seem so far away. We miss you."

She acted as though it were a choice. Just like his mom. Everyone did. It was frustrating and it was humiliating, his voice another horrible, inexplicable victim of the tragedy. It was not, however, a choice. Why couldn't they understand?

Measuring her words carefully, as though acknowledging a difficult truth, Rosa added, "I can't be there for you if you won't let me."

Pablo's gut began to burn. He hadn't asked her to be there for him. He hadn't asked anything of anyone, other than to be left alone. This was why. He didn't want to do this.

She had come to him. He hadn't asked her to come. Yet now she was acting as though she were doing him a favor, as though making thinly veiled demands more about her needs than his own were a selfless gesture for which he should be grateful. What he needed was time and space, understanding and patience. He did not need pressure.

Diverting his gaze, he slipped his hands from hers, his silence that much more pronounced.

She meant well. But she had gone too far.

She got it.

"I'm sorry, Pablo," she said, getting up to leave. "I'm really sorry."

11

After yet another day indoors, Pablo had to get out of the house. As though he'd spent weeks trapped under the snow, cabin fever had finally set in. What had been a refuge was now a prison. He had to move. He needed fresh air and sunshine, even if that just meant the final few hours left of it.

So he headed for the reserve.

Unfortunately, heading for the reserve meant walking through the village. It meant seeing people. Watchful, curious, prying people. The very people he was trying to avoid by staying locked up in the house.

His mother was right: sometimes the village was so small.

On the other hand, he knew it so well that he knew which routes were less likely to be frequented this time of day. Still, they would only get him so far. Unless he wanted to go completely out of his way, he'd have to pass through the center of town, putting himself at the mercy of circumstance.

It felt strange to be outside, novel even. The expansive sight of the sky, the familiar sounds of the birds, even the soothing breeze on his face, everything fresh and alive. He shouldn't have been surprised, but he was: life had moved on. Unlike in his bubble at home—where it seemed to have come to a standstill, where he was spending much more of it reliving the past than concerning himself with the present—time had continued its unstoppable advance.

As expected, people were out. He saw Señora Muñoz turning a corner with her roller cart. She must have been coming back from the shops. Some screaming kids ran by, paying him no mind as they headed to the playground down the hill. When a delivery truck turned into the alley, he had to step into a doorway while it squeezed past like an oil tanker in the Suez.

Just as he was getting ready to hightail it past the church, it hit him.

Stop.

Out of nowhere.

Stop.

Stop?

Now.

As though startled by something that had crossed his path, he came to a halt at the foot of the alley with the *panadería* where his family bought their bread.

From one moment to the next, it was as if he'd become confused about which way to go. Though in a rush to get to the trail, he found himself hesitating, caught off guard not by a rat darting into the alley but a thought just as unexpectedly popping into his head.

Stop.

Except it wasn't a thought. Not exactly.

It was more like a feeling, a feeling that gripped his mind and body alike. One that now seemed to be pulling at him from the inside.

The panadería.

Like the answer to a riddle.

He had to go to the panadería.

No, he thought, annoyed to find himself even entertaining the possibility, I'll get the *barra* later.

The panadería was open for a few more hours, so there was no rush. Stopping to get bread now would only slow him down. Plus, he'd have to carry it with him on the hike. It could wait.

As he turned to continue on his way, the hesitation asserted itself again. Stronger than before, it left him with the overwhelming sense he needed to buy a barra without delay. If the thought or feeling or whatever it was were to be believed, buying the bread couldn't wait after all.

Still, Pablo resisted, unleashing a small-scale war inside himself.

He didn't want to buy the bread yet. He wanted to get to the trail while there was still enough daylight to even bother. He could buy the bread later. What was the big deal? Why was he hesitating? It didn't make any sense. Rather than going round and round in circles, directing his attention first toward the panadería, then back in the direction of the reserve, then back to the panadería yet again, he needed to rein himself in. He needed to pick up where he had left off and pick the bread up later. It was that easy. No need to overthink it.

But that was it exactly, something inside him countered. Why overthink it? If for whatever reason—in spite of the apparent absence of one—he felt it would be better to buy the bread now, why not just do it? Then there would be no wondering. It would be done. Again, no need to overthink it.

Exasperated by the senseless deliberations, he threw in the towel. It wouldn't take more than a minute to buy the bread, and it wasn't as if one barra were really going to inconvenience him that much on the hike. He wondered why he had allowed something so insignificant to turn into such a needless struggle.

No sooner had Pablo walked into the panadería than he noticed something was awry.

Looking at the wall of bread baskets, which should have been full of at least several loaves, Pablo saw not a single one. There wasn't a barra in sight.

Alarmed, he shot Cristina a look that demanded, "Where's the bread!"

A good-natured, no-nonsense woman just a few years his senior, Cristina had a short, stout body and pale, pasty skin that bore an uncanny resemblance to the dough with which her family's bread was baked. It was as though she shared a common lineage with the Pillsbury Doughboy and flour, yeast, and salt had long been part of her DNA.

"What did you want?" she asked, blowing a few stray wisps of hair out of her face and dusting off her apron, both taken aback and mildly amused by the disproportionate urgency of Pablo's expression. "Your mom's gone, so I'm assuming just a barra for you?"

Pablo nodded.

"Let me look in back, but I don't think we have any more. There was a big group of Brits that came up late this afternoon, and they cleaned me out! But let me go double-check."

Under ordinary circumstances, Pablo wouldn't have been nearly as concerned. He probably wouldn't have cared at all. He would have returned home empty-handed, survived one night without bread, and not given it another thought. But these weren't ordinary circumstances. He wasn't standing in the panadería by chance.

"Last one!" Cristina proclaimed, as she triumphantly passed through the beaded curtain concealing the back of the store, barra in hand.

On top of it, the last one! Pablo thought in amazement, taking the bread into his hands like a father holding his child for the very first time, as though beholding some sort of crusty miracle.

Still unsure what to make of Pablo's disbelief, but indulgently playing along as though she shared it, Cristina added, "I guess today's your lucky day. And mine, too, because now I get to go home early!"

12

Picking his walk back up where he had left off, Pablo was soon at the foot of the steps next to the town hall. A spring trickling out of several spigots in the wall to his left, he bounded toward the tiers of houses overhead. The ascent was steep, an endless zigzag of interconnected stairs and ramps lifted right out of one of Escher's mind-boggling works leading him higher and higher.

Pausing to catch his breath, he looked down over the territory he had just covered. The majority of the village lay beneath him. White walls and terra-cotta roofs clung tightly to one another, like a flock of sheep huddled in defensive response to a predator lurking unseen in the ridges of orchards and scrub of the surrounding countryside. He could also see the huge reservoir that took up so much of the valley floor.

A steep, winding street later, he took the last flight of stairs of the village proper. Continuing along a trail that passed through corrals of bleating goats and clucking chickens, he came to the fire road that served as the park's boundary.

Rejoining the trail on the other side, he relished the feel of gravel crunching under his feet, each step reminding him of his freedom. The pine trees he came upon shortly thereafter did even more to soothe his spirit. Their inescapable, invigorating scent leaving him with no choice but to open up, breathe in, and let it out, he gradually began the process of releasing at least some of his sorrow and frustration.

He climbed with resolve, pushing himself even more than would have been required otherwise, given that the trail proceeded almost straight up the mountainside, one switchback after another. He didn't pause, as he might have ordinarily, to observe the songbirds he saw out of the corner of his eye, nor did he attempt to identify two falcons startled to flight as he interrupted their secret rendezvous. It was only when he left the small pines beneath him and came out into an area of the shrubs, flowers, and grasses characterizing most of the mountainside that he paused again to catch his breath. The refreshing scent of the pine competed with the delicious aroma of rosemary growing there in abundance, like two courtesans vying for the attention of their king.

To the south, the Mediterranean was clearly visible now, several kilometers away on the other side of a series of ridges. In places, Pablo could even see the coast itself, or at least the apartment buildings and hotels built along it, gigantic, inorganic blocks popping up improbably wherever the mountains dipped low enough. The town of which they were a part had a history spanning millennia, dating all the way back to the Phoenicians and the Greeks; sadly, with the exception of an occasional monument that had somehow survived in the shadows, that past had been indecorously paved over by a steel-and-concrete present.

Closer to the crest on which he was standing, Pablo could see the neighboring village wedged between two ridges far below. It was smaller than his and only a few kilometers away, the road linking the two a favorite for seniors taking their evening strolls.

The sky overhead was bespeckled with puffy white clouds. The only ones appearing at all menacing were the darker masses enshrouding the very top of the mountain, covering it like a hat protecting a bald head from the sun. Pablo wasn't worried. They were localized enough not to pose any threat, especially since he had no plans to go nearly that far. His destination was the cave, only about an hour up the trail; the peak was at least four.

After passing through the "rock circle," a flat area with a sandy floor surrounded by a circular wall of craggy rocks that created a natural sort of Stonehenge, he began another phase of the ascent. Again he traversed an area of pines, before leaving them behind in favor of more scrub. Thereafter, the trail became even rockier. Forced to watch his every step, he noticed the incredible variety of colors beneath his feet, as he had so many times before.

There were different shades of pinks, oranges, and reds, which in places were so deep and rich he couldn't help but think of dried blood, as though the very life force of the Earth had seeped to the surface, petrifying there as it did. He saw golds that reminded him of the riches at one time concealed beneath the mountain's surface, purples of which so many of the flowers seemed to have made resourceful use, and reddish browns the pine trees appeared to have incorporated into their bark, only to let them fall again in the form of large, bumpy cones. There were big chunks of blue gray, like pieces of the evening sky chipped off by some celestial hammer, as well as the pure white from which the snails he occasionally saw formed their curly shells and, for that matter, with which the walls of the village were immaculately washed.

Although all the colors in the entire fantastic palette were visible to the naked eye, they could easily—and, it occurred to Pablo, no doubt usually did—go unnoticed. A thin layer of dust subjugated their hues into a cohesive, deceptive harmony that failed to call attention to any particular one of them.

As another falcon glided overhead, Pablo entered a small clearing. Several slabs of rock were embedded in the earth at a precarious angle and surrounded by larger pines than what he had passed on the way up. He crossed the rocks, careful not to slip on their polished surfaces, and headed for the spring, which he could hear well before he saw it. Disdainful of the surrounding silence, like a child laughing loudly in a cathedral, it showed no respect for the sanctity of the place.

Bending down to a small pipe from which the spring tumbled into a rectangular, tadpole-filled pool, Pablo scooped some water into his mouth, repeating the gesture until he was sated. Even though it was late in the afternoon, the sun was still bright, the air hot and dry. The cool spring water came as a very welcome relief.

Stretching his back, he looked ahead toward the cave. During his ascent, some of the clouds lingering around the peak earlier had met him halfway, covering the path in a cool mist. For much the same reason as the water, it, too, was welcome, and soon he'd immersed himself completely in it. As he did, the cave gradually took form, even more intriguing than usual, given the mysterious cloak enveloping it.

Apart from the mauves, ochres, and golds of its rock, the cave wasn't particularly remarkable. Its entrance was wide enough for four or five people to stand shoulder to shoulder, and it was almost tall enough for a person of average height to stand upright. More so than its appearance, most of the cave's mystique lay in the stories Pablo had heard about it. It was said the Romans had mined gold there and that the cave itself was even mentioned in the Bible. It was also common knowledge that during the Arab period it had been inhabited by three holy men; Pablo had heard they were buried there—although he didn't know if that had ever been proven. Regardless, the place was one with a long, interesting history.

Turning away from the cave, Pablo directed his attention toward one of his favorite spots, where he hoped both to rest from the climb and, more importantly, to try to come to terms with at least some of what he was feeling.

Having taken not more than a single step, he stopped dead in his tracks.

As a light gust of wind dispersed the mist, there, turned the other way and not moving a muscle, sat an old man, his white, wavy locks matching the color of his shirt. In spite of himself, Pablo thought of the holy men. It was as if one of them had materialized, roused from their centuries-long repose deep within the cave.

Just as quickly—like when he had been on stage—a flash of recognition.

The stranger from the store.

Clearly he had been there a while—and gotten there first. Pablo wasn't sure what to do. Make himself noticed or quietly slip away, retracing his steps and leaving the man to himself?

As is so often the case in life, Pablo was struggling with a decision he didn't have to make.

"Hello," said the old man, turning slightly over his shoulder, without otherwise changing position.

Pablo jumped.

"Sorry to startle you! One of the holy men brought back to life!" the stranger quipped with a knowing smile.

Again Pablo was visibly caught off guard.

The old man laughed, gesturing for him to sit down.

"I see you're familiar with the history of the place. It's certainly a fascinating one, going all the way back to the Phoenicians and lasting thousands of years, during which the cave was mined for gold and silver. Apparently, it was just one of many in the region, their riches such that it's even been said they gave way to the legend of King Solomon's mines."

For the first time in days, Pablo found himself distracted from his troubles. He'd never met anyone who knew so much about the cave.

"Then, of course, there were the Sufis."

Pablo looked at him inquisitively.

"The holy men. Mystics normally associated historically and culturally with Islam, though many of them profess not to adhere to any particular dogma and, as a result, were often at odds with authority, including Islam itself. Apparently the Sufis in question ended up in this cave because they'd been forced to flee some authority figure or another who deemed their teachings contrary to the words of the Prophet and, therefore, a menace to society—not to mention a mortal sin, I would guess. Fortunately, the men escaped. Somehow they found themselves here and took refuge in this very cave, from which they began sharing their wisdom with anyone who came seeking it."

The old man paused, he and Pablo peering through a large opening framed by branches of nearby pines. As the mist that had obstructed their view was swept away, wispy spirals ascending like smoke, it unveiled a spectacular landscape. The valley was now visible far below, mountains rising up on the other side of it and, again in the distance off to the left, the sea.

"I'm sorry for your loss," the man said.

Like a right hook out of nowhere while his guard was down, the words, simple but heartfelt, hit Pablo hard. Even the stranger knew?

"You've been through a lot, my friend. And you've done right to take refuge in silence."

Pablo looked up at the old man, astonished. Good that he had gone silent? When everyone berated him for it? When even he couldn't explain why it had happened? Now a total stranger was telling him he had done the right thing? Pablo wanted to believe him, but what did the old man even know about his situation, really?

"I did the same thing when I lost my daughter three years ago. Granted, my silence was more of a conscious decision than it would seem yours is. But still, it's the same idea."

Pablo was stunned. The old man had a daughter? He had lost a daughter?

"In her case, it was a long battle. I'm not sure what's worse. The shock of losing someone unexpectedly, as you did. Or, the drawn-out torture of watching someone you love slowly fade from sight. All part of the cycle, I suppose. The lessons we're here to learn. Not always easy to see it that way though, is it?"

Reflective, the man again turned toward the breathtaking view. The breeze stirred his hair like it did the needles on the pines.

"Take your time, my boy. Take your time. We all have our own way of dealing with things. Listen to what your heart is telling you, and honor that. Your loved ones are eager for you to get back to your old self, because they care about you and they're worried about you. Some of them might even see their own sadness reflected in yours, and it might be too much. They might not know how to cope. Be patient with them just as you'd have them be patient with you, and do what you need to do to take care of yourself."

So the old man did understand.

And he didn't judge.

"Speaking of the silence, I've had my share. I'll turn it over to you now," he said as he stood to go, gently stretching his back. "In the meantime, if you need someone to lend you an ear—or, for the time-being, just some company—I believe you know where to find me. Speaking of which, you'll be glad to know the spinach was still frozen by the time I got home!"

Pablo smiled.

"Listen to what you hear in the silence," the old man added, almost by way of afterthought. "Pay attention to it. Trust it."

And with that, he headed back down the mountain.

13

A few nights after their evening gone awry, Rosa stopped by with more food, this time by way of peace offering. Pablo felt bad, too, about how things had gone on their previous visit. It helped that he'd since gotten out of the house and had the interaction with the old man. He was in much better spirits than Rosa had found him the last time around.

It helped that much more that one of their favorite TV shows was on. A welcome distraction, it not only gave them something to do, but alleviated Rosa of the pressure of delivering a rambling one-sided monologue.

As with any of the other countless reality shows on TV, it was easy for them to get sucked into *Operation Victory*, a talent contest that had already launched the career of more than one new pop star. Sitting on the edge of the couch with their plates on the coffee table, they watched the next contestant walk onstage.

It only took Pablo a few notes to recognize the song. It was one of his favorites, one he was always singing to himself, in fact. It came as no surprise, then, that while eager to hear the contestant's rendition, he felt a little protective, as though hoping something near and dear to him weren't about to be desecrated.

Rosa nudged him knowingly when she, too, realized what the song was.

Initially, Pablo had little cause for concern. To the contrary, the singer made a good first impression. He looked more or less at ease. It sounded as though he had a decent voice. The selection seemed to be a suitable one for him.

Things quickly took a turn for the worse. Glued to the screen, following along as the contestant worked his way through each measure, it wasn't long before Pablo grew restless, given plenty of reasons to find fault. Listening ever more intently, like the most unforgiving of armchair critics, soon he was picking the performance to pieces.

He winced when the contestant landed conspicuously short of a dramatic, defining note, falling flat before picking himself back up. When he made the same misstep not long after, Pablo recognized it as a clear indication he wasn't breathing properly. Pablo sighed when the singer got tongue-tied on a challenging bit of phrasing, faulting him for not having worked it out beforehand. And he protested indignantly when it became clear the contestant had no intention of budging from the mic. Planting himself there as though mortified of taking so much as a single step in either direction, he refused to use the rest of the stage at all, never mind make the most of it, never mind own it outright.

There were other issues, too, a long list of things Pablo felt the contestant could have done better. Yet his most serious grievance, what for Pablo was far and away the most egregious flaw of the entire performance, wasn't something the singer did but—much like his refusal to inhabit the space around him—something he didn't do.

Simply put, he wasn't feeling it.

Rather than pouring his heart into the performance, the longer it went on, the more Pablo sensed the contestant was holding back, merely going through the motions. It was as though he'd realized halfway through that the song wasn't so suitable for him after all and that, to the contrary, he'd been overambitious with his selection. Now he was just trying to get through it. But if he wasn't feeling it, the audience wouldn't either. And then, what was the point?

The longer they watched, the more painful it became. Even Rosa, normally the more forgiving of the two, having spent no time onstage, was unable to overlook the singer's more serious missteps. Soon Pablo was worked up as though he were somehow personally invested in what was transpiring. Increasingly, his reaction was out of proportion for something that, on the surface at least, had nothing to do with him.

But then again, maybe it did. There was no denying something had struck a nerve. Clearly there was more at play than his love of the song or any shortcomings, real or imagined, in the contestant's rendition of it. What? Why was he letting himself get so worked up?

Because he could do better.

Much better, in fact. And he wasn't being arrogant in thinking so. He was simply being honest.

How he longed for the chance to prove it.

Indeed, the more he watched, the more he yearned to be the one on that stage, each ostensible wrong the contestant committed an opportunity for Pablo to have done it right. If the television screen had been a literal window as opposed to a metaphoric one, he wouldn't have thought twice about crashing through it. Making a grandiose entrance heralded by a shower of shards of glass, he would have taken the song away without skipping a beat. He would have infused it with enough passion and power to save it from the lackluster finish it was otherwise fated, left in the incapable hands of the uninspired contestant.

Then it hit him. A rude awakening that only made his frustration and longing that much greater. Overlooked as he watched the performance, forgotten as he gave himself over to the fantasy, once again he remembered.

He couldn't do better.

He couldn't do anything at all, in fact.

He had no voice.

"*¡Pero chico!*" Rosa exclaimed with a playful shove, snapping him out of his trance, as the program cut to a commercial break. "*¡Tranquilo!* It's just a TV show!"

Pablo smiled and rolled his eyes, masking his frustration, his fear and sadness. It was and it wasn't just a TV show. But she was right. It was silly to let himself get so worked up.

"Someone's got a lot of pent-up energy," she murmured, taking a drawn-out sip of wine. Moving in closer, she ran her fingers up the back of his hair.

Pablo tensed, all his nerves suddenly alive. He hadn't seen it coming, and at first he wasn't sure what to do with it, like someone uncomfortable with touch. But this was Rosa's touch, familiar and experienced. She knew what he liked. And it had been so long.

From one moment to the next, parts of Pablo that had lain dormant since the store burned stirred to life, setting off an altogether different sort of fire. His lips came down on Rosa's, his strong, nimble body pinning hers beneath him as one shirt button after another gave way to his dexterous fingers, efficient and precise. She was right. He did have a lot of pent-up energy. What she couldn't possibly imagine was just how much. And now she didn't have to. Now she was on the receiving end of it.

Pablo owned Rosa like moments before he had longed to own the stage. He savored the smell of her hair, the feel of her skin, the taste of her. He relished her writhing beneath him, the exquisite expressions of pleasure she was unable to suppress. She now the one caught off guard, her own pent-up energy was coaxed and teased from her, unleashed. Pablo, after all, knew her buttons just as well as she knew his.

As the friction intensified, the tension continued to mount, Rosa began slipping out of her pants.

It was then that, without warning, the brakes slamming on a runaway train, everything came to a screeching halt.

Rosa looked up at Pablo, confused and dismayed. Her hair mussed, shirt open, chest heaving. Beads of sweat glistened on her forehead. Her cheeks and lips were flush.

He'd lost himself in the moment. But then something had

snapped, tearing him out of it.

He couldn't do it.

Disappointed and embarrassed, Rosa refastened her pants. She redid the buttons on her shirt, misaligning them in her haste. She moved back on the sofa. Grabbing the remote, she turned off the TV, putting an end to the intrusive, meaningless chatter.

A long, painful silence followed.

"I just thought it might make you feel better."

Pablo understood.

But what it felt was sacrilegious.

Never mind that he just didn't want it. He had assumed he would, since he always did. And at first he obviously had. But then something had happened, something had broken the spell. He felt so confused. Ashamed.

Sex having proven an awkward, miserable failure, Rosa braced herself to deliver an awkward, miserable truth. Given how naturally it came out, it was clear she'd already given it considerable thought.

"Pablo, this isn't working."

Her words hung heavy in the air. She needed a moment to regroup after saying them. She needed to give him a moment for them to sink in, to ready himself for the ones that would follow.

"I wanted to be there for you," she continued. "But I can't tell what you're feeling, and I don't know what you need. Nothing I do seems right. Not even this. I just feel like I'm in the way."

What he was feeling?

What he was feeling was that his whole world was slipping away. What he was feeling was that everything he had ever known and loved was being taken from him, while he was helpless to stymie the tide. His father. The store. His voice.

And now his girlfriend was breaking up with him.

What he was feeling was horrible.

He understood her frustration, but he didn't know what to do. His heart ached with a relentless pain that he couldn't give voice. Still in shock, he struggled to make sense of feelings with which he didn't know how to cope, rage, pain, and sorrow like he'd never experienced.

Again it occurred to him that, in actuality, the conversation was as much about him not being there for her as it was about her not being able to be there for him.

As such, maybe she was right.

Maybe they couldn't be together right now.

"I'm really sorry, Pablo. I really am," Rosa said, wiping away the tears she hadn't been able to hold back. "You will get through this. I know you will."

Pablo found little comfort in her words, knowing full well that, for the time-being at least, they were the last he'd be hearing from her.

14

It wasn't until late the next morning that Pablo woke up.

He felt as though he had a hangover. The store had burned. His father had died. And now he had broken up with his girlfriend.

Or rather, she had broken up with him.

Sleep. Escape. Forget.

But he had to wake up.

No, there was more to it. He needed to actually get up. Now.

He could feel it.

He didn't want to. Like a little boy pulling the blanket over his head to hide from the day, he resisted. He tried to will himself back to a world where, if he were lucky, he'd remember, feel, think nothing. Or, maybe instead—if he were even luckier, which he often was—maybe he'd find himself someplace else altogether, someplace where none of it had ever happened.

Get up.

It was unrelenting. Waves of anxiety urging him to action.

He didn't understand the rush. He resented it. He wanted to ignore it.

But there was no time to waste.

Heading for the shower, he defiantly indulged in its enveloping, luxuriant warmth, almost as much of an escape as slumber itself. He brushed his teeth, unable to turn away from the mirror, Narcissus transfixed by how worn and weary he looked as opposed to how beautiful. For the first time in days, he shaved. He went downstairs and put on a pot of coffee. He walked into the living room and organized the records into deceptively neat piles. He picked up the wrappers and tissues off the floor. He folded the blanket.

Pouring himself a cup of coffee, he heard the garage door.

Right on cue.

Somehow he had known. Except he hadn't. Not exactly.

Neither did he know what to make of it, nor would he have time to give it any more thought. For now.

A car door slamming. A hand on the doorknob.

It had only been a week and a half since his mother had left, but it felt like an eternity. Not that he missed her; at least not that he was willing to admit. It simply felt as though much longer had passed than actually had, time warping, slowing and stretching, in his self-imposed solitary confinement.

"*¿Hijo? ¿Estás allí? Soy yo . . .*"

Pablo let a spoonful of sugar cascade into his cup, grains of an hourglass, time itself, dissolving into oblivion. He was glad he had cleaned up not only himself but the house as well. He would have heard about both otherwise.

"Ah, there you are," Carmen said, setting down her purse on an empty chair and bending over to give Pablo a kiss on each cheek. "*¿Qué tal cariño?*"

Pablo mustered a smile.

"I needed a few things from up here. And I wanted to make sure you were doing OK."

Pablo took a drink of coffee while his mother assessed the state of affairs. She opened a cupboard to check what was left. She looked in the refrigerator to see if anything was there at all. She poked her head in the living room, as though fearing what she might discover.

"His music," she reminisced with a smile, before walking

over to the coffee pot and pouring herself a cup. "I should have known."

Pablo got up from the table and went into the other room. His fingers flipped through the albums with the resolve of someone searching for a contact in an old Rolodex. When he found what he was looking for, he took it out, set it on the turntable, and put the needle on the record.

As music filled the house, tears filled his mother's eyes.

"You know just the right song, don't you!" she scolded, wiping her eyes. "He was always singing that one. I loved it when he sang that one."

Pablo sat back down, his own eyes clouding over as he clutched his coffee.

Several measures passed, a lone voice and a simple, poignant melody transporting them both elsewhere.

"*¿Cómo te va, hijo?* How are you holding up? Are you doing OK?" Carmen asked, taking hold of his hand, squeezing it. "I know you've been hiding out, but I hear you headed up to the reserve?"

The village was so small.

More silence followed, the music filling the space between them. Carmen gently released her grip and shifted her attention back to her cup. If she looked closely enough at the smooth, caramel-colored surface, like a fortune-teller reading grounds, maybe she'd find the right words.

She took a deep breath.

"Pablo, things aren't going well with the store. The insurance company isn't on our side. They keep wanting me to prove things and show them documents and justify numbers. They keep debating what's covered by the policy and what's not—even though it looks like it's all right there in black and white to me. I'm really worried. I don't know how this is all going to end."

Pablo reached across the table, reciprocating his mother's gesture of shortly before and taking her hand.

Their eyes met, more tears welling up in hers.

"There's something else I'm worried about," she said after

another silent exchange. "Mercedes said things aren't going well between you and Rosa—she said you broke up?"

Pablo took back his hand.

"How long is it going to be like this, *hijo*?" his mother pleaded. "Can't you see what you're doing? Can't you see your family and friends are worried sick about you?"

Pablo got up from the table and took his cup over to the sink.

"We're all suffering," she continued, undeterred. "I'm grieving, too. He was your father, but he was my husband. We need to be there for each other, but you're shutting everyone out."

He wished she hadn't come.

"I'm going to grab some things, then I'm meeting some of the gals for lunch. I really hope you'll think about coming down to Málaga. The kids keep asking about you, and the change of scenery would do you some good. I'm sure of it."

15

Before his mother came back downstairs, Pablo had left.

She was right. He needed a change of scenery. He desperately needed some fresh air. He needed to clear his head and stretch his legs.

Making his way to the reserve, he came to the top of the steps leading out of the village. Turning to his right, he set foot on a path likely to go unnoticed by someone unaware of it, enshrouded as it was in dense vegetation.

Ducking under some low branches as he rounded the corner, he found himself in a sort of miniature Garden of Eden. Like so many other places in and around the village, at some point in a long-forgotten past the mountainside had been terraced there. The narrow path Pablo now followed ran along one of the stone retaining walls. A meter above him was a plot of gnarled, centuries-old olive trees while, to his right, just below the trail, was the garden itself. A beautiful, well-maintained group of four or five small plots, it was shaded by a few large magnolias and boasted a surprising variety of vegetables, including corn, tomatoes, and hot peppers. No matter how many times he walked by, Pablo never failed to notice something new, its caretakers always hard at work on whatever was next.

Pablo followed the path along an empty irrigation canal not much wider than the trail itself, reemerging into the sun. It was hot, but he wasn't worried. Over the course of his hike the path would meander in and out of the shadows of the mountainside, as well as the shade of orchards and pine groves.

Rounding another corner, Pablo headed toward one of the many curves that delineated where one flank ended and another began, the boundary demarcated by a deep, rocky crevasse. As though following the fingers on some great earthen hand, he walked in and out, along canyon after canyon, never out of sight of the boundless, bright-blue sky overhead.

Eventually coming to where the irrigation canal had been blocked, he saw that the water was being diverted into an olive grove. Although he didn't know the specifics, he did know that each land owner was allowed to irrigate their parcels at specifically designated times, in accordance with rules that dated back hundreds of years—if not to the very founding of the village itself.

Now accompanied by the pleasant trickle of the man-made stream, Pablo arrived at a ruin hidden among a dense, unkempt olive grove. A steep segment of trail followed, at the top of which was yet another sharp turn, bringing him to the most dramatic part of the hike. It didn't matter that he had seen it all countless times before. It was breathtakingly beautiful.

Hundreds of meters below, he could see the road to the other village, making a tight *S* as it wound around one curve, inward toward another, and back out again, skirting the edge of a sheer, rocky gorge that divided two massive flanks. At the tightest part of the curve, he could also see a couple of cars parked at the picnic area next to the old stone bridge, which maintained its hold on each side of the gorge like a suture binding a wound.

As dramatic as all that was, it scarcely compared to what Pablo beheld off to his left, provoking in him a profound, reflective reverence.

An immense cleavage bore deep into the mountainside, a zigzagging series of soaring bluish-gray cliffs, vast sections of whose faces had been worn away like old layers of paint scoured by wind and rain, exposing brilliant rusts and golds hidden just beneath the surface. Bright-green pines, as well as bushes and flowers, grew wherever they could manage to keep hold, often clinging tenaciously—even miraculously—to vertical precipices or imperceptible spaces between rocks, where they were somehow able to not only take root but flourish. Covering entire sections of the canyon floor, dwarf palms unfurled their leaves like fans in the hands of elegant Andalusian *damas*, while massive boulders and piles of rubble lay scattered about like fallen heroes.

Above and beyond it all, among the jagged limestone and marble peaks in the chasm's furthest reaches and highest heights, hidden like the mysterious, life-giving treasure it was, the spring to which the village owed its very existence was found.

It wasn't possible to hike to the spring's source, perched in some out-of-reach recess high atop impregnable cliffs. Instead, the trail ended at the beginning of the irrigation canal, a picturesque, cascading succession of crystal-clear pools set among lush, riparian vegetation. Pablo had made the spectacular trek countless times. Often resorting to narrow metal walkways drilled right into the cliff faces, the trail dangled precariously high above the floor of the rocky gorge, a life-ending plummet far, far below.

Unlikely to go all the way today, he slowly resumed his walk, following the path until, as he was about to round another bend, it came out of nowhere.

Stop.

Subtle. Almost imperceptible.

So much so that at first he ignored it. But then it came again, more insistent this time, a mild tension throughout his body, like when he feared he was about to miss an opportunity.

Stop.

So he did. Dead in his tracks.

Then came a clear sense of what to do next. Not quite a voice. More than a feeling. Intangible, yet unmistakable.

He sat down in that very spot. In the middle of the trail.

He never could have explained it if someone had been there to ask—and never would have done it, if someone had been there to watch. Yet in that singular, out-of-the-blue moment, he was lucidly aware that, for whatever reason, he was supposed to sit down right then and right there. It didn't matter that it was completely exposed. It didn't matter there was no place to sit other than on the ground itself, the seat of his pants already dusted with dirt.

Surveying the precipitous, rocky mountainside he'd traversed only moments before, the trail since having crossed over to the opposing flank, he inhaled a deep breath of scrub-scented air. It felt good to sit, particularly since he'd been walking for well over an hour, having made several steep ascents. On the other hand, he wasn't tired, and ordinarily he wouldn't have stopped at all until later on. He had no idea why he'd been compelled to do so now, and he felt self-conscious sitting there for no apparent reason.

When one of them slipped on a rock that sent several others cascading down the side of the cliff, doing away with the cover afforded them while frozen in place, a group of mountain goats took off in a panicked display of stunning dexterity. As Pablo watched, they sliced across a bare, almost vertical patch of mountainside he would have deemed impossible to traverse, even by creatures as well suited as the goats for bounding up and down the treacherous terrain. No sooner did their hooves come into contact with the sheer, sandy escarpment than they were forced to take off again, the ground billowing toward the valley floor the instant they placed any weight on it. Rather than fright, it was as if the herd had somehow taken flight. Clouds of dust shot into the air, engulfing the startled beasts and drawing even more attention to them, until, mere moments later, each member of the small drove found footing on more solid terrain and bounded out of sight.

In all his years observing them, Pablo had seen the incredible animals do many impressive things. But none compared to the drama he had just watched them perform. He was astonished, elated to have had the good fortune of finding himself in just the right place at just the right time to witness something so spectacular. Seeing the animals at all would have made him happy. Watching them execute such a breathtaking maneuver was more than he could have hoped for.

Awestruck and inspired, Pablo got up. Dusting off the back of his pants, he took another look at the mountainside before him, now as peaceful as if nothing had happened. Even as he turned to be on his way, he still couldn't believe what he had seen.

But it wasn't just what he had seen. It was why he had seen it. Out of nowhere, an unmistakable awareness of something he needed to do. Too strong to ignore. Just like the bread. Something inexplicable that ended up making perfect sense.

Except he had no idea what, if anything, it actually meant.

Or why it mattered, assuming it even did.

All the same, he couldn't let it go. And as he continued to ponder what had happened, mulling it over again and again, repeatedly his thoughts turned to the old man; specifically, to his parting words at the cave.

"Listen to what you hear in the silence," he had said. "Pay attention to it."

16

Pablo felt strange as he got onto his motorcycle. He was anxious, unsure what he was even going to do when he got there. But he knew he had to go. And, his apprehension aside, he was eager to.

Unlike the first time he rode down the driveway, Pablo found the old man outside. Victor was atop a ladder, his face and hands buried in the thick, leafy grape vines that hung on the trellis over his porch.

Like a bear climbing a tree to get at the honey in the beehive buzzing in the branches, Victor had set his sights on the gorgeous bunches of voluptuous grapes he'd been allowing to ripen over the past few weeks. His prudent restraint not only ensured he harvested the grapes in their prime, but it delayed the inevitable encounter with their devoted caretakers: the hornets.

At any time of day—even at the hottest, brightest hours of the height of summer, when no one in their right mind went outside for any reason, let alone gave any thought to doing any sort of physical labor—as though they were either oblivious or somehow immune to the severity of the elements, an innumerable group of the delicate yet fierce creatures glided up and down the vines. Like obsessively dedicated farmers, they refused to waste so much as a moment that might be devoted to the painstaking care of their precious crops.

Other than the fact he was moving slowly, Victor seemed unfazed by the presence of the grapes' winged custodians. His focus instead was on the fruit itself, a bunch of which he had selected for picking. Carefully holding it in place with one hand, he cut its thin, leathery stem with a pair of scissors he held in the other.

"Perfect timing! Would you be so kind as to take this?" he called out to Pablo, who left his bike behind and rushed to the old man's aid.

They were beautiful: each one of the bunch a large, translucent, succulent jewel. Their pale-green color almost seemed to downplay just how incredibly sweet their crisp and juicy flesh was sure to be.

Pablo did as asked, adding the freshly cut cluster to one that was already sitting in the basket at the foot of the ladder.

"Just one more," Victor said, as he surveyed the vines for the bunch that would complete the day's harvest.

Glad Victor was the one on the ladder and not him, Pablo watched as the sleek, angular creatures swirled up and down the vines in erratic but deliberate bursts that left them in constant motion, like live wires throwing black and yellow sparks.

"They know I don't mean them any harm," Victor remarked as he cut down the third and final bunch, seemingly reading Pablo's thoughts. "And worse come to worst, there's always aloe to soothe the stings."

Victor took the grapes inside to wash them off, coming back out a couple of minutes later with a glistening bowl of them. He sat it down in the middle of the table, encouraging Pablo to help himself.

"I'm glad you stopped by," Victor remarked. "You're doing better than when we last crossed paths. I can see it."

Pablo smiled. Any hesitance he felt about showing up unannounced was all but forgotten. The old man was friendly and relaxed. He made Pablo feel welcome.

"I trust that means you've been taking care of yourself. I remember what it was like. Everyone wants to help. They mean well. But they all have their own ideas of what you need and how you should be feeling."

He had been through a similar loss. He understood. Even better he was a stranger, so he had little context and few, if any, expectations.

Maybe that was why it happened.

Whatever the reason, without warning, it did, like a mature pomegranate whose insides have swollen to the point they can no longer be contained, the skin literally ripping down the middle as ruby-red seeds fly forth.

Or, in this case, words.

"You told me to listen. I have been. And I've been hearing things."

Pablo was even more surprised by the sound of his voice than the old man. He almost questioned whether he had imagined it. Yet again it wasn't a conscious decision. Yet again it just was. Reengaging with his voice felt at once perfectly natural and self-consciously novel, as if he were borrowing someone else's. Though it had yet to register entirely, it was also an unimaginable relief.

Victor waited a moment before responding, honoring what had just come to pass, without explicitly acknowledging it.

"Of course you have. After what you've been through, inevitably your heart and mind are awash in a host of emotions, memories, even regrets."

"Yeah, but that's not what I mean—not those kinds of things."

"Oh?"

Pablo paused to find the right words.

"No. It's like I know things. Not even important things. But I know them—or I almost do, even when I don't have any reason to. I don't know how to explain it."

"Ah yes," Victor smiled. "Those things."

Pablo hadn't shown any sign of helping himself to the grapes. Having waited as long as courtesy dictated, Victor took some for himself, discovering they were worth every bit of the effort.

"When we stop the chatter, when we sit back and just listen, sometimes we hear not only what's being said around us," he remarked, "but inside as well. We hear our inner voice. That voice without words. Our intuition."

Pablo thought back on his experiences. Not quite a voice. More than a feeling.

"It just started happening."

"You mean you just started paying attention. No, my friend, you can rest assured that your intuition has always been there—even though you may not have paid it any mind or given it a name."

"I don't know. I mean, how would I know? What is it?"

Victor once again fell silent. Popping a few more grapes into his mouth, he looked into the sky as though his answer were slowly forming there, taking shape like clouds coalescing from crystalline drops of vapor.

"As I said, intuition is that voice inside you. It's 'going with your gut,' 'feeling it in your bones,' or 'listening to your heart.' You see? All those expressions refer to your intuition. It's not thinking, but feeling."

"Don't think?" Pablo questioned.

"Ha! You're taking my words a little too far!" the old man countered lightheartedly. "Of course you have to think. I wish more people would! And, for that matter, in a deliberate, rational way. Reason, after all, is an essential, invaluable tool. But not only is it far from infallible, it's far from the only one we have at our disposal."

"Like our intuition."

"Exactly."

Victor having given him plenty of food for thought, Pablo finally partook of the food on the table, taking a cluster of grapes.

"Does everyone have it? Intuition, I mean," he wondered.

"It's not really a question of having it or not. True, we talk about 'our' intuition, but that's more a reference to an experience than it is to something tangible that's possessed per se. But, yes, I would say everyone has the ability to be open and attuned to their intuition."

"Then why doesn't anybody talk about it?"

"People do talk about it—all the time," Victor contested, "even though they don't always realize it."

"Oh yeah, going with your gut and all that."

"Expressions such as those, but also, for example, our tendency to explain certain otherwise inexplicable decisions by saying that something 'just felt right' or—when we find ourselves at a loss for any other explanation—by blankly offering 'I just knew it.' Similarly, when someone's going around in circles, grappling with a difficult decision, we advise them not to 'overthink it'; in other words, perhaps, to open up to what their intuition might have to say and not rely solely on reason, particularly once its limits have been reached."

"Its limits? What do you mean?"

"We insist on using reason when it's no longer appropriate. Like a drug we won't stop taking even when it's no longer helping our symptoms, we get hooked on it. And when we do, that overdependence sends us running around in circles, chasing our tails like dogs."

That struck a chord. Pablo had no trouble understanding how dwelling on something too long could leave a person going round and round, getting nowhere.

"What's worse is that not only are we overdependent on it," Victor mused, "but when we do put reason to use—or at least attempt to—we're often horrible at it. Indeed, except when employed by the most adept of practitioners, reason becomes as malleable as clay in the potter's hands!"

"But something's either true or not, isn't it?"

"I'm not talking about truth itself changing," the old man cautioned. "What I'm saying is that often we're not very good at using reason to get to it. I'm saying that what we suppose to be true is, just as often as not, based upon flawed logic, on our inability to effectively use this tool with which we've been blessed on the one hand and cursed—given our ineptitude and overdependence on it—on the other. And yet, at the same time, somehow we manage to be incredibly gifted at manipulating it to serve our needs—to spin it into whatever conclusion it is we'd like to see!"

Taking another cluster of grapes, Pablo took a moment as well. He needed to mull over everything he'd just heard.

"Now that I know about my intuition," he eventually asked, "is it going to keep happening?"

"Of course. But how much is largely up to you."

"Why do you say that?"

"Because just like any faculty, you can choose to develop your intuition or not."

"Really? How would I develop it?"

"By doing exactly what you've been doing," Victor explained. "By listening—to that little voice, to that impulse in your gut, to that feeling in your heart. You just keep listening."

"In a way, it's similar to dreams. Many people have no recollections of their dreams when they wake up. Once they make a conscious decision to pay more attention, that starts to change. As it does, they quickly realize that holding onto their dreams is difficult, so they begin writing them down, paying even more attention. That, in turn, fuels the cycle, and soon the combination of intent, observation, and action opens up a whole new world of insight. Fostering an awareness of your intuition works in much the same way."

17

Just because Pablo had gotten his voice back didn't mean he felt like talking.

Victor was right: silence was a perfect refuge.

That didn't stop him from calling his mom and even chatting with his sister, well aware they'd both be tremendously relieved to know he was speaking again.

Otherwise, in the days following his visit with Victor, not much changed. His mood had lightened, but he continued to be overcome by unpredictable, crippling waves of grief. He reminisced about happy times with his father, slipping into a languid melancholy where he did nothing for hours. He watched TV. He drank beer. He listened to records, now occasionally joining in under his breath. He slept a lot, slumber continuing to prove an ideal escape.

He desperately wished his father were still there. He longed to be behind the counter at the store, going through the motions of yet another ordinary day. He thought of Rosa in much the same way and for similar reasons.

While being alone still felt like more of a blessing than a curse, things began happening to suggest the tide might have turned; that it might be doing him more harm than good.

So much time on his hands. So little social interaction to

ensure he didn't get drawn so deep into his head that he lost perspective, his grip on reality. The silence could be a perfect refuge, but it could also be a dangerous trap.

One morning he woke up just as he had every morning since the fire. Fading in and out, he made the ascent back from his subconscious like a migrating stork on thermals, gently circling higher and higher. No one to answer to. Nowhere to be. No need to rush.

Opening his eyes, he took in his surroundings, surveying the room as though looking for something that might have changed since he had last left it behind.

The window to his left, the blinds working hard to hold back the light filtering through the cracks. The desk to his right, an empty water bottle where he had left it eons ago, sure to reveal a perfect ring of dust when he eventually picked it up. A couple of pens, some loose change, and a pile of papers. A postcard of la Sagrada Familia from his cousin Juan, haphazardly affixed to the wall. Next to the trash can on the floor, a duffle bag and a pair of cleats, their laces still tied. And directly in front of him, the closet, its cracked door offering a glimpse of the chaos inside, like a prank can of spring-loaded snakes, liable to burst all over the room as soon as someone dared to open it.

As he began to get out of bed, he paused.

No sooner had he done so than he regretted posing the question.

But by then it was already too late.

Which side?

It made no difference. Obviously. Yet now that he had asked—too tired to stop himself—his mind ran with it.

His natural inclination was to get out on the right side, like he always did. But was that what he really felt? Looking to the left, he realized that side was exerting a pull, extending its own invitation. Maybe this morning wasn't like all the others. Maybe, for whatever reason, today he was supposed to get out on the left side.

Or maybe not.

Now that he gave it more careful consideration, he could feel the pull to the right. Stronger. As he turned back that way, his whole body seemed to open up to it, to be drawn in that direction. He was sure of it.

But then he caught himself.

What was he doing?

Chastising himself for having succumbed to such a ludicrous debate, he jumped out of bed on the same side he always did, and headed downstairs.

A few days later he found himself in a situation every bit as maddening.

Jorge had stopped by. Although it hadn't been easy, he had coaxed Pablo into meeting up the next day at the soccer field. Other than the hikes, Pablo hadn't gotten any exercise. Kicking the ball around would do him some good.

It happened as soon as he came to an intersection, the first of what would be a long series of decisions. He could continue straight ahead. He could go right. Both options would get him where he was going, and neither was significantly faster.

Rather than just picking one and getting on with it, he hesitated. He couldn't help but think of the bread. And the goats. He thought of the morning he'd been compelled to prepare for his mom's arrival, even though he had had no idea that's what he was doing. What about now? Was his inner voice guiding him toward one alley over the other?

He looked to the right. A short jaunt up to a small plaza, a spectacular blue sky soaring over it like a dome atop a cathedral. He should head in that direction. He could feel it. Couldn't he? Looking straight ahead, at a flat lane enlivened by bright-red geraniums grateful for the shade, he wasn't so sure. His conviction of a moment earlier was undermined by the distinct impression he should head that way instead. Conflicted, again he questioned what he thought he felt, his mind soon spinning in dizzying revolutions that only stopped once he was forced to admit: he had no idea.

The fact that the village was a labyrinth didn't bode well for the rest of Pablo's walk.

When he eventually made it to the soccer field, he found Jorge ready and waiting. They had lucked out. The group of kids there when they showed up left shortly after. Pablo and Jorge had the field all to themselves.

"Why don't you just talk to her?" Jorge asked, kicking the ball back Pablo's way and quickly adjusting his glasses.

"I don't know . . ."

Pablo hadn't stopped thinking about Rosa. Nothing about the breakup felt right. He didn't believe it was what she really wanted, and it definitely wasn't what he did.

"What don't you know? You weren't talking, now you are again. So make use of your newly rediscovered talent and go to talk to her!"

Jorge saw Pablo and Rosa as the perfect couple. He'd often wished he could have what they had with a girl of his own. As far as he was concerned, they were bound to get back together.

"Things just felt so weird the last time we saw each other."

"Because they were! But only because you were in such a bad place. Things are different now."

Always the rational thinker, Jorge made it sound so simple. Why did it feel so much more complicated?

"You're probably right," Pablo admitted, his foot making contact with the ball at the wrong angle, sending it into the stratosphere, soaring far over Jorge's head.

"Nice one!" Jorge taunted as he ran after the ball. It had landed on the fire road and threatened to roll down the hill if he didn't move fast.

He was right, Pablo thought. They had broken up because he wasn't talking, because he couldn't share what he was feeling.

But now he could.

And so he would.

18

In the days following his outing with Jorge, Pablo again retreated into the silence. He didn't go see Rosa. He didn't talk to anyone else.

What he did do was continue to get a sense for things he couldn't explain. Insights that appeared to make no sense initially, but whose outcomes left no room for doubt. Like the previous incidents, sometimes what he experienced was akin to a voice; sometimes it was more like an impulse or an inclination, a gut feeling. Whatever its form, however he would have attempted to describe it, it repeatedly defied reason.

But along with those mystifying experiences were ones he could only attribute to an imagination run amok. What he thought were cues from his intuition either led nowhere or seemingly proved mistaken, baseless and illusory.

One day, he felt compelled to see Rafa. It was almost as though there were some sort of urgency to it. Try and try as he might, he couldn't get the idea out of his head. He attempted to justify it. Maybe he simply felt guilty for having shut him out since the fire, and now he felt a need to make it right. Whatever the cause, the feeling was unrelenting. Finally, he had to act.

Rafa and his grandfather were coming out the front door

when Pablo showed up.

"*¡Hombre!*" Rafa's grandfather called out as soon as he saw Pablo.

"Well look who finally crawled out of his cave!" Rafa exclaimed. "What's up?"

"*Nada*. Where you guys headed?"

"I just talked my grandson into picking up some things I left down at one of my plots."

"Want to come along? It's going to be a great time!" Rafa joked, with a smirk.

"Sounds like it!" Pablo replied, playing along. He was more than happy for an excuse to be outside. "I'm in!"

Rafa's grandfather was a short man in his late seventies who was nonetheless spry, alert, and in good health—despite a smile conspicuously lacking teeth—no doubt due to the fact he stayed so active both physically and mentally. When he wasn't working on his land, which was considerably more extensive than his humble appearance might suggest, he was sure to be socializing with his friends. Most of them were still around, too, always up for a game of cards or dominoes. Although small in stature, he had a big presence, always radiating an infectious happiness. You simply couldn't help but feel good around Rafa's grandfather.

"So what's going on?" Rafa asked, as the threesome made their way toward the plot, his grandfather putting a trail of dust between himself and the youngsters.

"Oh, you know," Pablo said vaguely. "It sucks. And then Rosa broke up with me, too."

"Yeah, I heard."

"What about you? Are you still hanging out with that girl from town?"

"Which one?"

"Which one! The one you told me about the last time I saw you at the store! She had really big lips?"

"Oh, yeah—her. Well, it's kind of hard to say," Rafa hesitated, struggling with how to characterize the situation, which was a complicated one. "Sort of. But the thing is, she's got this amazing friend . . ."

"Ha! I bet she does! Again Rafa? Really?" Pablo chided, both astounded by and envious of his friend's endless exploits.

"No, but seriously," Rafa laughed, unable to deny it was a familiar scenario. "This one is so hot! If you saw her, you'd totally understand!"

"Of course I would—I always do!"

The walk to the orchard didn't take long. In addition to almonds, the large plot had olive, carob, and fig trees. Rafa's grandfather had a sincere love for them all, and he rarely missed an opportunity to share his fascination with anyone who would listen—something altogether inevitable when he had a captive audience.

"Three thousand years!" he would say, emphatically shaking his hand high in the air, as though the gesture inspired even more awe than the words alone might have. What he was referring to, with just as much wonder and respect as each time before, was that the almonds had probably arrived with the Phoenicians who founded Málaga itself. It was even possible, he would add, that the trees had arrived still earlier, though that had never been proven for sure.

"The Romans," he would continue, "cultivated them as far back as the third century BC—BC! That's *antes de Cristo!* But, of course, it was the Arabs who covered the region with them."

He also liked to remind people that bitter almonds contained a substance that, when it came into contact with water, produced a poison so toxic a dose of twenty almonds could kill a man.

"On the other hand," he would offer, while his audience considered the previous ominous bit of trivia, "five or six can keep you from getting drunk!"

Pablo had heard that before, too. Unfortunately, in his experience at least, it had proven little more than a disappointing myth.

When he ran out of facts about almond trees, Rafa's grandfather would move onto the other species, his next most likely subject of praise being the olive.

"Oh yes," he would say with even more veneration. "Once again, we can thank the Phoenicians, since they brought them to these lands as well. However, like the Arabs with the almonds, it was the Romans who spread their cultivation far and wide. They were so successful, in fact, that they exported olive oil all the way to Rome itself!"

At some point, Rafa's grandfather was almost guaranteed to remind them that, in addition to being a symbol of peace, the olive branch appeared in the Bible many times, including when God announced the end of the great flood by sending Noah a dove with an olive branch in its mouth. And after touching on the various places in Greek mythology where the olive tree was also important, such as its use in making the crowns placed on Olympian victors, he would finish his summary of its glorious history by noting there was allegedly no other wood that would sprout new growth with such ease.

"If you get it wet, watch out! You'll have an olive branch growing out your door!"

Once they came full circle back to Rafa's grandfather's house, they all went their separate ways, since Rafa already had plans in town. Pablo was glad to have caught up with him, but he couldn't help but recall the sense of urgency he'd felt earlier in the day. He wondered what it had been about, since nothing seemed to have come of it.

He didn't get it. At times, feelings in his gut and stirrings in his bones seemed to provide him with perceptions and guidance that reason alone was powerless to explain. At others, what he thought was the voice of his intuition seemed little more than his imagination, leaving him feeling foolish, if not delusional.

How to know the difference?

It was time to pay Victor another visit. He was the one who had told him to listen. He was the only one who might understand.

19

There was someone else Pablo needed to talk to first.

He felt bad about how things had gone between them, about how it had abruptly, unnecessarily ended. He felt guilty for not being able to share with her what he had been feeling, for not being able to let her help.

He missed her.

Even still, although he could feel it was what he needed to do—although he had, in fact, decided it was what he was going to do—for several days Pablo had bullheadedly resisted. It was only when, like metal succumbing to the laws of physics and submitting to the unseen pull of a magnetic force, the insistence of his inner voice overcame the resistance of his shame and fear that he was finally compelled to go see Rosa.

Walking through the town hall plaza that afternoon on his way to the day care center, Pablo discovered Rosa standing with a small group waiting to catch the bus down the mountain.

His heart jumped. Was she leaving? She couldn't. Not yet. Not when he had finally mustered the courage to pay her a visit.

As though she felt the weight of Pablo's stare, Rosa looked up. Their eyes met. She nodded.

Pablo returned the gesture, unsure what to do next. Go say hello or continue on his way? Caught off guard, he felt drawn to her, yet hesitant, suddenly a school boy too shy to approach a pretty girl. What was he going to say? All the words he'd rehearsed a hundred times in his head—the apologies, the explanations, the entreaties—escaped him.

While Pablo grappled with his indecision, a mechanical rumbling approached the plaza's entrance. Each of the cobblestones underfoot began to tremble, like thousands of ice cubes being shaken from their mold. In the next instant the bus rounded the corner, unleashing the chaotic frenzy that inevitably accompanies the comings and goings of the masses.

Realizing he was about to miss his chance, Pablo darted over to Rosa.

His mind filled with questions, with things he wanted to say. Where are you going? How have you been? I'm sorry. I miss you. Forgive me.

Unfortunately, he was just in time to learn that he was too late.

"*¿Te vas?*" he asked, dispensing with formalities.

"Yeah, I'm going down to Málaga for a few days."

"Oh."

Passengers getting off the bus hurried to gather their belongings from the storage hold, while those waiting to depart rushed to do the opposite—many with an urgency suggesting they feared that, if they didn't move fast enough, the bus might leave without them.

"I guess I'll see you when you get back."

"Yeah, OK. See you," she said as she stepped up into the bus, unsure what to make of their brief, awkward interaction.

The bus departed soon after, squeezing into the narrow alley where it began its circuitous route out of town. In a precarious maneuver with almost no margin for error, it came within mere centimeters of the centuries-old Moorish tower, the walls of which had been scraped and gashed and streaked by countless instances when that margin had in fact been breached.

It wasn't until the tail lights vanished that Pablo discovered he was alone. The plaza, which only moments before had been a veritable circus—a cacophony of voices calling out and engines revving up, of doors eagerly thrown open and unceremoniously slammed shut, of joyous hellos and reluctant good-byes—had emptied out every bit as quickly as it had filled up. Even the old men almost always watching from the town hall veranda were nowhere to be found.

As he turned to go, Pablo was overcome by an unsettling sense of remorse. He shouldn't have waited. This was one instance in which he hadn't doubted what he was feeling. His inner voice had been clear.

If only he had listened.

20

Victor was sitting outside when he heard the telltale sound of his young friend's motorcycle. Setting down the sheet of paper he'd been reading, he secured the entire pile with the colorful tile fragment he used as a paperweight, lest the wind give into the temptation to browse through its contents.

Greetings were exchanged while Pablo took a seat, and Victor went inside to put on coffee.

To pass the time of what would be only the briefest of waits, Pablo picked up the book he'd noticed on his first visit. Letting it open to wherever its pages might fall, he came upon a man with the most curious of names: Averroës. The accompanying illustration depicted a striking figure with a majestic turban, well-kempt beard, and pensive, piercing gaze.

"So, in addition to your cave-dwelling philosophers, you're interested in the greats of the Islamic Golden Age as well?" the old man joked, catching him red-handed.

"Who's Averroës?" Pablo asked, the red now shooting from his hands to his face.

"The Commentator!" Victor enigmatically declared, setting down a tray with everything they would need once the coffee was ready.

"What do you mean?"

"His commentaries on Aristotle, which, after being translated to Latin, were almost single-handedly responsible for reintroducing Aristotle to the West. No small contribution! Although in Islamic philosophy he's much better known for his defense of reason, specifically as espoused by Greek philosophy, which had long been of paramount importance to Islamic thinking. However, it had come under attack from an immensely influential predecessor, Al-Ghazali. Al-Ghazali argued that revelation trumped reason, which he considered of only limited worth in only specific circumstances. Averroës, on the other hand—who, interestingly enough, was from just down the road, from Córdoba—insisted reason did in fact have a very important place. He maintained that, rather than contradictory, reason and revelation were complementary, two means to the same end."

Victor ducked back inside, returning with a silver *cafetera* whose full-bodied, satisfying aroma filled the air even before Victor had filled Pablo's cup.

"Fascinating to think that the battle between reason and revelation, science and religion, if you like, has been waged for so long—since the ancient Greeks, if not longer. And that this very land was the setting for such an important chapter of that debate, home to such an influential figure, someone of such importance not only to East but to West, to Islam and Christianity alike."

"The battle's pretty much over now, though, don't you think?" Pablo remarked, while Victor poured his coffee. "The only people who go to church are the old folks, and technology moves so fast it's hard to keep up."

"No doubt about that," Victor readily allowed, pouring his own cup. "But as far as the age-old debate, I think it might be a little premature to declare reason the undisputed winner."

"Why do you say that?"

"Because even today our own personal experiences regularly force us beyond its boundaries. Reason comes up short. We continue to observe and experience—to feel—things for which we're unable to imagine, let alone deduce, any sort of rational explanation. Or, when we do, those explanations just aren't good enough."

"Like when?" Pablo wondered, a breeze billowing through the nearby trees like a group of horsemen galloping around the bend of a trail.

"There's a perfect example."

"What?" Pablo asked, looking around as though Victor had seen something he hadn't. "Where?"

"Right here!" the old man gestured into the ostensible emptiness, taking childish delight in the irony. "The wind! If your knowledge that it's caused by the difference in the density between two air masses prevents you from finding wonder in a gentle breeze, does it also stop you from being awestruck when it envelops you on the mountaintop? When you feel its power, fearful that it well might carry you away? Or when you behold the inconceivable havoc it's capable of wreaking—the immeasurable force of something you can't see or touch, something that has no discernible form yet is capable of such astonishing devastation? Do you feel no sense of mystery then? Do you truly fail to sense something that defies the limits of your intellectual understanding of the physics involved?"

Pablo said nothing, listening as Victor continued.

"Then, of course, there's the miracle of birth—the glorious mystery of life itself! And its enigmatic corollary, death. Does your rational understanding of the biology of reproduction, of a sperm fertilizing an egg, take anything away from the indescribably profound moment in which you bear witness to another human being coming into the world? Or, instead, does what you feel forever alter your perspective in a way that no medical text could ever rival? On the other end of the journey, when you lose someone you love, are you satisfied with the physiological explanation that—regardless of whatever complications may have led up to the final moment—their heart simply stopped beating? Is that all you need to know? Is that all there is to know? Or, does the experience provoke in you feelings and questions for which reason alone is unable to provide satisfactory answers, leading you to keep looking, to seek them elsewhere?"

That struck close to home.

"Deductive reasoning almost never offers a man on his deathbed any reassurance as to what to expect on the other side, never mind insight about the meaning of the life he's leaving behind. And when a young mother throws herself onto her child's casket, rarely is the raw, blistering emotion she feels in her heart at all assuaged by the logical calculations of her mind. Inevitably, reason is impotent before her grief-stricken cries!"

Again Pablo couldn't help but think about when his father died, remembering how many times in desperation he had asked why. Over and over again. Coming up empty-handed each time, he never found any sort of explanation that might have somehow made his father's untimely demise make even the slightest bit of sense.

"And, what about love?" Victor laughed, visibly pleased with what he considered perhaps the best example yet. "Science tells us that falling in love is a chemical reaction in the brain! Socrates and Plato called it a mental disorder! And while the latter is undeniably harder to dispute than the former"—he laughed more heartily still—"it certainly seems to me that reducing love to mere physiological processes is a poignant example of reason failing to grasp—its inability to grasp—the breadth and depth of an integral part of the human experience."

"But there probably are chemical reactions going on when you're in love," Pablo proposed, unable to see why Victor might not find the idea credible.

"Of course there are," the old man allowed with no hesitation. "Lots of them! Probably more than we even know! For that matter, not just in your brain! From head to toe, the juices are flowing—no doubt about it! But that's not the point. The point is that there's so much more to love than those physiological processes—that the recognition of physiological corollaries to an experience does not inherently represent the totality of that experience. Neither does it negate other dimensions on which we might not have as firm a grasp. Oh yes, love is indeed a perfect example of a case where reason reaches its limits, where it has to stay behind in favor of some other way for us to make sense of our experiences as human beings, of the world in which we live, of our very realities."

Victor paused, taking a long, slow drink of his coffee.

"The bigger point, perhaps, is that as a result—and thankfully—the world, our everyday lives, continue to astound. At least until the day reason finally succeeds in explaining everything—which seems unlikely, given the more answers it finds, the more questions it uncovers. Never mind that a world without mystery would be sorely lacking!"

Pablo finally put down the book, helping himself to more coffee. Without pausing to consider whether he might be overstepping his bounds, he found himself asking, "Are you interested in Islam because your family used to be Muslim?"

First the Sufis. Now Arab philosophers. It was curious.

"Because we used to be Muslim!" Victor laughed. "Who told you that? Not that it's not true, but if you look in the history books that could probably be said for half the country! If you recall, my boy, the Moors were here for seven hundred years!"

"So your family did convert?" Pablo found the notion fascinating. The Arab period was the stuff of legend, an archway here, a cistern there, mysterious mystics buried in caves. Now it seemed to have come to life before his very eyes.

"Oh, quite possibly, hundreds of years ago! Who knows? An interesting bit of trivia at most. So much of religion is fluid, dependent on time and place, culture and politics. People kill each other defending their beliefs, but so often they forget how they inherited those beliefs. They forget that a king or a khan or a caliph came out of nowhere and forced them to choose between conversion or death. They forget their mosque was a church or their church was a mosque—and a pagan temple before that! So, yes, while it's interesting to think that part of the Spanish side of my family might have been Muslim, at this point it doesn't really matter."

"So you're not entirely Spanish? My mom said you lived here when you were a boy, but then your family left? And sometimes it sounds like maybe you have a little bit of an accent?"

"Ah, yes! *Mon petit accent*, as the French would say. Actually, as the French *do* say," Victor laughed again. "You're right about that. We were only here when I was very young. So, even though I've spoken Spanish all my life—sometimes more, sometimes less—I suppose the accent comes and goes."

"Then where did you grow up? Where'd you go when you left Spain?" Pablo didn't want to pry, but since Victor seemed open to sharing, he figured it was OK to ask.

"A more difficult question than you might think. Actually, you'd almost be better off asking where didn't we go," Victor replied, as though the question were exasperating. "We were always on the move, a band of vagabonds. I suppose you could say London was home base, but there was Paris, Stockholm, Istanbul. There were the years in Shanghai. There were stints elsewhere. Like I said, we lived all over."

Pablo was blown away.

Paris? Istanbul? Shanghai? Names he'd heard of. Places he'd seen in movies. Faraway, mythical places. Places that, in a sense, were even further removed from his experience than the Arab period, a distant past that still permeated his present, albeit in subtle, overlooked ways. But those places, rolling off Victor's tongue as easily as addresses down the street, they were exotic, as foreign to him as the moon in the sky. Who was this man who had not only visited, but called them home? Where else had he been? What else had he seen? And done? Once again, Pablo's own world, his tiny corner of a little province, felt so small.

"What's ultimately most important though is wherever I am right now."

"I was wondering about that, too. I mean, why are you here? My mom also said that your family owns a lot of land in the village?"

"Your mother seems to have done her homework! Yes,

well, probably the simplest answer is that I came to take care of some administrative matters, but I'm staying for some personal ones."

"So you'll be here a while?"

"More likely than not, but only time will tell. All I know for sure right now is that I'm looking forward to walking in the mountains, enjoying the fresh air and glorious sunshine, and tending to my garden."

Victor looked off into the distance, his expression almost wistful, incongruous with the upbeat tone of his comments.

"But enough about me—let's talk about you. What have you been up to? Have you been going with your gut and listening to your bones?" he asked, the glimmer returning to his eye.

"Actually, I have," Pablo confessed, grateful for the segue. He told Victor about the perplexing obsession that had followed his initial experiences, the ensuing confusion and doubt.

"The more I paid attention, the more it seemed like there was to hear. So then I started wondering if I was making it all up—and sometimes I really think I was. But other times what happened was definitely real—even though there was no logical explanation for it. It got really overwhelming."

"It seems that you've overdone it my friend," Victor commented.

"Why do you say that? I followed your advice—I tried to listen."

"Yes, but maybe a little too hard!" Victor joked.

"What do you mean?"

"I mean you've been overthinking it. I mean that instead of allowing yourself to slowly become more attuned to your inner voice, you've turned it into some sort of intellectual challenge, something to get a hold on by working hard enough at it, a puzzle to figure out. But that's not how it works. It's experiencing the mystery, opening yourself to how it feels. It's immersing yourself in the subtleties and nuances as it rattles your bones or whispers in your ear. It's not thinking, but feeling."

"But that's what I've been trying to do," Pablo protested, disheartened by Victor's assessment he'd been going about it all wrong. "It's just that sometimes I don't get what I hear."

"Ah, yes," said Victor, as though they'd stumbled upon a familiar problem. "By trying so hard to hear the voice of your intuition, you discovered other voices competing for your attention as well."

"Other voices?" wondered Pablo. "What other voices?" If the idea of one inner voice seemed odd enough, the revelation there might somehow be many—ones that were in competition, no less—almost seemed cause for concern.

"Of your desires, your hopes, your fears . . . any number of them, I would guess, although those are certainly the most obvious ones."

"Then how am I supposed to figure out which one to listen to? I don't understand—it's so confusing. It's like there are all these people talking to me, but I can't see their faces and I don't recognize their voices. So, I don't know who to trust."

"All those voices can indeed make you crazy. It's like listening to a noisy radio playing several stations at once. Especially when you're overwhelmed, the other voices can cloud out your intuition. Fortunately, there are ways to distinguish its voice from the others—to tune into just that one station, so to speak."

"How?"

"First of all, you take a deep breath. You have to calm yourself, so you can calm them as well. When you do, just like when those insects in the flowers pause from their work and, instead of whirling blurs on the air, we're able to see their true forms and colors, you'll be better able to recognize each of the voices for what they really are."

"OK, but once all those voices are calm or whatever, I still don't get how I'm supposed to figure out which one's my intuition."

"You can start by asking whether your own doubts or desires are at the root of what you're hearing. In other words, are you somehow invested in what those voices have to say?"

"How can I tell?"

"You consider each of them as honestly and objectively as you can."

"And which one is my intuition?" Pablo asked, still not sure he followed.

"The one that is not a manifestation of your own desires, doubts, or fears. The one that, rather than speaking on behalf of yourself, almost seems to come from someplace independent of or beyond your self."

"I kind of get it," said Pablo after a moment, sensing something familiar in what Victor was describing. "But I don't think I understand completely."

"Of course not, and that's OK," Victor reassured him. "You have to experience what I'm talking about in order to genuinely internalize it. The good news is that you already have—don't lose sight of that. And, more importantly, don't forget what those experiences felt like."

"You mean like the hike?"

"A perfect example. When you felt compelled to sit down in the middle of the trail, was it because you had some sort of desire to stop? Did you stop because you were tired or wanted to enjoy the view or had some other motive?"

"Not at all. I was just walking, and I suddenly got this weird feeling that I was supposed to stop."

"And is it safe to presume that neither did you stop because you were afraid of continuing nor because you were overcome with doubts about what might happen if you kept going?"

"Of course not," Pablo replied, the very idea seeming laughable. "I was just taking a walk, like I always do. What would I be afraid of?"

"Exactly. It wasn't that for some reason you wanted to stop, nor that you were afraid to continue. Stopping and sitting, when you heard your inner voice urge you to do so, wasn't about your own desires or fears, or any other motivation stemming from yourself. It was rooted in something else, something beyond or independent of your own will. At the same time, though, it came from within you. And, because when it did you were calm, clearheaded, and open, you were able to feel, acknowledge, and act upon it."

"OK," Pablo continued, "but why would my intuition stop me so I can watch some goats? What's the big deal?"

"The big deal? I don't know. Is there one? Does there have to be? What if there's not? Would that rule out the possibility your intuition played a role?" Victor countered, sharing none of Pablo's concern. "Although I must say that when you first described it, it sounded as though it was in fact a very big deal at the time! Regardless, although what happened on the hike or with the bread or any of your other experiences may seem trivial, they're the ones of which your days—your very life—are comprised. As such, they're not exactly inconsequential."

"I don't know," Pablo hesitated, still not convinced. "Buying bread really doesn't seem like that big a deal."

"Not unless it's the last loaf, right?"

Pablo couldn't help but laugh.

"It's like electricity," Victor maintained, unwavering. "It's always there, ready to power appliances big or small. By the same token, your intuition is always there, ready to offer guidance in situations that may seem of little importance just as readily as it is in those that could prove life changing."

Victor lifted the top of the cafetera to see how much coffee was left, before adding, "I suppose it's a question of what kind of life you want to live, of how present you want to be."

"How present?"

"Take right now. How present are you really?" Victor challenged, moving in closer and narrowing his eyes. "Are you totally focused on our conversation or only partially engaged, preoccupied by other things that might be on your mind? Are you just waiting for the conversation to be over, after which you won't give it much more thought, or are you eager to grasp all it might have to offer?"

"Oh, no, no—I'm definitely listening," Pablo insisted, fearing Victor doubted the extent and sincerity of his interest.

"But that's just it—it's not only about listening!" Victor

proclaimed, zeroing in on the heart of the matter like a bullfighter about to make his *estocada*, or death thrust of the sword. "It's about using all your faculties—not just your hearing and your sight and all the other usual suspects, but your intuition, as well. After all, just because your experiences thus far have been limited to seemingly mundane happenings of little consequence, doesn't mean your intuition won't eventually be instrumental with regards to ones with further-reaching ramifications."

"You think so?" wondered Pablo. It was hard to imagine how something that still felt like little more than an intriguing novelty could ultimately prove to have some sort of monumental importance.

"Absolutely—but only if you let it. Again, it's a choice. No one is going to force you to open your eyes, listen to what you hear, or, most of all, be attuned to what you feel, including your intuition. You have to make the effort."

21

As he rode his motorcycle down the mountain, Pablo was surprised by how excited he was to get out of the village. He felt good, nothing before him but the exhilarating freedom and boundless possibility of the open road.

The road in question was the Mediterranean Highway, a mighty, rolling thoroughfare bordered by the glistening, deep-blue waters of the sea on one side and the arid heights of the coastal ranges on the other. There were perfect rows of olive trees, horse farms, and greenhouses and even occasional patches of unadulterated scrub.

The closer Pablo got to his destination, the more the scenery changed. Farms, orchards, and pastoral hillsides were replaced by more recent, less picturesque additions to the landscape: vacation complexes being hastily erected on any parcel deemed remotely suited to serving as a building site. Entire mountaintops were being leveled into bare plateaus where developments were being crammed like books piled onto overcrowded shelves.

Having seen it all before, he did his best to ignore it, speeding past a proliferation of garish billboards promising unimaginable luxuries at unheard-of prices. Shutting out an endless succession of flags, banners, and streamers heralding one unattended party after another, he focused on the road, especially since the number of cars seemed to quadruple from one moment to the next. Not long after, the mountains parted like the curtain on an opening act, and the city came into view below.

Pablo hadn't been to Málaga for a couple of months. It always seemed much further than it was, as though instead of an hour, it were an entire world away. And, in a sense, that was true. His world consisted of the village, the town in the valley, and the one on the sea, with the beaches and clubs. He didn't really have much need for Málaga and, if it weren't for the fact that his sister lived there, it would have come up on his radar even less.

María lived not far from the Plaza de la Merced, Málaga's largest and perhaps most culturally significant square, given that its most famous citizen, Pablo Picasso, was born in a house on one of its corners. Countless cafés, bars, and restaurants occupied the ground floors of the surrounding buildings, four- or five-story structures with simple, classic façades. On weekends, hordes of revelers not only overtook the nearby establishments but occupied the plaza itself into the wee hours.

Far from indulging in late-night debauchery, Pablo was in Málaga to spend the afternoon with his family. His mother still hadn't convinced him to stay for an extended period, but at least she'd scored this partial victory.

Leaving his motorcycle where he always left it—in the side street next to the kebab shop—he turned the corner to walk the short distance to the apartment building.

There she was, outside waiting for a gyro.

"Rosa!" he called out in disbelief. Although seeing her in the village was the most natural thing in the world, running into her in Málaga felt so much more random.

"Pablo? What are you doing here?" She looked as though she'd seen a ghost.

"Lunch at my sister's. My mom finally convinced me to get out of the village."

Rosa nodded but said nothing, the surprise still registering.

"Looks like the whole village is here!"

Pablo turned to find Rafa coming out of the restaurant.

"Sorry I took so long—there was a line," he explained, flashing a smile. "What are you doing down here?"

Pablo repeated what he had just told Rosa, before wondering out loud, "Did Pepa come, too?"

"She changed her mind at the last minute," Rafa explained as he reached for his order, which was now dangling at the end of a server's outstretched arm.

"She had a test," Rosa added.

"Oh," said Pablo, as Rafa began pulling back the foil on his gyro. Rosa expectantly looked inside the shop for hers.

Pablo wasn't sure what to do. Under ordinary circumstances, he would have paused to chat with his friends. But these weren't ordinary circumstances. Other than his ill-fated attempt at the bus stop, he and Rosa hadn't talked since the breakup. They weren't supposed to have crossed paths in Málaga. He felt as though he were crashing a party, the entire situation distressingly awkward. The only thing that felt right was to be on his way.

"OK, well, I should get to my sister's. I'll see you guys up in the village."

"Yeah, OK. *Nos vemos*," Rafa said, covering his mouth with one hand.

"See you," said Rosa, almost as if Pablo had said something to upset her.

Walking toward his sister's, again Pablo regretted not having gone to see Rosa when he knew he should have. Again he kicked himself for the oversight, for silencing his inner voice. All the worse that he hadn't been able to say anything just now, since Rafa had been there, too.

It would have to wait.

22

If the commotion on the other end of the intercom were to believed, the family gathering was already in full swing. Turi and Trini met him at the elevator, each claiming one leg in the battle for their uncle's attention. Already struggling to keep up with not one but two conversations, he almost thought twice about stepping into the apartment. Perhaps all the time alone had made him forget what to expect at a family get-together.

Things didn't slow down once inside. A soccer match blared on the TV. Familiar voices in the kitchen chattered and exclaimed and laughed over chopping, clanging, and whirling, all muffled by the jet-engine suction of an oven fan. Kids ran around the apartment in a constant state of hysteria, not only Turi and Trini, but a couple of others, too.

Pablo's expression betraying his struggle to shift from mountaintop hermit to son, brother, and uncle, his brother-in-law, Miguel, quickly came to the rescue, handing him a beer. Pablo felt like an astronaut touching down in the Plaza del Sol after spending months alone orbiting the Earth. He'd be fine, but he needed a moment—and *una caña*—to acclimate.

Miguel's cousin Daniel was there, as was his wife Lola, which explained the unidentified youngsters carousing with Pablo's niece and nephew. Introductions took place, updates were given about the game, and niceties exchanged about his trip down. Out of nowhere, his mother appeared at his side, in a single breath welcoming him, letting him know she was glad he was there, and making sure he didn't need anything. Before he could get a word in edgewise—other than perfunctory *yeses* and *nos*—she'd disappeared back into the kitchen, already calling out something about not letting the *croquetas* fry too long.

Although Miguel and María had a spacious apartment, the dining room wasn't particularly large. As such, when the time came to eat it was with no small effort that everyone squeezed around the table, the children banished to their own in the living room.

Conversation was loud and lively. Given that two couples with two children each were in attendance, the kids' achievements were repeatedly lauded, while again and again the never-ending challenges of parenting were decried. The women periodically got up to check on the little ones, taking them more food or settling minor spats, while the men inevitably turned the subject back to soccer, the only part of the conversation in which Pablo had much to say. Even then, he kept mostly to himself, still not up to shouting over the others to be heard.

"I hope you're not getting too comfortable up there by yourself," Carmen said midway through the meal, as she took another piece of bread.

"Feel free to stay down here as long as you like," he retorted, prompting smirks around the table.

"Sounds like Pablito is enjoying having the bachelor pad all to himself!" Miguel observed.

"Yeah, well, I'm about to ruin the party. Your sister and brother-in-law are kicking me out."

"We're not kicking her out," María was quick to interject with a roll of the eyes, pouring herself a glass of wine. "Miguel's parents are coming from Madrid. We told *Mamá* there was room for everyone—they're not even going to be here that long, and his mom loves her—but she doesn't want to stay."

"I'd only be in the way. Besides, I've been down here long enough. I'm ready to get home."

Pablo was glad for the advance warning. Miguel was right. Although he'd hardly been in the best of spirits, he had relished—and gotten used to—having the house to himself.

Once the table had been cleared and everyone was settled back in the living room, the moment came that Pablo recognized as the end to his familial obligations. All eyes once again glued to the TV, there was no reason he had to stick around any longer. In about fifteen minutes, half the room would be asleep.

"You're leaving so soon?" his mother protested, as he headed for the door.

"*Mamá*, everyone's nodding off, and I want to see Sergio before I go home."

"OK, then. I'm just glad you came," she said, brushing something off his shirt and handing him his helmet. "Be careful on your way back, and I'll see you in a couple days."

23

Pablo's friend Sergio had moved from the village to Málaga a little over a year earlier, and he and his girlfriend Tere had recently opened a small café on a side street off the Plaza de la Merced. It wasn't easy, given the larger competitors on the Plaza itself. Nonetheless, they'd been able to carve out their own niche of loyal customers who appreciated the more intimate, off-the-beaten-path charm of the place.

Pablo had told Sergio he would try to stop by, and was glad when he saw him smoking a cigarette on a bench outside the café. The two exchanged greetings, and Sergio ushered Pablo inside.

The locale was a simple one consisting of just four tables, not including the bench and two tables out front. A display case full of sandwiches, desserts, and beverages ran along the back. Behind it, Tere, an attractive, petite blonde, sat on a stool, presiding over the establishment like a queen waiting for her subjects to approach the throne. Overhead was a small menu board, while random photos, announcements, and event flyers were posted on the wall to the right and, to the left, abstract paintings by a local artist were on exhibit.

As a lever snapped back and forth like someone cracking a whip, followed by dramatic steam-engine bursts of vapor and, finally, the gentle trickle of midnight-black into star-white, Pablo and Sergio started catching up. An espresso later, the two young men struck out on their own, stopping by Sergio's apartment, where Pablo marveled at the extensive collection of music Sergio had downloaded from file-sharing sites on the Web.

Eventually noticing time slipping away, the two friends begrudgingly disconnected from the virtual world and reengaged with the material one, heading for Larios Street, formerly Málaga's main avenue, now a vast pedestrian zone. As they made their way there, Pablo noticed lots of construction was still underway on the narrow side streets. Many of the elegant nineteenth-century façades were being refurbished as the whole area continued to undergo an extensive, prolonged facelift.

Sergio led Pablo to a restaurant on the Plaza de la Constitución, the heart of the city and a perfect place to people watch. And there were lots of people. Not only Spaniards, but lots of tourists as well, some in hand-holding pairs, others in camera-toting groups, most having stepped off the cruise ship docked in the port for the day.

Málaga had plenty to offer visitors, from Larios Street itself, lined with countless stores and enlivened by almost as many street performers, to the quaint alleyways adjoining it, an endless succession of smaller shops, inviting bars, and bustling restaurants. The Picasso museum, housed in a beautiful sixteenth-century palace, was also a major attraction, as was the Alcazaba, a fortified mountaintop complex from which a long line of Moorish rulers had governed for nearly five hundred years. There were countless other attractions as well, including the massive Renaissance cathedral, a well-preserved Roman amphitheater, and a renowned museum of modern art.

At the moment, however, Pablo was perfectly content with his seat on the square. In fact, he was transfixed, as though seeing it all for the first time, when in reality none of it was even remotely new to him. The majestic buildings peering proudly onto the plaza. The vast space of the plaza itself, simultaneously looking up to and making room for the sky. The endless streams of people, locals and foreigners, young and old, guys and girls. Everywhere he looked, it seemed, still more beautiful girls! At times he was so distracted he could hardly focus on his conversation with Sergio.

When Sergio ran to a kiosk for more cigarettes, Pablo was momentarily left to himself. He took another sip of beer and glanced down the bustling pedestrian street. The entire scene was so alive. As his eyes darted from one curiosity to another, his pulse quickened and his thoughts began to race.

"I don't know what you're still doing up in the village!" Sergio had chided.

Pablo was suddenly, profoundly unsure himself.

He hadn't seen it coming. He didn't know what to make of it. He almost felt guilty, as though he were indulging in thoughts he wasn't sure he was supposed to have. He'd always taken it for granted he'd be in the village.

That wasn't to say he'd never thought about leaving. Of course, he had. It was only natural. His sister and his friends like Sergio had moved to Málaga. His cousin Juan had gone all the way to Barcelona and tried to convince him to come along. His parents had always made it clear he could go to college—an idea he still occasionally entertained, though it never really seemed that imperative.

He was happy in the village.

At least he had been.

He looked around again. So much energy and excitement, possibility and promise. Like vines rising up from the ground, they snaked upward, seducing him, forcing him to open his eyes, to see the familiar in an unfamiliar way. He'd always taken Málaga for granted. He'd never seen it like this before. Like the tourists, he, too, an outsider appreciating for the first time what had drawn them from afar.

The village was so small.

Once Sergio came back, another beer gave way to an aimless, leisurely stroll that included spontaneous stops in motorcycle and music shops, as well as random encounters with several of Sergio's friends. Eventually coming full circle, they returned to the café for a parting coffee.

As he rode out of town two espressos later—following the road along the water, as opposed to heading straight for the highway—he passed the cruise ship that, like some sort of Trojan seahorse, had sent the countless legions of tourists into Málaga's city center, overtaking it for the day.

Where had they come from? What had they seen? Where were they headed next?

Before proceeding along La Malagueta, with its health-conscious city dwellers running up and down its luxuriant sands, he made his way past the old lighthouse. Peering out toward the vast, mysterious horizon, it, too, seemed to be urging him to direct his own gaze into the unknown.

He pulled over.

He didn't know why. He just knew it felt right.

Imperative, even.

He got off his bike, still not sure what he was doing exactly. For a moment he was torn. He needed to get home. Stopping felt like an unnecessary indulgence.

He took a deep breath, slowing his thoughts just enough to regain perspective. Why was he in such a hurry? Whatever he had to do back in the village, five minutes wasn't going to matter.

He walked over to the beach, taking off his shoes and making his way toward the water. The soft sand felt good on his feet.

The sun was sinking lower in the sky, streaking it with violets, oranges, pinks, and blues. He sat down, again peering toward the horizon. Waves lapped the shore, and a warm breeze came off the water, salty. A seagull squawked overhead. Even that was soothing. All of it was. It was perfect, in fact.

For a moment there was nothing else.

24

A few days later Pablo rode up to the house and saw the car in the garage.

She was back.

He walked in to the swish of the washing machine, its agitator defiantly jerking back and forth like a child refusing to budge. The windows had all been thrown open, the house breathing a long-overdue sigh of relief. The vacuum cleaner was running and something was baking, the fresh aroma stirring Pablo's stomach to life. She couldn't have been home long but, true to form, his mother hadn't waited a minute to get to work.

"*¡Hola, Mamá!*" he called over the drone of the vacuum.

"*¡Hola, hijo!*" came in return from the living room. "*¡Oye!* Can you put the records back? I started to, but they're all mixed up."

"*Sí, Mamá.*"

"And if you have any other clothes you want washed, will you bring them downstairs?"

"*Sí, Mamá.*"

The vacuum cleaner stopped, its whirl replaced by the centrifugal sound of the cord being sucked back into the machine, ending with a painful snap.

"I need your help Friday," she said, coming around the corner with the vacuum, pausing to give him two kisses.

"With what?" he asked, following her into the kitchen, where it smelled even better than when he'd walked into the house. He wondered what she was making.

"The store. The insurance company is sending someone up to assess the damage. I'd like for you to be there. I need a second pair of ears."

The store. It was odd. Just like his mom, seemingly out of nowhere it was back. Although he hadn't realized it until then, he'd essentially put the store out of his mind, relegating it to some far-off, intangible place and time from which it might never return. It was as though they'd scooped up its ashes and interred them along with his father's.

It was too painful. He hadn't wanted to think about that night. He hadn't wanted to think about the store itself, the loss of it.

He no longer had a choice. Now, for the first time since the night of the fire, he was going to have to go back.

He wasn't sure he was ready.

25

Pablo didn't stay home for long. His mother hardly ever sat still, her activity and chatter obliterating the peace and quiet that had been his sanctuary.

Walking up the alley, he wasn't sure where he was headed. He might go find Jorge or Rafa. Maybe he'd head up to the reserve. Or, he could turn back around, grab his motorcycle, and go down to town. It really didn't matter; he just needed to be out of the house.

Wandering past the pub on the way to the main plaza, something caught his eye.

Backtracking to do a double take, his heart skipped a beat.

His mom wasn't the only one who was back.

The last place he wanted to go was a crowded bar. It almost defeated the point of getting out of the house. But he had to talk to her.

The pub was a warm, traditional place with basic, almost nondescript tables and chairs, exposed wood beams, and two large kegs in the wall behind the bar. The lighting fixtures, as well as the bars on the windows, were all done in a traditional wrought-iron style that vaguely recalled the Middle Ages. Although not a restaurant, per se, a variety of tapas was on offer, including *jamón serrano*, several legs of which dangled overhead. A little inverted umbrella stuck into each caught the grease that, otherwise, might have fallen like pigeon droppings onto unsuspecting patrons.

The thunderous roar of animated conversations, raucous laughter, and heated debates assaulted Pablo as he made his entrance. Chairs slid across the floor like chess pieces on a board, moved over and over to accommodate never-ending comings and goings. The sound of glass on glass rose above it all, the bartender busily clearing away drinks emptied almost as fast as the pistachios served alongside them were cracked from their shells. A light cloud of smoke did its shape-shifting dance over the lively, festive scene, alone, perhaps, in appreciating the muffled music below it.

Rosa was sitting on a stool at the bar. She and Pepa were laughing hysterically.

"*Muy buenas*," Pablo called from behind them.

"Oh, hey," said Rosa, wiping a couple of tears from her eyes as she regained her composure.

"You're back," Pablo observed, after kisses were exchanged all around.

"Yeah, I got back a couple days ago."

"You know what, I think I'm going to take off," Pepa said, her hair falling forward as she reached for her bag.

"*¿En serio?*" Rosa asked, disappointed. "Come on, at least stay for one more."

"Yeah, don't leave on my account," Pablo insisted.

"No, it's not that," she assured him. "I told my mom I'd go down to town with her."

"OK, *guapa*. We'll talk tomorrow then," said Rosa, setting off another flurry of kisses.

"*Sí, sí, hasta mañana*," Pepa said as she turned to go, only to get held up by a group of friends near the door.

His stomach tied in knots, Pablo braced himself for a difficult conversation. He'd known her almost all his life, but Rosa suddenly felt like an intimidating stranger.

"Can we talk?"

"Sure," she said, finishing her beer. "Do you want one?"

"Actually, I do."

"*Dos cañas, porfa,*" Rosa called to the bartender. "So what's up?"

Pablo didn't know where to begin.

"I don't know. I guess . . . I guess I just feel bad about how things ended between us."

"I know. Me, too. But it was really hard for me when you shut down like that. I didn't know where you went or when—or even if—you were going to come back."

The bartender set down the beers.

"What happened was so, so horrible," she said, pausing to take a deep breath. "But it felt like you didn't even want me around."

He had never meant to make her feel that way. His heart ached to know he had.

"I'm really sorry. I couldn't feel anything. Or, actually, maybe I felt too much, and I just couldn't make sense of it. And then everyone kept looking at me like 'why won't you say something.' But the words just stopped coming. It wasn't until the shock started to wear off, that's when I kind of started making sense of what happened."

He wanted her to see he hadn't meant to drive her away. He wanted her to understand how painful and confounding his struggles had been, how alone he'd felt.

"It takes a long time to get over something like that, Pablo. A really long time."

He took a drink of his beer, building up his courage.

"Do you think . . ."

Second guessing himself, he hesitated.

"Do I think what?" Rosa asked.

He could spend forever looking for the right words. He'd never find them. He just had to come out with it.

"I want to get back together."

Now that he'd said it, it was as if the entire bar had been silenced. The only sound that mattered, the only frequency to which Pablo was tuned, was Rosa's.

But Rosa had gone quiet. Looking straight ahead, she

focused on her glass, drops running down its side as though it, too, had gotten caught up in the emotion.

"Pablo," she eventually said, reluctantly, "I don't know."

"I didn't mean to shut you out. I really didn't."

He wanted her to understand. He wanted her back.

"I know, Pablo. I know. I believe you—it's not that. Honestly, it's not."

"But?"

She hesitated. Again she considered what she was about to say. She took another drink.

"Pablo, things happen for a reason. You're still going through so much. And since we broke up, I've been giving a lot of thought to what I want. I'm just not sure. You're so important to me, Pablo. You really are—and you always will be. But I don't think we're supposed to be together right now."

Pablo felt as though someone had knocked the stool out from under him. Blindsided. He couldn't believe his ears. It hadn't even occurred to him she wouldn't want him back. Not deep down inside. Naive though it might have been, in his mind what had happened was a horrible misunderstanding, a wrong that would be righted once they talked it out.

He felt like a fool, his heart broken a second time.

He didn't know what to say. Rosa looked at him, then back at her beer.

"You don't even want to talk about it?" he asked, more to break the silence than anything else. She had given him her answer.

She smiled slightly, but said nothing. Her expression reminded him of so many he'd seen at the funeral. He didn't like it. He didn't want it.

He turned to leave, still clinging to the hope she might say something to stop him. He longed for her to have a sudden change of heart.

She didn't.

Making his way to the door, Pablo absent-mindedly acknowledged Rafa as he came in but didn't stop to talk.

He had to get out of there.

26

It was strange to be back at the store. Or what was left of it. Like peeling off a scab to discover how little the wound has actually healed.

Carmen and Pablo had made small talk on the short jaunt there. Both were nervous, though neither wanted to admit it. It helped that the adjuster was already waiting for them when they arrived. They were forced to put up a convincing front.

Carmen fared better than Pablo. As far as she was concerned, she had no choice: she had to be all business. In her mind, the store's very future was at stake. She couldn't afford to miss a beat. So she carefully watched the adjuster's work. She questioned his assumptions. She corrected and clarified his understanding of the facts. She looked over his shoulder, and she breathed down his neck.

It was a good thing she had the situation under control—the adjuster practically squirming under her thumb—since Pablo was of so little use.

Stepping foot in the store was like stepping back in time. The sight of it shocked him, the family's livelihood charred almost beyond recognition, in shambles. The space itself was like a bombed-out church, a holy place desecrated. It took him not only back to the night of the fire but to the time before.

He relived the store's happy past. He again bore witness to its tragic destruction. He feared for its uncertain future. Even if he had tried not to, the lingering smell of smoke, the sight of whitewash turned black, the heart-wrenching devastation inside would have made it impossible.

He beheld the largest of the fallen rafters. Was that the one? Was that where it had happened? It felt like visiting a crime scene, face-to-face with despicable horror, forced to look it right in the eyes.

While his mom and the adjuster carefully navigated fallen plaster, twisted metal, and broken glass on their way to the back room, Pablo stayed behind. His eyes went up and down each aisle, imagining the chaotic, contorted shelves restocked with goods. He saw new panes on the coolers, and he heard their distinctive hum as though it had never been interrupted. The door swung open, a different bell picking up where the old one had left off, heralding a familiar succession of beloved faces.

It pained him that his father's wouldn't be among them. When he failed to see his own, he wasn't sure what to make of it.

Once his duty had been fulfilled, Pablo left the store behind without looking back. He needed to put as much space as possible between him and it. He needed to shake it off, to get back to the place he'd gotten to after weeks away from the horror, that tenuous but comparatively safe distance. Not that it would be easy. No matter how far he ran, he'd carry the store with him, painful memories and difficult emotions having shot back to the surface like blood to the skin.

Easily tracking him down, Pablo was pleased to discover Jorge had some time on his hands. Soon they were driving down the mountain.

Pablo felt better once they got to the valley floor, as if grounded in a literal sense. Yet as the dark, waxy leaves of row after row of avocado trees flew by, he was still agitated.

"Keep going," he said.

"I thought you said you wanted to grab a beer in town."

"I did. But now I feel like we should keep going. Don't turn—just go straight."

"So you want to go down to the coast?"

"Yeah, let's do that. Let's go to the coast."

The town rose out of the plains like an actor taking to the stage before an empty audience, ignored in the distance. The highway's invitations east to Almería and west to Málaga were declined without explanation, and the mall came and went without seducing them with any of its worldly temptations.

The hustle and bustle of the seaside town followed. Chaotic, narrow one-way side streets. Banks and hotels, cafés and restaurants, shops, kiosks, and lottery vendors who never took off their shades. All of it rendered in a soulless architecture that failed to think outside steel-and-concrete boxes, the town's history reduced to rubble by both civil war and a notion of progress that favored fish and chips over fishing villages.

Jorge found a parking spot along the promenade, which local officials had dubiously touted as "the most beautiful beachfront walkway in Europe." Regardless of how well it truly fared in comparison to its countless counterparts across the continent, there was no question it served as a pleasant buffer zone between the beach and the hotels and apartment blocks lining it.

Pablo and Jorge left the car behind and cut through the green space, passing through the tall, majestic palms, smaller, fragrant pines, and manicured flower beds that acted as a gateway to the vast expanse of sand.

No sooner did the water come into sight than Pablo made a break for it.

"*Pero tío*, what are you doing?" Jorge exclaimed.

Before he knew it, Pablo had left most of his clothes behind, just like he had his friend. His jaw dropping to the sand like an anchor to the seafloor, all Jorge could do was double over with laughter.

"What are you doing?" he called out between guffaws.

Pablo didn't answer. He didn't even hear. Not over the

sound of the waves. Not over the deafening confusion of his thoughts or the overwhelming convulsions of his tears. Saline like the sea itself, drop by drop they became part of it, as though welcomed home.

And then a cry. Of defiance. Of anger, frustration, fatigue. Of hope and determination.

The cold water enveloped him. It consoled and cooled him, like it might an iron taken out of the fire. It offered to carry him away.

Looking to the horizon, Pablo let his body rise and fall to the rhythm of the waves. The offer was tempting, to find a current and go wherever the water might take him. He could hear it beckoning. He could feel its pull. He longed to surrender.

In time, he headed back to shore, ignoring shocked looks and suppressed laughter as he emerged from the sea. Struggling with only modest success to hold up his saturated underpants, he lumbered up the beach.

"What are you doing?" Jorge asked, laughing again as he handed him his shorts. Pablo may not have been embarrassed by the attention, but he was.

"I have got to get out of here," Pablo said with calm resignation, as much to himself as to Jorge. "I have to get out of here."

"What do you mean?"

Still confused by Pablo's unexpected antics, Jorge didn't follow.

Pablo took off his underpants and quickly put on his shorts. Spreading his shirt out on the sand, he lay down and stared up at the sky. Puffy white clouds rushed inland like an armada of airborne ships, while gentle waves cast ashore a light salty spray. After the shock of his dip in the sea, his nerve endings felt as though they were on fire. His mind was in overdrive.

"I just don't know what I'm supposed to do."

It was like knowing he had to sing a song with all his heart but having no idea what the words were. It was like preparing to give the performance of a lifetime, without ever having seen the script.

"I still have no idea what you're talking about."

"I've got to get out of the village," Pablo said, turning to look Jorge in the eyes.

"Really? Leave?"

Jorge hadn't seen that coming, especially from Pablo.

"Where're you going to go? You mean like Málaga?"

Málaga was the natural choice. It was, after all, where almost anyone who left the village went, at least as the first stepping stone. It was close. His sister was there. Sergio was there. Other people he knew were there. It made sense.

"I don't know," Pablo mused, as nearby a scuffle over the remains of a melon broke out between a pair of impossibly immaculate gulls. "I don't know where. I don't think that's even the point. I just know I have to leave. I can feel it."

27

Clinging tenaciously to the curves in the mountainside, struggling upward, plummeting downward as though in an uncontrollable free fall: few things felt better than the freedom of speeding along the twists and turns and ups and downs of the open road. Aggressively tackling it all, Pablo left his preoccupations scattered in his wake like trash thrown out a car-door window, leaving everything—the village, his problems, the future—behind. No matter what was on his mind, the intoxicating combination of the power of his motorcycle, the wind in his face, and the surroundings rendered a blur never failed to help him forget, leaving him as clear and open as the road itself.

All the better, given the question he was grappling with today.

Could he really leave?

Again he thought about all the people who had, whether for school, jobs, or just to get out. Thinking about them now, his imagination ran away with itself like they had from the village, filling him with a mix of admiration, envy, and longing.

What would his mom say? Would she let him go? What if she tried to stop him? He'd never even mentioned wanting to leave. There had never been any reason. If he did now, he'd be catching her completely off guard.

What about the store? Who would replace him? There were always people looking for work, but could he put his mother into the position of having to hire someone new, given everything else she had to worry about to reopen? On the other hand, maybe it would be perfect timing, just one more part of a fresh start.

Then there was the village itself, which he couldn't help but contemplate as he raced along the stunning rural routes surrounding it. The rugged mountains, whose sharp, barren peaks were visible in all directions. The endless orchards of almonds, olives, and grapes. His favorite places, where he was always sure to run into friends. And, of course, the nature reserve, with its spectacular views and the beloved goats, eagles, and other wildlife that called it home. If he were to leave, he would really miss all that.

Again he wondered, could he actually do it?

28

The mallet dropped down hard on the almond, its shell splintering into countless pieces, reluctantly surrendering the tear-shaped jewel for which, until then, it had served as such effective, ostensibly impenetrable armor.

"So, you were just out for a ride?" Victor asked, as he tossed the almond into a bowl with the rest of his slowly expanding trove.

"Yeah, I wasn't going anywhere in particular," Pablo responded.

"Of that you can never be sure!" the old man joked, a knowing sparkle in his eye.

"Actually, that's what I needed to talk to you about," Pablo conceded, a translucent, golden strand of honey glistening on the end of his teaspoon.

"About where you're going?"

"Yeah. I guess. I mean, something like that." Pablo wasn't even sure where to begin. "Something happened. You were right—like with the bread or the goats, but way bigger."

"Something?" Victor asked, his eyes not straying from the task at hand. Methodically selecting another almond from the burlap sack next to him, he rolled it around until it came to rest in a relatively stable position.

"I think I have to leave."

"You *think* you have to leave?" Victor echoed, again letting the mallet fall.

"I don't know how to explain it. I guess it first hit me in Málaga, and then afterward at the beach. And when I was in the water, I really felt it, then, too. But what's weird is that it's not specifically about any of that. I just feel it. That's what I was trying to say—it's like the bread or the goats, but way stronger. I don't know . . ."

"Don't know what?"

"Could I really do it? It almost feels like I have to. But it's so out of the blue. There's a lot I'd have to figure out. What would my mom say? What about the store? And where would I go? I don't even know."

"That's just it, you don't know," Victor agreed. "So no need to consider the situation based on questions to which you don't—and can't possibly—have the answers. You don't know how your mother will react. You don't know who will fill your place at the store. You don't know the answers to those or countless other questions, innumerable what-ifs, about where you're going or when you're coming back or if you even are! And for now, that's OK. All that matters is that you feel compelled to leave. Trust that, and take it one step at a time."

Another impact revealed yet another treasure certain to prove a tasty treat later on.

"So, what are your options?"

"I have no idea. I feel a pull, but I honestly don't know where. It's weird. I'm not sure what to do."

"Something," said Victor nonchalantly, as he reached into the sack for another almond. "Anything."

"Yeah, but like what?" Pablo asked, hoping for more tangible guidance.

"Anything," Victor reiterated with a shrug.

"I don't get it." Pablo wished Victor would set aside the almonds and focus solely on their conversation. Even so, unable to resist the temptation, he helped himself to a few.

"The issue is much less about *what* you do than it is about your simply doing *something*—anything that might get you started."

"Anything?" asked Pablo incredulously.

"Yes, anything. Use your imagination! You feel a pull, open yourself to where it takes you. Get a job in Málaga. Look at colleges. Plan a trip. Go home right now, pack your bags, and hitchhike across the country! It doesn't matter. Your intuition is doing its part, do yours! There are countless roads out of the village. You just have to set foot on one, which in turn will lead to others, until you eventually find one that truly resonates. The point is simply to do something—anything—to kick things off. It's the same with any new endeavor. When you open one door, others will follow. As Aristotle said, 'Action is the secret to happiness'!"

Another whack exploded in the space between them, after which Victor added, "We could sit and stare at the almonds in their shells all day, but unless we make the effort to break them open, we'll never enjoy what's inside, right?"

29

Pablo had sat and stared at the postcard for months. La Sagrada Familia, its mosaic-covered spires clawing at a bright-blue Barcelona sky. He'd laughed when he got it. His cousin Juan didn't seem like the type to send postcards. But he had joked about Pablo coming to Barcelona since even before he left. Apparently the card was another ploy to get him to consider it.

He never really had. The idea had never seemed realistic. Juan was the one who ran off and had the big adventures, not him. He'd taken it for granted that his obligations at the store and his relationship with Rosa precluded any serious consideration of a life elsewhere, the one possible exception being school. He'd never even left Andalucía, which, geographically at least, was much closer to Africa than it was to Cataluña, far away in the north. Could he, a young man from a village of less than two thousand people, really make a life for himself in a city of millions? Did he even want to try?

He hadn't before.

He got out of bed and took the postcard off the wall. Getting back into bed, he flipped the card around in his hand, over and over. As if holding it made what it represented that much more tangible, ideas began to flow and possibilities started to take shape.

Maybe now he did.

The fact Juan was there made it infinitely more attractive. He never even would have considered it otherwise. Juan could probably help him get a job. He could probably help him with a lot of things, finding someplace to live, figuring out his way around the big city, meeting new people.

Maybe he should give Juan a call.

He hesitated. Even the thought of it made him anxious, his stomach tensing. Why? What was the big deal? It was just a phone call.

Going round and round a few more times, he picked up the phone. Even now, having thought it through, having reminded himself repeatedly that he was simply exploring his options, he couldn't escape the feeling he was flirting with danger.

He dialed. Juan answered.

"So you're finally coming up here?" he joked.

"I don't know," said Pablo. "Maybe."

"Maybe? *Maybe!* You mean you're thinking about it!"

Juan was so excited it was hard for Pablo to keep up, but the bottom line was clear: the warehouse where Juan worked was getting ready to go through another round of hiring. Pablo's timing was perfect. There were no guarantees, but given that Pablo had connections, it was more likely than not he'd get the gig.

Assuming he wanted it.

Juan, after all, had given Pablo much more to consider than the potential job offer.

It wasn't that he had reneged on any of the wonderful things he'd said previously about Barcelona; rather, instead of impressing his younger cousin, he was now trying to prepare him. Revising his description of paradise, he told him about long, grueling hours on the job, a high cost of living, and dirty, dangerous streets that reeked of car exhaust, putrefying garbage, and the rancid odor of urine. He didn't want Pablo to expect the streets to be paved with gold. In the village, life transpired at an entirely different pace and with an almost innocent simplicity nowhere to be found in a large, cosmopolitan city like Barcelona. So, his apparent change of tune wasn't actually a change at all. He was simply telling the rest of the story, hoping to help his cousin have somewhat realistic expectations, to the extent expectations are ever based on any semblance of reality.

"So what do you think?" Juan asked.

"I don't know." Pablo was as overwhelmed as excited. "It sounds great, but it's a big decision. I need a little time to think about it."

It was perfectly understandable. He was only being prudent. All the same, Pablo felt like a child backing off a naive wish upon realizing the grown-up realities surrounding it.

Juan wrapped up their conversation by reminding Pablo that jobs in the warehouse didn't come up often. When they did, there were a lot of people vying for them. If Pablo didn't jump at the chance now, it could be a long time before another came along.

30

Descending through the silvery rows of olive trees that evening, a trail of dust billowing up behind him, Pablo discovered Victor sitting outside. On the table in front of him was a plate of cheese, a half-eaten barra, and an open bottle of rioja.

"Hello there!" he said, greeting Pablo with a familiar smile and closing a book he'd been reading.

"*¡Buenas!*" responded Pablo, taking off his helmet.

"What brings you this way this time of day?" asked Victor cheerfully.

"I have to talk to you."

"All right then, but first things first. Coffee? Tea? What would you like?"

"Could I just have some wine?"

"Oh, of course! Maybe I've already had too much myself! Let me go get a glass."

A small flock of swallows circled noisily overhead, corralling its insect prey in midair, each of the birds partaking of their last meal of the day, as though they, too, were guests at Victor's table.

The old man returned and poured Pablo some wine. As he did, Pablo indulged in a quick bite, one hand concealing a mouthful of rich, semicured manchego while he told Victor about the opportunity in Barcelona. Misgivings momentarily upstaged by possibilities, he quickly tapped back into the excitement of that morning.

"That sounds wonderful!" Victor exclaimed, as though it were a done deal.

"Do you think so? I think I want to do it—but I'm not sure."

"Not sure about what?"

"My mom. The store. You know, the things we talked about the other day. Barcelona, too. Especially Barcelona, actually. On the one hand, it sounds so exciting. On the other, it's really daunting. What if I don't like the job? Juan says it's brutal. And what if I get all the way up there and don't even like living in the city?"

"A lot of what-ifs! But aren't you overlooking the most important question?"

Victor's words hung heavy in the air, somewhere between invitation and challenge.

"What do you mean?"

"Come now," Victor admonished. "You know exactly what I'm getting at. You're still talking about what you think. What's your heart telling you? What do you feel?"

Pablo hesitated, as though he'd been avoiding asking himself that very question, not to mention naively hoping Victor, too, would fail to bring it up.

"Rather than falling into the all-too-familiar trap of letting your doubts and fears sabotage the opportunity, approach the situation one step at a time," Victor reminded him. "Problems and possibilities are similar in that there's no point in doing much about either until they materialize. The only thing that matters now is how you feel about going—or at least applying for the job, which you may not even get. As such, there's only one question left to ask yourself."

"What's my intuition telling me?"

"Ha! I'd say we're well beyond that!" Victor retorted, not about to let Pablo so easily off the hook. "You could hardly contain yourself when you told me the news. The question is whether or not you believe it."

"Believe it?"

Pablo was thrown.

"Yes, believe it. When you felt your initial experiences were of little consequence, I suggested your inner voice might eventually come to bear upon circumstances that wouldn't seem so trivial. Now it is. But the role you allow it to play depends on how much trust you've built up in it. Maybe you're not there yet. Maybe you're not ready to make important decisions based on what you feel. It's not easy to let go of a lifelong reliance on reason alone! These things take time. Either way, I suspect that's what's truly at the root of your hesitation."

Victor was right, thought Pablo. It wasn't that he hadn't heard his inner voice. It was that he'd been afraid to trust it, instead dwelling on the unknowns. In his defense, though, it was only natural he might hesitate to trust something he had yet to fully understand, something he was still at a loss to explain.

"But what is it? I mean, what is it really?" he asked.

"It?" replied Victor.

"Yeah, intuition. Even though we've talked so much about it, I can't really say. But at the same time, it feels so natural—which makes it even weirder."

"You're right. It is in fact both entirely natural and undeniably mysterious," Victor reassured him with a knowing smile. "As for your question, as for what it is, that's something that can be approached any number of ways. I suspect you could find as many answers as you could people to ask. You, for example, you equated intuition with knowing something was going to happen, right? Something akin to a premonition?"

"I guess so. I didn't really know how to define it."

Victor took out a match from a box on the table and lit a couple of candles, the air momentarily charged with phosphorous.

"*Intuēri*," he said cryptically, as the flames began to give off a gentle glow.

"*¿Cómo?*" wondered Pablo, not certain he had heard correctly.

"Intuēri," Victor repeated, this time more deliberately. "'To look at,' in Latin. That's the root of intuition, which seems as good a place to begin as any if we want to get to the bottom of what it is."

"To look at," echoed Pablo thoughtfully.

"If we were to go a step further and look in the dictionary," Victor continued, "we'd find lots of other definitions as well. Anything from 'knowing' or 'sensing without the use of reason' to other concepts such as 'idea,' 'instinct,' 'sixth sense,' and on and on."

"So which one is right?"

"Which one?" Victor shot back with a laugh. "They all are, of course!"

"What?" Pablo objected, dismayed. "How can they all be right?"

"Because there isn't a single contradiction on the list," Victor replied, encouraging Pablo to see his point. "They're all just different facets of the same phenomenon, light refracted through the same jewel."

"I don't get it," Pablo protested. "An idea is not the same thing as your sixth sense. I mean, what is intuition exactly?"

Two bats, apparently having taken over for the swallows, as though some sort of aerial changing of the guard had taken place, darted along unpredictable, jagged paths overhead. At times they came so close to the table their wing beats were audible, like miniature helicopters erratically chopping through the air.

"I suppose if you want to go beyond dictionary definitions," Victor began, as though reluctantly preparing to indulge his young friend and take things to a whole different level, "you have to leave behind the dictionary."

"OK. I guess. But what does that mean?" Pablo still didn't follow.

"It means that, ultimately, intuition is not something that

can be simply and succinctly summarized with words, no matter how eloquent or articulate one might be. The Sufis—remember, the holy men in the cave—they believed, as in fact Sufis still do today, that many of life's mysteries had to be experienced firsthand in order to be truly understood, as opposed to merely transmitted intellectually, be it through a book, a lesson, or what have you—though any and all of those might be helpful. The same is true for intuition. Although we can talk about it, and although—as the Sufis also believe—it can certainly be of help to have someone with more understanding help you find the way, in the end, it's something that has to be experienced personally."

Pablo took another drink of wine, letting Victor's words sink in. He then asked, "If you can't even really explain it, how do you know it's real?"

"I'm sure many people would say you don't!" Victor readily allowed, a mischievous, even provocative, twinkle in his eye. "Which, no doubt, goes a long way toward explaining why so many people disregard their inner voices—never mind their feelings in general. We live, after all, in an age of reason, one in which science—though I'm neither a luddite nor foolish enough to suggest it doesn't have its place—science has spoiled us. It's deceived us, really, with the expectation that everything has a logical explanation that can definitively lay to rest any and all questions. By extension, anything that cannot be readily explained rationally is inherently suspect. Any claims it might have to any basis in reality are tenuous at best, if not entirely illegitimate. Indeed, if permitted to do so, science would single-mindedly claim a monopoly on the foundation of our beliefs, of what we consider real. Yet, inside ourselves, even in this glorious, triumphant age of reason, with all its advances and changes and pomp and circumstance, we're still not convinced."

"Why do you say that?"

"Because if we were, we wouldn't continue to look elsewhere for answers."

"Answers to what?"

"To life's fundamental questions! We continue to look anywhere and everywhere we think we might find them. Indeed, we don't have to venture far to discover all sorts of belief systems that, although they have little or no apparent basis in reason, nonetheless serve as potential alternatives for the answers we seek."

"I get it," said Pablo, now clear where Victor was headed. "You mean like religion."

"Certainly not the only one, but undeniably a rather striking example."

"You think so?"

"Absolutely. What better example of something that can't be explained in rational terms, yet in which millions upon millions of people profess a blind—yet incredibly powerful—faith? No doubt as to the reality of something that cannot be proven logically? Something that, despite what many would consider that rather notable shortcoming, plays a very real, active role in their day-to-day lives, shaping their beliefs, affecting their decisions, charting their paths forward. Religion not only persists, but in many places it prospers, growing right alongside science, unthreatened by something that would seem such a menacing contradiction. How would that be possible if we truly believed science had all the answers, that we no longer had any need to look for them elsewhere? No, if we were convinced it did, religion would be dead."

Presented with such a monumental statement, one that felt almost sacrilegious, despite arguably being more akin to a defense of the divine than an indictment of it, Pablo needed a minute to sit with it, to let its ramifications sink in.

"So how does all that relate to my intuition?" he asked, after helping himself to another piece of cheese.

"In just about every way, I'd say!" Victor insisted. "In a nutshell, though, perhaps you can see that our inability to explain something rationally doesn't necessarily mean it has no basis in reality. Perhaps it does, but we haven't figured it out yet. Perhaps it's beyond reason altogether. In either case, in the absence of reason, we have the experience itself—what we observe and what we feel—to attest at least on some level to its authenticity, just as you've seen with your intuition."

31

"You're going to Barcelona?" Jorge asked in disbelief. "You're actually going to do it?"

They had met up at the bar with outdoor seating, the clock tower in plain sight a short distance away and the day-to-day of the village transpiring around them. People came and went. Two little boys kicked a soccer ball back and forth, careful to avoid the cars that occasionally came in one side of the square and went out the other. A cat slept in the sun, while pigeons cooed overhead.

"Hopefully. I'm not sure yet. I told Juan to submit my name, so we'll see."

"So you'd really leave the village? You'd really go all the way to Barcelona?"

"Yeah, I would."

Pablo felt good, emboldened, since telling Juan he wanted the job. Although Juan had reiterated it was more likely than not he'd get it, it could be a week or more before they knew for sure. There were other candidates, and it didn't help that Pablo couldn't apply in person. Fortunately, Juan had proven himself to be a reliable, hard worker, and his word carried a lot of weight. It was always better to hire someone who came highly recommended than a stranger off the street.

"What about Rosa?"

"What about her?"

"Aren't you going to try to get back together?"

"What are you talking about? I already did! She doesn't want to."

"You can't give up that easy."

"Jorge, she said no. What am I supposed to do?"

"I don't know. I'm just not convinced it's over."

"Great. When she tells you she wants to get back together, let me know. She can come up to Barcelona and we can have a nice, long talk about it!"

The man working the bar brought them both a beer.

"What about the store? What's your mom going to say?"

Pablo flinched, the question like an arrow piercing his Achilles' heel.

"I don't know."

"You don't know? What do you mean? You didn't tell her you were applying for the job?"

"No, she doesn't know anything about it."

"Not even that you're thinking about moving to Barcelona?"

"No."

"Oh."

Realizing he'd ventured into dangerous territory, Jorge decided not to probe further.

"I don't want to say anything in case I don't get it," Pablo confessed. "I don't want to bring it up, if it turns out there isn't any point."

"Right," Jorge replied, more to be supportive than because he agreed.

"It'll probably be a few months before the store opens back up anyway. My mom doesn't need me right now. I can go up north for a while, try it out, and come back if I have to."

"You think you actually would? If you got up there and you liked it, it seems like it'd be hard to turn around and come back to work in the store."

"I know, but I don't know what else to do!" Pablo

admitted, exasperated. "All I know is that I have to get out of here. I'm just figuring it out as I go along. And for now, if I don't have to tell my mom, I'm not going to."

An awkward silence followed, broken only when Jorge asked, "Isn't that your friend?"

Sure enough, there was Victor, crossing the plaza.

"*¡Oye, Victor!*" Pablo shouted, waving him over to their table.

"Well, look who it is!" Victor greeted them, setting down his bags.

"Victor, this is my friend Jorge. Jorge this is Victor."

"*Encantado*," said Jorge, shaking Victor's hand.

"Shopping?" asked Pablo.

"Just picking up a few things. What about you boys?"

"Jorge was reminding me what a nightmare it's going to be to tell my mom if I get the job in Barcelona."

"Have you heard anything?"

"Not yet. But my cousin said I should know anytime."

"Barcelona. Such a wonderful city," Victor reflected.

"What do you mean? Have you been?" Despite all Victor's other travels, Pablo had never asked if he'd been to Barcelona.

"Oh yes, several times. Didn't we already talk about that?"

"No! You never even mentioned it! I can't believe you never told me!"

"I can't believe you never asked!" Victor retorted facetiously. "What about you, young man? Have you ever been to Barcelona?"

"Me?" Jorge replied. "Oh no, I've only been to Madrid. My parents have though, and they said it was amazing."

"It's worth it for the works of Gaudí alone! But then you have Las Ramblas, the Barri Gòtic, the modernist architecture in the Eixample. Really, so much to see and do."

"I can't believe you never told me you've been," Pablo said again, dumbfounded by the ease with which Victor cited highlight after highlight.

"You never asked," Jorge reminded him, goading him on.

"Well now I'm wondering what else I should have asked."

"Ha! You can rest assured we still have plenty of unexplored territory!" Victor laughed. "And if you'd possibly consider coming by tomorrow morning to help me clear some debris off my roof, I'd be happy to answer any additional questions you might have."

"Sure. I don't have any plans."

"Wonderful, I'll see you then," Victor said, picking up his bags and turning to go. "Nice meeting you, Jorge."

"Nice meeting you, too."

One friend turning to go, yet another turned up.

"There's Rafa," said Jorge.

"Where?" Pablo asked, setting down his beer.

"There—coming out of the post office."

"Rafa!" Pablo yelled across the plaza.

Rafa stopped and looked in their direction. Though for a moment he seemed to consider crossing the square to say hello, apparently he thought twice, instead gesturing to a watch he wasn't actually wearing.

"*¡Vale!*" Pablo called out. "See you later!"

Looking down at his empty beer, Pablo wondered if he should order another. Before he could even pose the question, Jorge gave him the answer.

"All right, I've got to take off. I have to go study."

"Now? Can't you do it later? Let's see what's going on in town."

"I can't. I'm meeting Pepa."

"Pepa? What do you mean you're meeting Pepa? I guess Victor's not the only one who's been holding back! I didn't even know you guys had the same classes."

"We don't. But she's having some trouble with her math course, so she asked for my help."

"And you weren't going to tell me?"

"What do you mean?" Jorge protested. "I just did!"

"Uh-huh," said Pablo with a wry smile, his eyebrows arching in accusation.

"What! It's nothing! Seriously, I'm just helping her study. It's no big deal!"

"Not yet," Pablo taunted. "It never is in the beginning."

Speechless, Jorge turned beet red. Every drop of blood in his body had risen to the surface, his hopes rising right along with them.

32

“I had a friend who fell three stories and lived to tell about it, but I’d rather not risk it—especially being here on my own,” Victor explained from down below, while Pablo cleared a large branch and some other debris from the roof.

“Three stories!” Pablo exclaimed. “And he lived?”

“Not only did he live, but despite both feet being reduced to bags of bones, he learned to walk again, too. And quite well, I might add, without any assistance. Eventually I even saw him dance a tango with his wife.”

“*¿En serio?* That’s incredible!”

“Indeed, it was,” Victor reminisced. “Never underestimate the body’s miraculous healing power. Or, for that matter, the determination of the human spirit!”

Once the work was done, Victor brought out a pitcher of lemonade made with fruit from his own trees, and the two took seats on the porch.

“So, my friend, how did it feel to tell your cousin you were interested in the job?”

“At first I was really nervous. I couldn’t believe I was doing it. But as soon as I told him, I felt great. It was like a huge weight had lifted, and I knew I’d done the right thing.”

“Then you almost certainly did. No sooner do you make a

decision based on what you feel in your heart, than you find yourself awash in an unmistakable sense of peace. You have the inexplicable yet undeniable assurance that—as you said—you've done the right thing. Or, the opposite might be true. You have a horrible feeling in the pit in your stomach urging you not to do something and, as soon as you decide against it, the pain dissipates—and you subsequently learn that you made the right decision."

"So you do have reasons to believe your intuition," Pablo observed. "If things work out like you thought, you know you weren't imagining them."

"Sometimes. But reason isn't the reason, so to speak. Logic isn't what gets you there—to those reassuring feelings or those validating outcomes. Inevitably they come after the fact, if they come at all."

Having worked up a thirst, Pablo practically downed his first glass of lemonade in one gulp. Victor poured him another before offering some words of caution.

"It's very exciting, but try not to get too attached. Don't put all your eggs in one basket. Stay open to other possibilities, too. In hindsight, you might look back on Barcelona as just the beginning."

Pablo hadn't thought of that, and it was disconcerting to do so now. As much as he hated to admit it, there was no ignoring the wisdom in Victor's advice. On the other hand, as long as it hatched, one egg would be more than enough.

"What about you? If you've been so many amazing places, why are you staying around here?"

Pablo had asked the question before, but he wasn't convinced he'd ever gotten the full answer.

"First of all, I would argue that this, too, is an amazing place," Victor was quick to insist, taking a drink. "If it weren't, you're right—I probably wouldn't be here. But I understand why you're asking. You're getting ready to run off and see the world. Why would someone want to spend an extended period in the very same out-of-the-way village you're trying to leave behind?"

"Yeah, I mean you've been so many cool places."

"But that's just it. You see, your eyes are just now starting to open, both to the world at large and the world within. You're beginning to realize not only how much more is out there but that it can be yours—and you're feeling called to embark upon that journey. I've taken it. Naturally, it's not one that ever ends, and I certainly don't mean to imply I've nothing left to learn. To the contrary, I hope to be learning until the very day I die! Still, more so than venturing back out into the world, what I most long for at this point is to focus inward. I long for the time and space for contemplation and self-reflection."

"Did you want to get away because of what happened with your daughter?"

No sooner had he asked the question, than Pablo regretted it. Victor, however, was unfazed.

"Oh, I don't know. Like I said, that was a few years ago. Of course, like I also said, it may as well have been yesterday. So, maybe, partly. But there were other obligations and distractions . . . the inevitable demands of daily life. Sometimes we simply need to retreat. And in that sense, coming down here was less about what I was getting away from and more about what I was coming to find. Solitude. Someplace I could reflect. Someplace to meditate, write, read, walk, garden. I had to come anyway. My family had the house. It's very simple, but it meets my needs. So, I decided to stay a while."

"I hope I haven't taken up too much of your time while you've been here."

"Don't be silly! Of course not," Victor reassured him with a dismissive wave of the hand. "This is a very exciting time for you, and it's exciting for me to watch you find your way. I'm delighted our paths have crossed."

33

Juan called a few days after their conversation. The job was Pablo's for the taking.

He could hardly believe it. It was actually happening.

He was going to Barcelona.

There was, however, one thing standing between him and a new life up north.

He had put it off. He'd done his best to put it out of his mind. Now he had to put his best foot forward.

He had to tell his mom.

Pablo made his way downstairs. Before he could see her, he heard her in the kitchen unloading some bags. For him, the day was only just getting started. For his mother, it was already well underway.

He was only half awake. But he had to tell her now. He had to tell her before he thought too much about it and lost his nerve.

"*Buenos días Mamá.*"

"*Buenos días hijo.*"

"Great news!" she said as she lay three packages of lentils on the table, each assuming its own random, lopsided form. "I heard back from the insurance company. Everything is good with our claim, and we can move forward with the repairs!"

The news was great. The timing could hardly have been worse.

"Now I just have to get some estimates and get a contractor in. I already talked to Carlos, and he'll probably do it. Still, I want to check with a few different people to make sure he's the one."

Pablo hadn't seen his mother this upbeat since the fire. Was now really the time to tell her?

"How long do you think it'll take to rebuild?" he asked, intent on showing his interest, while buying himself some time.

"I'm not sure. You know these things always take longer than expected. The good news is that—even though it looks bad—the building is so solid most of the damage wasn't structural—other than part of the roof, obviously. So, most of the work will be gutting and replacing the interior. And since the space isn't that big, if I can get someone in there right away, hopefully we'll be up and running sooner rather than later."

We. Sooner rather than later.

He had to tell her.

Now.

"I talked to cousin Juan in Barcelona this morning."

"Did you? What'd he have to say?"

Pablo took a deep breath. His whole body had tensed, and his throat was dry.

"He said there's a job in the warehouse."

He paused to see if his mother had any reaction. When, showing none, she continued unloading the bag, he mustered his courage to add, "He said I could probably take it, if I wanted it."

Carmen stopped what she was doing, wheels now spinning as reality hit. This wasn't merely a causal morning conversation of little consequence. There was more going on here.

Leaving the bag for later, she turned to the coffee pot and started a fresh brew. She then opened a drawer, dug around briefly, and extracted an almost empty pack of cigarettes before taking a seat at the table with Pablo.

"Barcelona?" she said, pulling out a cigarette and lighting it.

Pablo couldn't remember the last time he'd seen her smoke.

"Yeah."

"Not exactly down the street!" she remarked as lightheartedly as she could, given the gravity of the news. Pablo was surprised.

"And I'm guessing that if you're mentioning it, it's because you do want this job?" she surmised, exhaling her first drag.

"Yes."

He felt the urge to explain, to justify and rationalize. But his gut said otherwise, his inner voice silencing his outer one. There was no need.

"You've changed since the fire. I'm sure we all have," she said, as much to herself as to Pablo. "I guess it's inevitable."

The comforting aroma of fresh coffee began to mingle with the pungent odor of spent tobacco.

"I always wondered if you'd ever get the itch. Seems like almost everyone your age does, but you've always been so in your element here—not like your sister, who was always down in Málaga every chance she could get. Of course, I've never wanted you to leave, but I can understand why you might want to see some of the rest of the world."

Her voice trailed off as she withdrew into her thoughts. For the moment she said nothing. Pablo could sense there was more.

"I held your father back. I can't make that same mistake with you."

Pablo was now even more surprised.

"Held him back?" He had no idea what she was talking about.

"It was one of our only real fights," she explained, inhaling deeply. "The only time I wasn't sure we'd make it through. Of course we did. But it wasn't easy, and it sure didn't get resolved overnight."

"What happened?"

"He had a friend in Granada who was opening a bar and needed a partner. I had no desire to leave the village and go all the way to Granada to live in the city. And I sure as hell did not want to own a bar. The food. The alcohol. The horrible hours. No way. We fought and fought, and in the end he let it go. Once it was over it was over—Antonio had too big a heart to hold a grudge. But even so, I'm not sure he could ever completely forgive me. I came between him and his dream. And don't misunderstand—I don't regret it. It was not a dream I shared. It was not something we ever talked about before getting married. It was way out of left field, and he waited longer than he should have to tell me. But I can only imagine how tempting for him it must have been, every time something went wrong here, to wonder how different, how much better it would have been if only we'd gone to Granada. But we didn't. We stayed, and we opened the market instead."

Pablo let his mother's words sink in until, unable to help himself, he asked, "And what if I go, what about it? The market, I mean?" He couldn't believe he was the one bringing it up, but he had to know.

"Looks like you're in luck there, too. Your *tía* Lucrecia called a couple days ago and said your cousin José is coming back from Madrid. It turns out he didn't like it there, which doesn't surprise me—he's not the big-city type. Anyway, she told me to let her know if we needed any help. Of course, I told her we didn't. But now it looks like we do. So, it just might work out for everyone. I guess one's coming back, so another can go."

Pablo was astonished. She was actually letting him do it. She was sad and thoughtful as she contemplated her only son's unexpected departure, but she wasn't going to offer any of the resistance Pablo had dreaded from the first time the idea of leaving had occurred to him. There would be no fighting, no endless discussions or begging or pleading. Maybe there had been so much drama since the fire she was simply too drained to put up a fight. Or, perhaps this was how she always would have reacted. Perhaps all the worst-case scenarios—all the what-ifs—had been purely of his own creation, self-serving scapegoats to prevent him from taking risks he hadn't been ready to take.

Whatever the case, the one remaining obstacle between Pablo and Barcelona had just proven to be little more than a chimera, and his whole life was about to change.

He gave his mother a long, warm embrace, lingering as if they were both contemplating the good-bye they would have to say in a not-too-distant future. She then got up to wash her mug, while he ran upstairs to shower.

Most of Pablo's activities over the next few weeks would be spent preparing for his transition. He'd have to decide what to take with him and start packing. There would be countless trips down to town to run an endless list of errands. He'd also be socializing as much as his busy schedule would allow, since once news got out of his impending departure, he'd be the man of the hour. All his family and friends would want to see as much of him as possible before he left the village behind for the big city in the north.

34

The "rock circle" wasn't technically a circle at all, but rather an area of craggy gray rocks that rose out of the earth at different intervals and reached to varying heights, spread over a small plateau. Although within its periphery there was a more-or-less circular area with a smooth, sandy floor, the rocks themselves extended in all directions. It more easily called to mind a lunar landscape than the natural Stonehenge it had become in Pablo's eyes. Still, given its situation high upon the mountainside, the peculiar shapes of the coarse, jagged formations, and the unique natural enclosure it seemed to almost deliberately create, there was something undeniably mystical about the place.

Pablo. Jorge. Pepa. Their friends, Ana and Santi, too. They'd all made the hike up the mountain to celebrate Pablo's good news. Rafa was supposed to join, but he'd had a last-minute change of plans.

Once they'd caught their breath and taken in the views, they spread out blankets and unpacked food and drinks. In no time, they were immersed in lighthearted musings about everything and nothing. Like wine from the bottles they'd brought along, the conversation flowed, branching off on tangent after tangent. Gossip about friends. An impassioned debate between Pepa and Ana about new music one of their favorite bands had just released. Plans for the weekend and rumors about a new club opening on the coast.

Eventually, the conversation turned to the main reason for the outing, Pablo's impending adventure.

"So your mom's letting you go?" Jorge asked.

"Yeah, I couldn't believe it. She was really cool about it."

"And when are they going to begin work on the store?" Jorge wondered.

"She finally got things straightened out with the insurance company, and she's already lined up contractors. I think they're supposed to do some preliminary stuff next week, but they won't be able to really get started until after Christmas."

"Just like you in Barcelona," Jorge remarked.

"Exactly," Pablo replied, unable to hold back a smile.

As she poured another glass of wine, Pepa asked, "Does Rosa know you're leaving?"

Pablo tensed.

Although he didn't want to let on to it, again and again he had asked himself that very question. Did Rosa know he was leaving? More importantly, if she did, did she care? Would it change anything? Even though she hadn't wanted to get back together, he couldn't help but wonder. It wouldn't feel final until he got onto the plane. Any secret hopes he still harbored wouldn't be definitely laid to rest until then.

"You're asking me? How should I know?" he joked, downplaying his feelings. "You'd know better than me, wouldn't you?"

"I haven't talked to her in a few days."

"What? You haven't talked to her! What happened?" Pablo asked.

"It's no big deal," Pepa responded vaguely. "Just a little spat. We'll get over it."

"No, seriously. What happened?"

If Rosa and Pepa weren't talking, it had to be about more than a little spat. Like conjoined twins sharing vital organs, Pablo was sure they couldn't survive more than the briefest of periods apart.

Pepa shot Jorge a look. Put on the spot, he diverted his gaze.

Pablo didn't fail to notice, scrutinizing his other friends. Everyone had fallen silent. No one would look him in the eye. He was the odd man out. What was going on? Why were they holding back, and about what?

"You guys, come on," he insisted. "What's up?"

Jorge deflected to Pepa. He wasn't going to be the one.

"What?" Pablo demanded.

"I wasn't going to say anything," Pepa began. "Really I wasn't . . . but, well, you should talk to Rosa."

"About what!" He desperately wished someone would just come out with it.

Never one to mince words, Ana finally did.

"Rosa and Rafa are dating," she said, popping some chips into her mouth. Santi jabbed her in the side, as if to say she'd overstepped her bounds.

"What?" Pablo was dumb struck, turning to Pepa to see if it was true.

"I'm really sorry Pablo, but it just didn't seem fair for you not to know," she confessed. "I honestly thought Rosa might have told you by now. I told her she should."

"Told me? When would she have told me? I haven't even seen her!"

He suddenly understood why Rafa couldn't make it.

"And you knew, too?" Pablo asked, singling out Jorge.

"No, I just heard! Literally, on the way here!"

Pablo was blindsided. Could it be true? How? When? He remembered seeing them in Málaga. Were they already together then? Was this why she hadn't wanted to get back together, because she had started seeing Rafa? The only thing stronger than his disbelief was his sense of betrayal.

"You might want another one of these," said Santi, handing Pablo a beer.

Pablo gratefully accepted what would be far from his last indulgence of the evening.

The alcohol once again flowing, the mood gradually lightened, everyone doing their part to move on from the bombshell that had nearly brought their excursion to a premature end. Though his thoughts inevitably returned to the news, Pablo didn't want to think about it. It was too much. For the time being, he, too, did his best to put it out of his mind.

"Oh my god!" Pepa exclaimed a while later.

"What?" asked Ana, playing along as though whatever Pepa had to say were as important as her dramatic cry suggested—which she was sure it was not.

"The sun! It's about to set!"

"Relax!" teased Santi, "it's not going to happen all at once!"

"You can relax all you want," Pepa retorted, stumbling to her feet and taking Jorge by the hand. "We're going to go watch!"

Jorge eagerly obliged, turning as red as the flaming sky above and obediently following Pepa out the back of the circle, conspicuously avoiding Pablo's gaze.

All Pablo could do was smile and take another swig of beer. Despite his own malaise, he was happy to see Jorge's luck had turned. It was about time. He deserved it.

35

It began one otherwise ordinary morning, whereupon the villagers woke up to discover that overnight an aptly named cold front had descended upon the entire region. The unseasonably mild weather and warm temperatures of the days and weeks before were blown away by a blast of frigid air that may as well have descended straight from the Arctic. Heaters were turned on, the smell of burning wood filled the air before the sun had even come up, and people found themselves rummaging through their closets in search of long-forgotten wool sweaters and heavy coats.

The cold was only half the story—and the less interesting half, at that. It turned out the temperature wasn't the only thing to drop precipitously that day.

The rain came down slowly at first, as though doubting it was falling in the right place, considering the reception it was given. Ordinarily, the porous, sandy earth soaked up water like a sponge, quickly filtering it deep underground into natural cisterns that fed the innumerable springs dotting the region like ATMs dispensing water instead of cash. Given the severe shortage of recent months, however, the desiccated earth treated the water—an entire windfall of which poured down from one instant to the next—as an ominous liability, rather than a desperately sought-after asset.

The saturation point quickly reached, that most precious of commodities, that life-giving force of which the entire region was in such dire need, was shamelessly squandered. Only the lifeless legions of gullies, canyons, and seasonal creeks benefitted, from one moment to the next infused with spirit, violent, cascading whitewater deluges resurrecting them from months of anemic repose in a miraculous flash. Roads and sidewalks were flooded. Drainage ditches and sewers were backed up. Unstable sections of hillsides were sent tumbling down, mounds of dirt and piles of rubble coming to rest in the most bewildering and bothersome of places—and raising the specter of larger-scale landslides still.

As if that weren't enough, the proverbial icing on a cake whose candles were unexpectedly about to go up in smoke: the lights went out.

Rainfall-induced blackouts were only slightly less common than the rain itself, even though the mountain villages had every imaginable modern convenience and were hardly frozen in some technologically backward past.

Except when it rained just a little too hard.

Sitting alone in the dim interior of the house, Pablo listened to sheets of rain and gusts of wind wreak havoc on a distant, inconsequential world outside. Over and over he revisited the news about Rosa and Rafa, still struggling to believe it. The reality had yet to sink in. A fresh wound still bleeding, it hurt as much now as it had when he found out a couple of days earlier. He felt humiliated. He felt betrayed. He wondered what, if anything, to do about it.

When the phone rang, he jumped.

The timing of Juan's call could hardly have been better, a sympathetic ear right when Pablo needed it. Juan patiently heard his cousin out, a safety valve for his anger.

But that wasn't why Juan had called.

"*Primo*, I'm in love!"

His own predicament suddenly upstaged, Pablo gave Juan his full attention.

"What! In love? Congratulations! Who is she? Where'd you meet her?"

"At a club. She's been here visiting her sister. She's *gallega*, from La Coruña."

"So she doesn't live in Barcelona?"

"No. And, actually, that's what I wanted to talk to you about."

"What do you mean?"

"Pablo, you're never going to believe this, but . . ."

"But what?"

Juan paused to get up his courage.

"I have to be with her—I just have to. And . . ."

"And?"

"I'm moving to La Coruña!"

Pablo said nothing, struggling with whether he'd even heard correctly.

Juan was right. He couldn't believe it.

"Pablo?"

He wasn't going to Barcelona. That's what this was really about.

He was not going to Barcelona.

He was going to be sick.

"You're leaving?" Pablo finally managed to say. All that mattered was confirming he had understood correctly. "You're not staying in Barcelona."

He hadn't expected it, not remotely. But it wasn't out of character, not in the slightest. After everywhere else Juan had been, why stop with Barcelona? It was only natural he'd keep going, that his trajectory wouldn't end until he'd reached the furthest reaches of the Peninsula. Even then, who was to say he'd stop there? For the right girl, he could catch a plane to Paris. Or board a ship to the New World. The sky was the limit.

"No, but it's OK—you don't have to worry about the job . . ."

It was as if the needle playing the soundtrack of Pablo's new life had just slid across the record. Letting out a scratch worse than nails on a blackboard, it came to a halt only after jumping off the spinning disk altogether, resting on the edge like a semitruck dangling over a cliff.

There was no way.

"And I've got a friend you can stay with until you get settled . . ."

Pablo was no longer listening.

He wasn't going if Juan wasn't going to be there. End of story. His move had been predicated on that since day one. He never even would have considered Barcelona if it weren't for Juan. Maybe later. For now, it was way more than he was up for taking on himself. And it wasn't about the job. It never had been. The job was a means to an end, a stepping stone. He was going to Barcelona because Juan had been so insistent he come, offering so many assurances and so much support.

But now he wasn't even going to be there.

Pablo would have plenty to say to Juan later. For now, he couldn't bear long-winded explanations about how Juan had only just met the gallega when Pablo called originally about Barcelona, or how things had moved much more quickly between them than he ever could have imagined—let alone possibly foreseen. It might have eased Juan's conscience, but for Pablo it only made things worse.

He ended the call.

Was it even possible? Was he really not going to Barcelona?

After all that had happened. After all the risks he had taken, the seemingly resounding validation he had gotten, and, perhaps most importantly, the incredible trust he'd placed in his intuition—leaving him with no doubt that Barcelona was where his future lay—was it really not going to happen? Had what was supposed to be his greatest triumph instead turned out to be his most humiliating disappointment?

It was unfathomable. Hadn't his intuition been guiding him toward Barcelona? Wasn't that the incredible, life-altering lesson he had learned when, overcoming his doubts and fears, he made the jump from merely hearing his inner voice to actually trusting it?

But now Barcelona wasn't working out. And if Barcelona wasn't working out, had he been wrong about everything? All along? Every feeling and decision and conclusion along the way was now called into question. Everything. The biggest question of all was what he was supposed to do next.

His disappointment, while profound, paled in comparison to his frustration. It was like a couple of days before when he learned Rosa was with Rafa. Now like then he felt betrayed. By his cousin. By circumstance. Most of all, by his inner voice, his trust in which was reduced to nothing, like one of the neglected old buildings in Málaga's center that, prior to the boom, would collapse without notice, from one moment to the next turning to rubble.

36

Sitting in the shade of a large carob next to his garden, like a judge considering an impassioned case for delivering a death sentence to intuition, Victor listened as Pablo enumerated every occasion in which he believed he had heard his inner voice, trusted in it, and, ultimately, acted upon on it. Each of those instances was being called seriously into question, and Pablo was all but demanding some sort of justice.

His hands folded in his lap, Victor remained silent throughout his young friend's frustrated diatribe, neither making a gesture, responding to any questions—which, at any rate, were entirely rhetorical—nor offering any advice. He was acutely aware that what Pablo needed most was simply to be heard. Besides, given his emotional state, there was no way he would have actually been open to anything Victor might have said. As far as he was concerned, Victor may as well have been the very embodiment of intuition itself.

Instead, the old man let Pablo's words fill the space between them like the dense mist overlaying the valley floor. Fortunately, the words, too, were susceptible to the dissipating effects of the advancing morning, which took stealth advantage of the ensuing silence, enveloping the two friends in an invigorating freshness that rose up from the ground, permeated the air, and infused the light with a crystalline vitality.

"I'm truly sorry," Victor offered, once Pablo had regained his composure.

"Thanks," Pablo replied, not only exhausted, but now self-conscious. "I just can't believe that after everything that's happened, I've gotten nowhere."

"I can certainly understand why you're upset, but—even given the circumstances—do you really believe that?"

"What else am I supposed to think?"

"Once again, I'm not sure that's the question. You can think whatever you like. Whether your thoughts are rooted in any semblance of reality is something else altogether," the old man remarked. "And given all you're feeling, I for one have my doubts they would be. No, rather than what to think, I'd say the real question is what to do."

"But that's just it—I have no idea," countered Pablo.

Victor paused, looking into the chaotic harmony of the tree canopy overhead as though to help formulate his response. Each branch reached for the sky as it fought for its place in the sun, competing with the others while complementing them, part of the same twisted, tangled, perfectly balanced whole, an ecstatic, verdant expression of life itself.

"It's simple, really. Just like any other challenge, you confront this one head on."

"And what challenge is that?" Pablo asked, doubting it was one he'd want to face.

"You have to decide whether you're ready to go beyond simply trusting your intuition to having faith in it."

Pablo could hardly believe his ears.

"What's that supposed to mean?" he challenged. "If trusting my intuition has gotten me nowhere, why would I want to have faith in it? And besides, what's the difference?"

"If you've truly gotten nowhere, you're absolutely right," Victor replied. "As for the difference, I'd say trusting is believing in what your intuition is telling you here and now. It's more immediate, concerned with the potential action at hand.

Faith is further reaching—it requires more of you. It's going beyond taking the guidance your intuition provides in the moment and believing in where it will lead you ultimately."

Unconvinced, Pablo diverted his gaze. Halfheartedly struggling to make sense of Victor's comments, he discovered that as the sun gradually burned off the mist, he could make out an occasional carob or olive tree, their faint silhouettes teasing him through the brume like a pair of kohl-adorned eyes from behind a muslin veil.

Go from trusting his intuition to having faith in it? Do more as opposed to less, when what he had done thus far had amounted to nothing? Far from being won over to Victor's perspective, the more he thought about it, the more resentful he became.

"But what does that mean? My faith in what? Yeah, I know—my intuition. But I don't even know what my intuition is. Not really. And even you can't tell me. For all I know, it's just my imagination! What I do know is that it has let me down. And that makes me wonder if I ever should have listened to—let alone trusted or now have faith in—it in the first place!"

Pablo's voice was trembling.

"If I'm not going to Barcelona, what was the point? What was the point of any of it? All it did was set me up for an embarrassing failure. And now you're telling me it's another challenge. Well, I don't want to deal with any more challenges. I just want to get out of here!"

"Pablo," Victor began, "it's not that, by following your intuition, you're suddenly going to avoid all difficulty, that you'll never get caught off guard by any of the countless surprises life can throw your way at any time. Instead, rather than somehow rendering you immune to life's challenges, what your intuition can do is help you deal with them."

"So, how do I deal with this?"

"You deal with this by not losing the faith you had when you decided to pursue the job in Barcelona. You deal with this by remembering how right it felt both when you made that decision and afterward, as things began to fall into place. You trust that, even now, things are continuing to fall into place—remembering that you can't always know what it will look like when they do. In the meantime, now, like then, you take action."

"But what if I'm still stuck here?"

"Then it's your own fault!" Victor shot back, not mincing words. "As long as you equate not going to Barcelona with not going anywhere, then, yes, you'll almost definitely be stuck in the village. But if we stop focusing on Barcelona, what's happened over the past few weeks? You felt the call to leave and acted on it. Your mother supported your plans. Your cousin came back right when you needed him. You've been set up to leave—and you still are. That hasn't changed."

"What's changed is I don't have anywhere to go."

"Because you just got the news. You're disappointed, which is only natural. All your hopes were pinned on Barcelona. Once the shock subsides, however, you'll have to let it go, if you want to open yourself to what's next."

37

Pablo felt like a ship that had set sail with great fanfare—champagne shattering, streamers and confetti flying, faces beaming and hands waving—only to return the very next day to the very same port, forced to call off its highly anticipated voyage and finding itself right back where it started.

Content for the first few days to hide out, as though reliving the period after the fire, Pablo lay low at home. He felt like a celebrity waiting for a scandal to blow over. He didn't want to explain over and over again what had happened. Neither did he want to respond to questions about what he was going to do instead. Being the center of attention leading up to what should have been his departure had been great. His moment to shine clearly having past, now all he wanted was to stay as far away from the spotlight as possible until everyone had forgotten about his little spectacle.

If he didn't want to talk about what was next, it was because he himself had no idea. He still wanted to leave eventually, but having made the jump and fallen flat, he'd lost his nerve. He didn't have a backup plan. Málaga wasn't calling any stronger now than it had been before. Hitchhiking across the country seemed extreme. Nothing felt right. He needed some time. For now, his place was in the village.

"There's no shortage of work," Carmen explained, "but I can't pay you both, especially not after the market being closed for so long. And I can't take the job away from José just because your plans didn't work out. Naturally you can help—and I expect you to help, if you're here—but I'm not sure what it will look like now that José has taken your place."

"But it's our store," Pablo reminded her, disheartened.

"It's our store, but it was your decision. You gave up your place, and I had to fill it. I'm sorry Barcelona didn't work out, but you took the risk and now you've got to live with the consequences. You've got to figure out what you're going to do instead, because I can't afford to have both you and José on the books."

Pablo felt cheated, even though he knew he was the only one to blame. He hadn't thought it through, and his mother was right: it wouldn't be fair to take the job away from José. It wasn't his fault Barcelona hadn't worked out.

Pablo felt as though he'd crossed a line that would forever delineate a before and an after; one that, as though exposing divided loyalties, henceforth rendered him some sort of demicitizen. The fact that every time he ran into anyone who somehow hadn't heard the news, they reacted with the same disbelief—"I thought you were supposed to be in Barcelona!"—only drove the point home that much further. Neither did it help that, as far as he was concerned, they were right.

"Maybe you should do construction for a while," Jorge suggested one day. "There's so much going on, I'm sure you could find something. You know Nacho's father owns a company, so you could probably just talk to him."

Pablo had no desire to do construction. He hated the idea of getting up before dawn only to spend all day slaving away in the sun. But Jorge was right: thanks to the housing boom, the industry was full of opportunity. He probably wouldn't even have to go down to town, since there were countless sites in and around the village. It was merely a question of finding someone who needed help. And, as Jorge had correctly pointed out, he probably already knew someone who did.

Giving it more thought over the days that followed, slowly but surely, Pablo came closer and closer to convincing himself construction was the right next step. The industry was thriving. The jobs paid OK. He had connections.

It made perfect sense.

38

Although the house was empty, there were enough clues about to suggest its owner was somewhere nearby. An open door beckoned anyone to come and go as they pleased. An unseen radio chattered away to no one in particular. A glass of water was either half full or half empty, depending upon the disposition of the beholder.

Pablo followed the sound of metal scraping stone until he discovered a modest structure just over the crest of what quickly became the literal edge of Victor's land, plummeting into the valley below like a falcon in free fall. The old man was going in and out of the shed with small shovelfuls of rubble, which he dumped into a wheelbarrow waiting outside.

"I didn't know there was another building on your land," Pablo remarked.

"You can't see it from the house," Victor concurred, more dirt falling with a gravelly thud atop the accumulating pile. A billow of dust shot up into the air, a mushroom cloud spouting a powdery barrage of ashen spores.

"So, tell me more about that new job."

"I don't actually have one yet, but my friend's dad owns a construction company. I think I'm going to talk to him to see if he has anything."

Unable to get a read on what Victor thought, since, although he vaguely acknowledged the comment, he didn't pause from his work, Pablo continued.

"I can't go back to the store, so I feel like I should be figuring out something else," he added, hoping to elicit more of a response.

"Careful, my boy!" Victor warned, looking Pablo square in the eyes, "Often what you *should* do is one of the worst things you possibly *could* do!"

"What do you mean?" Pablo questioned, caught off guard by what seemed a paradoxical warning against doing the right thing.

"*Shoulds*," Victor insisted, becoming still more emphatic, "*shoulds* really aren't that much different from the paralyzing what-ifs! The only difference is that while what-ifs stop you dead in your tracks, *shoulds* send you erring down somebody else's!"

"Somebody else's?" wondered Pablo, still more confused.

"Oh yes," Victor contended, as another thud sent more dust airborne. "Rarely is there not someone looking over the shoulder of the *should* in question, a puppet master standing just out of sight pulling the strings, someone with their own agenda, be it family or society or tradition—or any of a thousand other people, entities, or beliefs. And although it's always wise to consider different points of view, doing something for no other reason than because you should is often merely another way of renouncing your own responsibility—not to mention your own choice—in the matter, a way of overlooking what feels right and letting someone else decide for you."

"But that's the thing. I really feel like I have to figure out what to do," insisted Pablo. "That *is* what feels right."

"*Have to* and *should* are even more closely related than *should* and *what-if*!" Victor laughed, before easing off the point. "But Pablo, what I'm really getting at is that it's only been a few days since you found out you weren't going to Barcelona, hasn't it?"

"Yeah, I know."

"Why the urgency? Before you decide to completely reverse course, what about giving yourself some time to clear your head, so you don't make a rash decision you later regret?"

"I just feel like I need to be doing something," Pablo insisted.

"And getting a construction job is that something?"

"I don't know. I mean, maybe. Don't you think it's a good idea?"

"First of all, it's not my decision!" Victor retorted with a laugh. "Secondly, I haven't decided one way or the other! How could I? I'm simply asking how you settled on construction, since I've never heard you mention it before. But since you ask, yes, I suppose it does seem a little out of character."

Victor disappeared into the shed, leaving Pablo alone for a moment of soul-searching.

"I just feel stuck," Pablo confessed once Victor reemerged, making no attempt to hide his frustration. "I'm disappointed I'm not going to Barcelona, but I don't know what I want to do instead. I can't get my job back at the store, and I feel guilty sitting at home. So, like I said, I feel like I need to be doing something."

"And you've decided whatever it is," observed Victor, "you're staying in the village?"

"Not at all." Pablo was adamant. Then, realizing he hadn't been entirely honest, he qualified, "What I mean is, I still feel like I'm supposed to leave. But since I don't see how yet, I think I need to figure out what to do around here, just for a while."

"I thought you just said you still didn't want to be here?"

"I don't. It just seems like the best thing for now, until I can figure out another plan."

"You don't think that approach might not be a little counterproductive? You don't think that it might not be better to focus your efforts on what you really want, as opposed to what you don't actually want at all?"

"I know," Pablo conceded, "it sort of seems like a step backward. But I don't have any idea what's next."

Victor fell silent, as though engaging in some sort of internal debate, stroking his beard and shooting Pablo a cryptic sideways glance. Words having proven useless to get through to his young friend, to break down the walls he could see him raising as quickly as the most skillful of masons, the time had come for a different tactic.

"Come with me."

The shovel fell with a clang against the shed, and Victor set off in the direction of his garden; more specifically, the shelter of the large carob where he and Pablo had shared a highly charged conversation not long before.

"Take a seat," Victor instructed, peeling the gloves from his hands like skin from bananas, as he himself sat down on a soft patch of grass.

Pablo did as told, bewildered.

"Pablo, my son, you have got to slow down," Victor began, almost beseechingly, looking deep into his eyes. "When you move too fast, when you whip yourself into a frenzy of what-ifs and *shoulds* and *have tos*, you can't think clearly, never mind have any chance of opening yourself to your inner voice."

"Yeah, I know," Pablo began. It was, after all, a familiar theme. "It's just . . ."

"No," insisted Victor, motioning for Pablo to go no further. "Not now."

Still more perplexed, Pablo let it go, leaving his thought unfinished like the load in the wheelbarrow they had left behind at the shed.

"Are you comfortable?" Victor asked, taking stock of Pablo's position on the ground.

"Sure," Pablo replied, shifting in response to the awareness brought on by the question.

"Good. Now, sit up straight."

Realizing he had in fact been slouching, Pablo made yet another adjustment, becoming that much more aware of not only his body but his surroundings as well.

"Now, close your eyes and take a deep breath," Victor instructed, as he did the same.

Pablo let out an involuntary laugh. It was one thing to be forced to stop and catch his breath when he was rambunctiously chattering on and on, a welcome splash of cold water in his face, snapping him out of it. That he got. It was another to find himself sitting under a carob tree with his eyes closed, asked to take a deep breath for no apparent reason—with Victor sitting right in front of him, no less. It felt strange, uncomfortably intimate. And, as a result, it made him very self-conscious.

If Victor heard the outburst, he showed no signs of it. Instead, he took another deep breath, his eyelids betraying not the slightest hint of movement and the rest of his face showing not the faintest change of expression.

With a mixture of shame for his gaffe and relief to shut out the peculiar scene in which he was reluctant participant, Pablo followed Victor's instructions. He allowed his eyes to close and his lungs to fill, his attention, like his breath, shifting from outside in.

"And again," Victor said gently, catching Pablo off guard. He'd naively assumed that Victor had already ventured far off somewhere on his own, leaving him to fend for himself.

Pablo inhaled again and, almost in spite of himself, noticed a sense of relief. There was a tangible easing of the tension in his body and even the slightest calming of the tumult in his head, the true extent of which he had yet to appreciate.

"It's like with singing," Victor offered, drawing on something to which Pablo could easily relate. "Just as breathing properly is essential to producing and sustaining the notes, in our daily lives, too, it's fundamental to our overall well-being. It underpins the health of our bodies. It fosters peace and clarity in our minds."

"Now," Victor continued, after pausing to inhale deeply again, "without trying to breathe faster or slower or somehow control it in any way, just focus on your breath."

Though resistant to what at first seemed yet another peculiar request, sitting there with his eyes closed, nowhere else to direct his attention, Pablo discovered he was relieved to be told what to do next.

And so again he followed Victor's instructions, concentrating on his breath. He felt it come in and listened to it flow out, an aural tide of an invisible ocean on whose shore he was always standing, conscious of it or not.

At first it was easy. Almost effortless. His breath, after all, was tangible, something he could feel as it streamed in through his nose, expanded his diaphragm, and filled his lungs. Like Victor said, in that sense it was like singing, familiar. As waves of sensation washed over his body, muscles engaging, tension releasing, awareness heightening, the breath flowed back out into that unseeable sea.

All the more frustrating when he discovered he could only maintain his focus in inconsistent, momentary bursts, his mind quickly losing interest in what, on the surface at least, seemed such a simple exercise. Like a monkey swinging from branch to branch of tree after tree, it jumped to one, then another, and then countless other thoughts. Racing over an infinite succession of tangents, it was like a chain reaction bound not to stop until it burned itself out.

"When you lose your focus, simply acknowledge the thought that has caught your attention—without judging yourself for getting off track—let it go, and return to your breath," Victor advised, as though privy to Pablo's thoughts.

Doing as told, Pablo picked up where he had left off, regaining his focus only to be repeatedly astonished by the ease with which his efforts were undermined, his mind dubiously coaxed from the task at hand over and over again. It wasn't long before he felt impatient and discouraged, forgetting the part about not judging himself. The fact that Victor showed no signs of bringing the exercise to a close only made matters that much worse, as it extended into an unbearable eternity Pablo began to fear would never end. His mind now wandering freely, it desperately latched onto anything that might fill the void and pass the time.

Just when Pablo had nearly reached his breaking point, unable to imagine how he could sit there another moment, his foot asleep and his back contorted into an achy mass of knots, Victor let out a profound, deliberate sigh.

It was over.

"And now, slowly, at your own pace, come back to your senses, opening your eyes whenever you naturally feel ready to do so."

Pablo was then thrown for another loop.

Despite what he had thought was a categorical failure, an experience of little consequence, oddly enough, he didn't immediately feel inclined to open his eyes. It was as though he weren't ready to do so. He needed a moment. A moment to regroup. There was, it turned out, some sort of transition to be made after all, as if he had strayed further than he'd realized, drifted off to somewhere from which he now had to make his way back.

The sensation only compounded when he did open his eyes, for a disorienting flash he was almost taken aback by the world he rediscovered, as though he'd forgotten what to expect there.

"Welcome back," said Victor, his knowing grin conveying both amusement and satisfaction.

Pablo said nothing. Having shifted to relieve the discomfort, he was struck by how profoundly relaxed his body was. His mind, too, was decidedly more calm, unexpectedly opening him up to his surroundings. He couldn't escape the feeling they were more immediate, his perception of them curiously altered, more acute.

"I'd say you're now in a much better place to contemplate your future, my boy!" Victor laughed, like a chaperone watching a friend come to after a psychedelic trip. Slowly rising to his feet, he brushed some dirt from his pants and turned to get back to work. "Or, even better, not to think about it at all for a while!"

And with that, Victor leisurely headed back toward the shed, leaving Pablo to his own devices, including an invaluable new one now at his disposal.

39

A couple of somber holiday weeks came and went. While both feeling and honoring the tremendous absence left by Pablo's father, his family made a concerted effort to carry on with long-established traditions and make the best of a particularly difficult time.

They had very mixed success.

Once the new year was underway, Pablo decided to take Jorge's advice. Having failed to identify any more-promising possibilities, he would talk to their friend Nacho to see if his father needed help on any of his construction sites. Pablo was just looking for a temporary position to get him through the spring, by which time he hoped to have figured out a new plan to get out of town.

Nacho's father told him to have Pablo stop by one of their sites on the outskirts of the village. They were building a large house on a beautiful parcel abutting the nature reserve, and they could use a hand with some odds and ends. Since Pablo didn't have any construction skills to speak of, it was the type of work he could do. Although sure to be dull at first, Nacho's father was optimistic there would be more interesting work in the relatively near future, since a couple of men were talking about signing up for the extension of the Mediterranean

Highway under construction up the coast—much more difficult, dangerous work that had already claimed the lives of several laborers but that, consequently, was much better paid. If and when those men did quit, Pablo would be able to start learning some new skills and doing more relevant work. In the meantime, he could get started with his initial responsibilities the following Monday.

As he walked back down the road from the site, a canopy of live oaks shaded his way and the fresh, earthy fragrance of the soil filled the air, revitalized by the recent rains. Having landed a job and settled on a new path forward, he felt some relief. He would soon be learning skills that, once he had a season of work under his belt, would allow him to make a decent living. More importantly, in the event he failed to come up with a better plan, the new job would provide him with valuable know-how he could use to seek other work elsewhere. Until that moment, that hadn't even occurred to him.

Maybe that was how it was supposed to happen. Maybe he was supposed to stay put a while longer, learn a trade, and use it as a stepping stone out of the village. It wasn't Barcelona, but maybe it would be—or Sevilla or Valencia or Madrid—in time. After all, he reminded himself, the construction boom was going on all over Spain, not just his tiny corner of it.

If that wasn't how he had imagined things working out, it was because he was still holding on to the idea of leaving right away. But that wasn't going to happen. He needed to accept once and for all that, for the time being, he was staying put. Over the coming weeks and months, he'd figure out another way out of town. For now, he needed to be grateful for an opportunity that, if all else failed, could very well be the one that paved the way.

Passing the cemetery without so much as a glance in its direction, Pablo climbed the hill back to the village proper. As he approached the day care center, he made his now-habitual detour down a side street.

It didn't matter. Fate had other plans.

"Rosa."

Less a greeting, more a statement of fact.

"Pablo."

They had practically run into each other as she came out of the alley of shops. His heart was pounding. Her mind was spinning. The fact it was inevitable they'd eventually meet did nothing to assuage his shock. Or hers. The village was so small.

"*¿Qué tal?*"

It, too, just came out.

Rosa didn't reply. Like him, she needed a moment to regroup.

After a couple of failed attempts to find the right words, she realized that what she wanted to say was actually very simple.

"Pablo, I'm sorry."

He felt bad. He didn't understand. He wished they could still be together.

"And . . ." Her voice trailed off.

"And?" Pablo wondered. "What?"

She looked around, as though making sure no one else was within earshot.

"There's something I have to tell you. I just found out a couple days ago." She hesitated again, now seeming not only confused but agitated. "And, well . . . you should know before you hear it from someone else."

Before he heard it from someone else?

"Rosa, what is it?"

She wanted him to just get it. Miraculously. So she wouldn't have to say it. But that wasn't going to happen. As shame welled up in her insides like the tears gathering in her eyes, she was forced to face reality. He wasn't going to give her any choice but to say the very words she most wanted to avoid.

"I'm pregnant."

The words ripped through the space between them like the innocent turn of an ignition key detonating an unsuspected, devastating blast.

For Pablo time stopped, suspending him in the moment like an astronaut floating weightlessly in space. Rosa's peculiar energy as she delivered the cataclysmic news. The dreadful, fateful words she uttered as she did. Each time the loathsome sequence of events flashed before his eyes, the reflexive battle to deny its ramifications came a little closer to being lost. Slowly but surely, the truth made its way into his world like a pathogen against which he had no defenses.

"Pregnant," he said, rather than asked, struggling to even give voice to the word, to form its letters and pronounce its syllables, like someone who had never said it before. After all, in this context at least, he never had.

As he struggled to assimilate the news, he was seized by an equally mortifying thought.

"And you're sure of . . ."

"Of what?"

It took a moment to register.

"Of the father? That it's not yours?" Rosa responded indignantly, as though the very idea were ludicrous. "Yes, Pablo. I'm sure."

Another excruciating silence. It was hard enough for him to think straight. It was even harder to articulate his thoughts. There was too much to try to make sense of. He felt too much at once.

"It just sort of happened. I'm sorry, Pablo. I really am."

Just sort of happened? What was that supposed to mean? If up until then he had struggled to find the right words, they now rolled off his tongue.

"You and Rafa did not just sort of get together behind my back."

It hurt to say it. But he needed to. He needed to confront her with the truth.

She looked away.

"And you did not just sort of have sex."

Rosa winced as though she'd just been dealt an unfair blow.

"You and I aren't even together!" she cried out. "I didn't even have to tell you! I wanted to do the right thing and let you know before you heard it from someone else, but I shouldn't have even bothered!"

"Wanted to do the right thing?" contested Pablo. "You mean like when you told me you and Rafa were dating? The only reason we're even having this conversation is because we happened to run into each other on the street!"

"Well, now we've had it," Rosa shot back, any discretion she had hoped to maintain long since blown completely. "And there's no point in continuing it. I've given you the news. I've apologized. Whether you accept it or not is up to you. Either way, I've got to go!"

Tears streaming down her face, she turned and was off.

Pablo walked around the corner to the springs next to the town hall. He took a quick drink, then splashed his face with cold water, hoping to regain some clarity. Seeing her was hard enough. The revelation she was pregnant with Rafa's baby was shocking, as nightmarish as it was surreal.

He couldn't believe it was happening.

40

Pablo got almost no sleep that night.

He tossed and turned. His mind raced. His body sweat.

The sun was only just stirring in its sheets when he threw back his own.

It didn't matter that it was painfully early. Nor that he had hardly slept. He couldn't lie in bed another moment. If he didn't do something, he was going to go crazy. He had to move.

He got out of bed. He got dressed and grabbed his helmet, neither showering nor eating nor pausing to do anything else that might slow him down. He headed downstairs, and, before he knew it, he was on his motorcycle.

Nimbly navigating the twists and turns down the mountain, like a fugitive from the law who's got to be out of town before sunrise, he made the precipitous descent to the valley floor a thousand meters below. He sped past huge prickly pears bearing their namesake fruit, regal carobs with gnarled trunks and leaves in perfectly symmetrical pairs, and withered grape vines hanging onto impossibly steep, rocky slopes. Like a smudged black-and-white photo awaiting the dawn to revitalize its colors and redefine its forms, all of it was rendered a monochromatic blur.

Somewhere in the east the sun had now risen, but the neighboring ridges continued to hold it at bay, allowing the valley to rest that much longer. Nevertheless, minute by minute the dark sky was slowly but surely taking on the blue-gray hues of morning, a clear reminder the dormant landscape wouldn't be able to sleep the day away.

Pablo didn't know where he was going. He didn't care. All that mattered was that he was moving. And yet, when he got to the orange grove at the foot of the mountain, he had a decision to make.

Normally he wouldn't have given it a second thought. He almost always would have turned left, toward town, toward the coast, toward Málaga, even.

But now he felt unquestionably called to go right. He recognized it immediately, that voice, that feeling, that somewhere in between. He thought he'd put an end to it, pronounced its death sentence under the carob, chopped off its head and watched its extremities twitch with the last of its life-force. Yet here it was again, apparently having escaped justice and still on the loose. As though waiting in ambush on an orange-tree limb, it fell down upon him, overtaking him from head to toe. His gut seized by a peculiar urgency. His pulse racing even faster than it already was from being on the motorcycle. Every last fiber of his being possessed by an intuitive pull.

And so he surrendered.

If before he had only the vaguest idea as to where he might end up, now he didn't have any at all. It was as though someone else were at the wheel. He still didn't care. All that mattered was putting distance between himself and the village, between himself and construction, himself and Barcelona, Rosa, Rafa, baby, the store. Himself and his uncertain, confusing future.

He worked his way up the valley, the wind in his face and the dawn continuing to push back the covers of night. An avocado farm came and went on his left. Shortly after, a small village took form up ahead. Bypassing it, he followed the road along the reservoir's rim. With a combination of curiosity and discomfort, he beheld the wide band of exposed earth that lined the periphery of the enormous basin, calling to mind a thick ring of soap scum in a giant tub.

Looking to the upper end of the valley, he spied the dramatic divide that connected his region with the province of Granada. Even from afar, he could see the massive sheer, steel-gray outcrops that dominated each side of the road. Like two giant guardians on top of the world, they kept steadfast watch as they judiciously controlled access to and from the valley.

And they were beckoning.

As though having made a mistake by coming off his own mountain, Pablo found himself climbing another, one switchback at a time. The motorcycle revved faster and louder as if the engine might blow at any moment, forced to work harder and harder as it made the long, brutal ascent.

A small eternity of patient backs and forths later, riding through a series of almond orchards before coming out into an undeveloped expanse of open mountainside, he found himself in the presence of giants. Approaching the megalithic stone gods, their vertical faces soaring high above him, made him feel small. Peering over the edge to his right, he was surprised by the heights to which he'd unsuspectingly ascended during his climb, the valley floor now a bird's-eye view far below. The sky was right there, too, just out of reach, nothing between him and it.

He pulled over. As he did, getting off his bike and removing his helmet, the sun flooded the entire panorama before him. Spilling over the ranges near the coast, it set the valley floor awash in a gentle morning light that seemed expressly intended to reveal the singular beauty that made it the extraordinary place it was. As though roused from its slumber by a refreshing splash of cool water, the arid countryside extending as far as Pablo's eyes could see came alive with a thousand hues that, until then, had been enshrouded in darkness.

He saw with uncharacteristic clarity the silvery grays, rusty golds, and blood reds of the mountains, whose colors would change over the course of the day in ever-evolving concert with the sun. He beheld the greens and yellows of the vegetation, both in the geometric perfection of the olive, almond, and avocado orchards and in the random, paradoxical harmony of the pines, bushes, and grasses. Perhaps most of all, he marveled at the blues, the sky and water, in the reservoir and the sea alike. The boldest of the colors, they offered striking relief to the predominantly earth-toned palette. No others were so deep or so pure, all of the rest faded by the unsympathetic fury of the Andalusian sun. In contrast, the blues were as immutable as the villages' own impervious white, imparting an unlikely vitality that otherwise would have been sorely lacking.

It really was a beautiful place, Pablo thought. He did love it, after all, despite hoping to leave, at least for a while. Once he had, once he'd seen some of the world beyond its borders, perhaps—just like what had happened with José in Madrid—his curiosity would be satisfied, and he'd be content to return home. He didn't know. That was the point: he had to find out.

Eventually, the sense it was time to move again. With it, a pull even more unexpected than the insistence to turn right at the orange grove. He'd more or less concluded the pass itself was his destination, time spent contemplating the stunning view an inspiring early-morning excursion to find some peace of mind. But there was more to it. Rather than the end of the road, it turned out the pass was merely the start of it.

As though the stone guardians had stepped to the side, like the motto between the Pillars of Hercules on the Spanish coat of arms, Pablo got the message: *Plus ultra.*

Further beyond.

No sooner had he traversed the pass than the scenery changed dramatically. Rather than sharp peaks, staggered ridges, and sheer cliffs, after riding through a small, unremarkable village, he found himself on a wide plain of farmland. He saw low, rocky hills on which little grew other than random, determined trees and, to his right, the back side of the mountains in his own province, their summits peering powerlessly over the horizon.

The bitter cold had left the ground, much of which consisted of bare rows of tilled earth, covered in a silvery layer of frost. It glistened as the golden rays of the sun, which was now making its ascent, set it asparkle. Even the road, meandering through a forest of short, stout live oaks, was dusted with frost, forcing Pablo to take extra care—something he was glad to have done when a large quail scrambled across his path. The forest gave way to more farmland and, further still down the road, impossibly steep, surprisingly uniform hills that looked like giant gumdrops. Each was dotted with olive or almond trees in such perfect, evenly spaced rows that Pablo couldn't help but think of Velcro.

Not long after, he came upon another village, this one larger and more picturesque than the nearly shuttered, lifeless border town. A pure-white conglomeration rising precipitously out of two deep craggy gorges, it was crowned by an austere sixteenth-century gothic church. Breakfast long overdue, Pablo headed into town in search of some sustenance.

Sitting outside a *pastelería* with a chocolate-filled *napolitano* and a coffee, he watched the village stir to life. A truck unloaded a delivery on the other side of the street. A couple of professionally dressed women made their way to work. A rental car drove by, the blonde in the passenger seat wide-eyed, staring at Pablo like a tourist on safari gawking at an animal.

Across the plaza, beyond a fountain whose elegant spectacle was appreciated only by the sparrows flittering in its pool, Pablo saw a fort whose brick-red walls and pointed parapets looked strikingly out of place. In reality, the opposite was true. Clearly of Arab origin, the fort had no doubt been erected long before any of the present-day structures surrounding it.

Pablo felt strange being there. Strange thinking that such a short time ago he'd been at home in bed, no plans to do anything, never mind ride all the way over the pass. Never mind have breakfast in a village he'd never visited. It felt like a whole other world. He savored the anonymity. He relished his perspective as objective observer, captivated by everything he saw, be it as curious as the fort or as trivial as the pigeons pecking crumbs at his feet.

Asking in the pastelería, he learned the gorges were just around the corner, an overlook providing an impeccable view. Steep cliffs plummeted into a verdant stream that, over the course of eons, had carved them out of stone once buried deep within the earth. Walking down to the stream itself, Pablo listened to the gentle song of the water tumbling over the rocks. He observed the vegetation that grew along the banks. He watched the swallows who nested in the cliffs circle overhead, unloading their distinctive chirps in machine-gun succession, ecstatic for the new day.

Returning to the square, he got back onto his motorcycle. His lungs filled with fresh air, he felt invigorated. His heart uplifted by the natural beauty, he felt inspired. More relaxed than he'd been in weeks, he felt free, thinking little about the past and even less about the future, absorbed as he was in his present endeavor.

Trusting those feelings, like a leaf on the surface of the stream, he let himself be carried onward by the same currents that had guided him thus far on his impromptu outing.

A couple of kilometers down the road, Pablo discovered that, in addition to its historic architecture and natural wonders, the town boasted Arab baths built on the site of natural hot springs also used by the Romans. The sensual and salutary pleasures of hot mineral water being timeless, the baths were still very much in use today.

Speeding past without laying an eye on their majestic horseshoe arches, never mind dipping so much as a toe into their soothing and curative waters, Pablo forged ahead, the road soon leading into a wide valley of gently rolling hills in a beautiful patchwork of subtle hues. There were vast fields of golds and browns, as well as some that were a light green. Other sections were a faint lavender, and in others the ground was a sandy color. Bright stands of tall, narrow, white-barked poplars shot up along the middle of the valley floor, no doubt laying claim to a stream hidden there. Elsewhere, small, isolated oaks valiantly bore undying testimony to the ancient extent of the forest through which Pablo had passed earlier.

As beautiful as it all was, nothing could have prepared him for what came next.

Climbing over a hill and rounding another bend, he came upon a breathtaking landscape aflame with scarlet. As though face-to-face with a raging wildfire, he beheld vast swaths of poppies that were completely otherworldly, straight out of Oz—Dorothy herself likely to be dreaming *en español* somewhere among the astonishing proliferation of inconceivably brilliant opiate-laden buds. The fields seemed to be in a perpetual state of outdoing themselves, of bursting into even more dazzling crimson. The flowers were so innumerable that, like rivers threatening to overflow their banks, it took stone walls to keep them from spilling into the neighboring plots of olives and scrub, muted and drab in comparison, unfairly upstaged.

Pablo had seen poppies before; they were common throughout the countryside. What he hadn't seen was such an astounding, brilliant profusion of them as this. It was one of the most striking landscapes he'd ever encountered.

Flying through it all, he felt exhilarated. It wasn't the first time he'd made the trip, but this time everything was different. There was something about experiencing it on his own terms, not only on his bike, but within the context of a spontaneous exploit, that colored the entire trip. It infused the familiar with novelty. It heightened his attention to details that otherwise might have been lost on him, to what he saw and felt and the thought-provoking impressions to which it all gave rise.

One particular detail came in the unambiguous form of a sign. One that in a single word divulged where—unbeknownst to him—he'd been headed all along.

Granada.

A rush surged through his body.

Could he really go all the way to Granada? Just like that?

On a whim? It was so far. Except, without realizing it, he'd already traveled well over half, if not three-quarters, of the way. According to the sign, he was fast approaching the junction with the freeway. From there, it couldn't be more than another half hour.

If he was going with his gut, apparently he was going to Granada.

Not long after, he left behind the rural route in favor of the multilane thoroughfare, his curiosity and anticipation giving way to a mounting anxiety. Even when going someplace familiar like Málaga, he never liked riding near large urban areas. Riding straight into the heart of one he'd never navigated on his own was even less appealing.

But then he saw the Alhambra.

Sitting majestically atop the city as it had for over five hundred years, since the days when it was the seat of the last Moorish caliphate in Spain and Islam was still the religion of the land, Pablo couldn't help but feel a sense of wonder as he beheld the legendary compound. Within its august walls there was a fortress, multiple palaces, and extensive gardens. In fact, the royal residences on its grounds were of such beauty and had been so skillfully conceived and rendered that, taken together, they represented not only one of the pinnacles of the history of Islamic art and architecture, but arguably one of the most superb architectural achievements in the world.

Finding his way through the urban chaos and clamor, Pablo left behind a large square for a narrow cobblestone road. He felt as though he'd returned to a rustic locale in the countryside. The single-lane, tree-covered street followed a picturesque creek serving as a natural boundary between two historic neighborhoods. Each rose on steep hills on either side of it, connected by the elegant arches of two stone bridges.

Little could Pablo have known that, besides an inspiring symbol proclaiming his arrival, the Alhambra was also a beacon of sorts. Yet when the cobblestone lane opened onto another large plaza that proved to be his destination, that was exactly what he discovered. Looking up, he found the

Alhambra regally perched in plain sight just overhead.

Getting off his bike, he paused for a better look. If it had been impressive from a distance, upon closer inspection it was even more extraordinary, particularly given the perspective he now had of the massive tawny-colored, parapet-crowned towers of its fortress. The oldest section of the complex, it was situated closest to the edge of the high plateau. Behind it, following the wall along the ridge, one of the two main palaces could be seen. Its own smaller tower, as well as the wooden arcades running between its two wings, were readily visible, as were groups of tourists taking in the extraordinary views afforded of the city below. Set apart on its own grounds a short distance away, the white walls, dark wood trim, and terra-cotta-tile roof of another palace could be seen; in times gone by it had served as the equivalent of a country getaway for the sultan and his retinue.

Leaving his motorcycle behind, Pablo turned toward the buildings across the plaza, each built in a classical style with two-toned façades consisting of three stories of symmetrically placed windows. Many of the windows featured wrought-iron balconies below, and most had emerald-green wooden blinds hanging above, all in different states of being rolled up or down. In front of the buildings, a few cafés had set up outdoor seating under a long, vine-covered trellis. Pablo walked over to one and ordered a coffee.

If earlier he'd been surprised to find himself in the village, now he could hardly believe he was in Granada. It seemed so random. So out of the blue. And it was.

As he tore open a sugar packet and let the grains tumble into his coffee, he questioned whether he'd done the right thing, wondering if he'd gone too far, running off without letting anyone know. But the secrecy only added to his sense of adventure, like the guilty pleasure of a school boy who's cut class in favor of some forbidden and more alluring exploit. Besides, it wasn't as if he'd caught the ferry to Morocco. He'd just gone on a longer than usual ride. His mother would be surprised he'd left before she'd gotten up; otherwise, she probably wouldn't give it a second thought.

Only taking a sip of his *café con leche*—pulling away like a plane aborting a landing when it almost scalded the roof of his mouth—Pablo watched as people came and went. A young woman stopped by for her caffeine fix, as clear of purpose as a hummingbird sucking nectar from a flower, on her way a split second later. A plump old man in a button-down and cardigan read the newspaper through thick black frames, never looking up, not even when reaching for his coffee or patting the scruffy dog at his side. A clean-cut family of northern Europeans showed up, the parents and two children the very embodiment of health and prosperity, scanning the café for the best table. Once they'd ordered, the father buried his face in a guidebook, intent on ensuring he devised the best possible itinerary for their day.

After so much time on his bike, Pablo felt good sitting in one place, watching the ever-changing spectacle play out before him. A blue sky overhead. A gentle breeze bearing aromas of coffee and tobacco, an occasional waft of someone's perfume. It was exactly what he needed. So much so that it was only after a second café con leche that his curiosity roused him back to his feet.

Pablo had touched down in a part of town called the Albaicín. Although surprised to have found his way there with such ease, it was in fact where he had hoped to end up. He knew enough to know it was one of Granada's most interesting neighborhoods, a natural starting point for a visit.

It would have been easy given all the nearby churches, monuments, and museums, but Pablo wasn't interested in playing tourist. He just wanted to wander. He wanted more of what he'd experienced in the village after the pass, more of what he had felt as he'd ridden his bike through the countryside, carefree, inspired, and emboldened. He wanted to stretch his legs and spread his wings. Having lost himself in one discovery after another, he wanted to go even further, dive even deeper.

So he started walking.

On the surface at least, the Albaicín was full of similarities to the village, from the endless whitewashed walls that held it together like flesh in a pomegranate, to the narrow alleyways to which they gave form, rising and falling over steep slopes like a jilted lover's hopes. The little plazas were familiar, too, making space for the sun and the sky, for flourishes of green and blue where there was so little room for anything but white. Then there were the brick cisterns, the *aljibes*, vestiges of the technologically sophisticated system the Arabs had developed centuries before for distributing water throughout the city.

His initial impressions tainted by a natural inclination to focus on the familiar, it wasn't long before he began to get a fuller appreciation for his surroundings. It soon became clear this was not the village or the historic neighborhood in town or any other place with which he might be tempted to conveniently equate it, to make quick and easy sense of it. This place was different.

There was a greater variety of buildings. Some deviated from the predominant whitewash and distinguished themselves with warm hues or exposed brick. Others were adorned with elegant wrought iron or other ornamental flourishes like horseshoe-shaped entryways or magnificent Islamic mosaics—details much more elaborate than anything found in the village. The most impressive edifices of all were crowned by regal towers bearing proud testimony to a distant, glorious past.

The alleys themselves were different, too. Though often well-kempt like those at home, at times they were covered in bold graffiti crying out in defiant, impassioned protest or had pockmarked surfaces where layers of whitewash had been worn away. Some alleys opened onto plazas where weeds poked through cracks in the pavement and wind-swept debris accumulated in overlooked corners. Others still took the form of long, tunnel-like passages that seemed to venture deep into impenetrable secrets. Their walls soared high above passers-by, invincible barriers whose heights were both beauteously and ominously covered in multicolored shards of glass.

Other walls weren't nearly as effective at guarding their

secrets. As Pablo made one steep ascent after another, he inadvertently peered over enclosures harboring lush gardens full of colorful flowers and vibrant fruit trees. He saw lemons, pomegranates, and quince, apples, figs, and persimmons. The ground below hardly made less an impression; there were rows of rough leafy greens, smooth fiery reds, and shiny eggplant purples. It was like stumbling upon fertile plots of countryside in the heart of the city.

What Pablo had no way of knowing was that, rather than improbable aberrations in the otherwise manifestly urban landscape, the gardens were an integral part of the neighborhood and its history. Each pertained to a *carmen*, a term of Arab origin that literally meant "vine" but in Granada had come to mean "house with orchard." Construction of the *cármenes* was said to have begun after the Moors were expelled; their dwellings were demolished to make room for the large homes with expansive gardens that would replace them, many of which, as Pablo had now seen with his own eyes, had survived to the present day.

What had also survived was the Alhambra itself. Despite being perched a hilltop away on the other side of the Darro, it was omnipresent. It peered around corners. It discretely inserted itself into backdrops. It imperiously dominated entire vistas. The whole neighborhood, in fact, seemed to have its attention directed toward the august monument, which refused to relinquish center stage.

As though following the neighborhood's lead, after a couple of hours meandering Pablo took a seat on a bench to take in the view. His eyes glued to the Alhambra, his ears began to wander, picking up where his tired legs had left off.

A baby crying. Voices murmuring behind closed doors and cracked windows. A gate slamming. Dogs barking nearby, then a few moments later, further off in the distance, as if in response. Pots clanging deep within unseen kitchens, and water turning on and off at unpredictable intervals. The presumptuous ring of church bells at what was no doubt a divinely ordained time, and, finally, a hilarious interaction between a pigeon and a man in a second-story apartment, neither of whom Pablo could see.

"Coo, coo, coo," the man playfully mocked the unsuspecting bird. "That's all you ever say! Why not coo, coo, cah or something else once in a while!"

The man then broke into a gentle, carefree melody of his own, unconcerned as to whether his feathered friend would prove receptive to the unsolicited advice, and unaware of the huge grin now etched across Pablo's face.

Footsteps on cobblestones snapped Pablo's attention back to the alley, to a young professional in pressed jeans, a tucked-in polo, and expensive-looking sunglasses on his way down the hill. An old lady lumbered by, dressed and coiffed as if coming back from church, though two rustling bags of groceries suggested a different sort of outing. A pair of early twenty-something dreadlocked counterculturists shared a joint and had a laugh as they, too, made their way to their destinations.

It would have been hard to say how long Pablo observed the goings-on from his peaceful, picturesque vantage point. He probably would have sat there even longer, had it not been for the sound of a flamenco guitar. Grabbing his attention like the Pied Piper's flute might a mouse, it roused him to his feet and lured him in its direction.

Working his way through the maze of alleys, Pablo found himself ascending a wide staircase that led to an imposing church of whitewashed brick. To his right, a large plaza packed full of people afforded the best view yet of the Alhambra, itself outdone by an even more impressive backdrop, the massive, snow-peaked Sierras reaching into an incomparable blue sky.

He had arrived at the San Nicolás lookout.

Seeing his endeavor through to the end, Pablo let his eyes follow his ears. A guitarist sat alone on a far wall, an artsy, unpretentious fellow several years Pablo's senior with long curly hair, a short beard, and dark sunglasses. Given the distance he was keeping from the mobs of tourists, he seemed to be playing for no other reason than the sheer joy of it.

More eager to interact with the throngs of visitors was a

group of young artisans hawking their wares, jewelry, paintings, and other goods displayed on blankets and benches. Each vendor conformed to the same nonconformist look of scraggly unwashed hair, ragged T-shirts, and loose-fitting, free-flowing pants of the finest hemp, while those selling jewelry donned examples of their handiwork. Cigarettes and joints dangled from their lips as they joked with each other and chatted with potential patrons.

Pablo squeezed his way through the crowd to the edge of the lookout. It truly was breathtaking, a spectacular view of not only the Alhambra, but the Albaicín and the rest of the city below. However, having seen it all from a similar vantage point shortly before and eager to leave the crowds behind, he didn't linger long.

Heading back down the stairs, he wandered onto one of the neighborhood's main arteries, a row of cafés and restaurants that narrowed into a succession of shops whose owners and goods alike appeared Moroccan in origin. Amidst the musty smell of leather and the exotic, festive sound of Maghrebi music, brightly colored clothes, scarves, and tapestries hung from walls that also featured metal lanterns, mirrors framed with inlaid wood, and a surprising number of miniature bongos.

Pablo knew that many North Africans had settled in Spain during the economic boom of the last few years; but, he couldn't recall ever having seen any in his province, nor had he seen many in Málaga. It was interesting to come upon a lane not only full of Moroccan men—as though he'd taken a wrong turn and accidentally ended up in Fez or Marrakech—but the occasional Moroccan woman in a headscarf. Curious testimonies to the peculiar, cyclical nature of time, the sound of Arabic and the sight of traditionally dressed Muslims had returned to the alleys of Granada over five hundred years after their expulsion.

After stopping for another coffee and a bite to eat, Pablo arrived at a busy thoroughfare separating the old from the comparatively new, the Albaicín from the city center. There he encountered yet another transplant from the other side of the Strait, this one from a land much further off than his neighbors to the distant north, a legendary desert away.

The young sub-Saharan was selling DVDs, just as many men in similar circumstances sold not only DVDs but sunglasses or whatever other inexpensive merchandise they could get their hands on in the hopes of eking out a meager living. He was tall and lean, possessing a defined musculature that, curiously, betrayed no sign of hardship. His skin was a deep, perfectly smooth black, and his eyes and closely cropped hair scarcely differed in tone.

What most struck Pablo was the total lack of emotion borne by the young man's face. He looked entirely out of place, seized by a profound, unfathomable ennui, as if he scarcely bothered to hope for a sale from a people among whom he would always feel impossibly apart. And yet, almost assuredly having no other options, he sat on a wall, keeping an unfaltering, hawkish eye on his goods from a spot wholly exposed to the sun, indifferent to an area of shade only a meter away.

As Pablo crossed into the city center, the cathedral rose imperiously to his left, its massive tawny walls proudly coaxing him into a stroll around their perimeter. Looking up, he marveled at gothic spires and intricate, lacelike stonework. Closer to the ground, a sudden, sensual mix of a thousand scents—of vanilla, cardamom, and Assam, of orange, jasmine, and mint—jolted his olfactory glands into overdrive, like hallucinogenic drugs overstimulating an idle imagination. He had come upon the spice sellers, their countless wicker baskets of herbs, spices, and teas infusing the air with an intoxicating combination of invigorating fragrances.

Passing through a grandiose wrought-iron gate, Pablo threaded through the masses laying the cathedral siege. A young couple played gentle melodies on Spanish guitars, followed by a North African man writing the names of tourists in Arabic script. A street performer dressed in silver from head to toe scrambled to apply the finishing touches to his make-up, as though afraid of arriving late to his own show. And as he neared the end of his jaunt, Pablo overheard a tour guide explaining that it was within the walls of the Royal Chapel that Ferdinand and Isabel had been laid to rest, the monarchs who not only put a definitive end to Moorish rule in Spain, but sponsored Columbus on his expedition to what would prove to be the Americas.

After wandering through an old bazaar where silk had been both made and sold by Moorish merchants but today was little more than a claustrophobic grid of cramped alleys full of souvenirs, Pablo entered a labyrinth of narrow, densely packed commercial streets. He perused music shops and sporting goods stores, instantly enamored of an expensive pair of cleats. At an electronics outlet, he admired the latest big-screen TVs like a museum-goer might works of art. When he came upon an ice cream shop, he fell victim to temptation.

Cone in hand, Pablo walked a short distance and found himself in the city center, as though it had been his intention to end up there all along. The imposing façade of the central post office soared before him. Banks, a luxury hotel, and a Burger King jockeyed for exposure on the busy circle. Masses of people crossed the streets in aggressive waves, and vehicles sped by with reckless abandon and deafening roars, swirls of dust and billows of exhaust engulfing everything and everyone. This was the heart of the city, and Pablo couldn't believe how hard it was beating.

His own heart racing, Pablo stood amidst the chaos paralyzed with indecision, unsure which way to turn. Before he could give it another thought, the answer appeared to him, a literal vision etched on the giant clock face across the plaza. Having completely lost track of the time, he hadn't even noticed.

Daytime had ended. Nighttime had begun.

He should get home. He couldn't believe he'd stayed as long as he had. The village suddenly seemed far away, the return trip a long, tiresome journey he'd rather not make in the dark. All the same, he needed to eat. If he didn't now, he'd have to on the way back. Better while he had so many options.

Setting off for the Albaicín, he left behind the frenetic avenues that crisscrossed the city center, opting instead for side streets. There were fewer people, there was less traffic, and he was more likely to find someplace interesting to grab a meal.

Trailing pigeons that preferred to waddle a half pace ahead rather than go to the trouble of taking flight, he came upon on a plaza shaded by mature sycamores. A crossroads for the neighborhood, as people converged on its center, Pablo spied a lively bar through the foliage. Instantly recognizing his destination, he made a beeline for it.

When he arrived, a couple was vacating their table outside. Since no others were free, he didn't think twice about claiming it for himself.

He ordered a beer and began perusing the menu. It wasn't long before he felt the weight of someone's stare.

"Are you using this chair?"

As Pablo went to respond, his voice failed him. Like after the fire. But rather than devastation, this time the cause was disbelief.

She was absolutely gorgeous.

He hadn't seen her initially. She'd been turned the other way, part of a group that had pushed together the two tables next to his.

At a loss to explain his bizarre expression, she tried again, in English.

"Do you need the chair?"

"*¿Cómo? ¡No, no, perdona!*" Pablo laughed, snapping out of it. "*¡Soy español!* And, no, I don't need it. You can have it."

"Ah! The way you looked at me, I thought maybe you were an international student or something."

"No, no, I'm from here. Well, I mean I'm Spanish at least."

"But you're not from Granada?" she asked, getting up to move the chair. Pablo lent a hand.

"No, I'm just here because . . . well, I'm not sure what I'm doing here, actually."

"Such a confused boy!" the young woman laughed.

"It's just . . . well, it's a long story," Pablo offered, realizing how ridiculous he sounded. "And I guess since I haven't talked to anyone all day, I'm not making any sense."

"In that case, you should probably join us."

"Oh, thanks. But that's OK." He didn't want to impose.

"No really, we have some more friends coming, so we actually sort of need your table," she confessed, unable to hold back a mischievous smile. "We were waiting for that couple to leave, but you swooped down on it so fast we didn't have a chance to make our move."

"Ah! I'm sorry. In that case, I can just go to another—"

"*¡Ni pensarlo!* Stay right where you are! You have a lot of explaining to do!"

Before he could protest, the woman turned to her friends.

"*Chicos*, this is . . ."

"Pablo," he said, turning as red as a pitcher of sangria.

"This is Pablo, a lost soul who will be joining us for the celebrations."

A chorus of greetings came in response, as Pablo's table was annexed to the others.

"I'm Eva, and this is Arturo," the woman said, motioning to the guy now seated on the other side of Pablo. In his early twenties like most of the group, he was of average height and had a thin, lanky build. His mussy dishwater-blond hair looked as though it hadn't been washed for a day or two, and he wore a faded sweat shirt and ragged jeans.

Eva was also of average height, but that was the only thing average about her. Her olive complexion was flawless, her light-hazel eyes inquisitive and alert. Full, healthy locks fell below her shoulders, and she inhabited her well-proportioned body with confidence and poise. Pablo could only guess whether she was always so full of life or in such great spirits because of the gathering. Her lips seemingly etched in a perpetual smile, she was quick to laugh at each of Arturo's ongoing barrage of one-liners.

Pablo was mesmerized.

"It's Javi's birthday," Arturo explained, gesturing to a

chubby, bearded fellow at the end of the table. A drink in hand and a grin on his face, he was chatting with a couple of girls.

Eva and Arturo showered Pablo with questions, captivated by the surprise appearance of a stranger in their midst. For someone who had hardly spoken all day, Pablo quickly made up for lost time.

"We're going to karaoke after this," Eva commented, when Arturo got up to go to the bathroom. "You should come."

"Karaoke?" He had performed on many stages, but none had been in a karaoke bar. The very idea seemed laughable. "Oh no, I've got to—"

"Don't say you can't sing!" Eva insisted, assuming he was about to start making excuses.

"It's not that. Actually, I do sing, but—"

"Perfect! Then you're coming."

Three beers later Pablo was enjoying himself so much that he put up no resistance when the time came for karaoke. It was as though he'd intended to go all along—as if he wouldn't be further deferring an hour-and-a-half trip home.

When they got to the bar, the subdued lighting, screen acting as teleprompter, and festive atmosphere were all as expected, as was what followed. The group got settled, and once again the alcohol flowed. Each round washing away more inhibitions, one friend after another—in singles, pairs, and occasional groups—proceeded to make fools of themselves to their favorite tunes.

Although he couldn't help but laugh at what, for the most part, were ridiculous performances, all the same Pablo began to feel anxious.

They were going to try to get him to sing. He was sure of it. But he wasn't going to. He hadn't since before the store had burned. Other than under his breath, not a single note since losing his father. It wasn't that he was worried about whether or not he still could—although he did wonder how rusty he'd be. There was more to it than that.

He wasn't sure it was right.

Like Señora Muñoz dressing in black for a year after her

husband died, no small part of Pablo's hiatus from music had been out of respect for his father. Singing—especially now, to a bar full of drunken revelers—would almost feel sacrilegious. Even under different circumstances, it would have felt too soon, like saying he was done grieving and ready to move on.

But he wasn't.

The more he thought about it, the more uncomfortable he became. Maybe he should leave. They were going to ask him to sing, and he was being naive to think his excuses would fly. He should have thought it through before he joined them. They had been so welcoming, so much fun, and he would seem like a straitlaced bore. He shouldn't have come. He didn't know what time it was, but he should have hit the road long before.

"Pablo!" came a voice through the speakers, catapulting him from his reflections to center stage, the microphone now pointed at him. "You might have forgotten how to talk, but it's time to reclaim your voice and sing!"

Once again, Pablo missed a beat. Time stopped, and the bar was silenced. His expression went blank. It felt so direct, so deliberate, as though Eva realized full well the implications of what she had just said. Pablo looked at her, a question in his eyes. She smiled knowingly, a divine messenger sharing his secret.

With an embarrassed smile, he got up and went onstage. A song had already been selected. One of the women had chosen an emotional ballad she never would have come close to mastering, even if she were still sober. It would have been a perfect disaster. But not only did Pablo know it well, for his voice it was ideal.

Now relishing an opportunity that mere moments before he'd resisted with all his might, as though granted permission to do the unthinkable, encouraged to break a taboo, he took a deep breath. Not exactly sober himself, after a monumental day and the revelation just before, his heart was wide open. He shut out the bar and turned all his attention to the song.

His new friends continued their banter, their drunken voices initially drowning out his own, as he eased his way into a delicate intro. But then came a shift. Something was happening at the front of the room, and it wasn't just another comical performance. The stranger from nowhere was about to take them somewhere, each note he sang, every phrase he enunciated creating more tension, generating more expectation. He was genuinely feeling it. And he really could sing. It was as if he'd duped them all by downplaying his talent. No one had seen it coming, and soon the whole group was hanging onto his each and every word.

But Pablo wasn't thinking about them. Whereas ordinarily he'd be playing to the crowd, presently he didn't care if they listened closely or ignored him completely or sang along to every lyric. This wasn't the festival. He hadn't even expected to be onstage. What he was doing had nothing to do with impressing strangers at a bar.

As though using a broken appendage for the first time since removing the cast, he reengaged with his voice tentatively, paying careful attention to its cues and respecting its limits. When he felt his cords begin to constrict as he went into his upper register, he pulled back. Faltering slightly when he went to belt out a powerful note, again, he eased up. Otherwise it was like riding a bike. Once more he was quickly attuned to his instrument.

The emotional intensity of the song notwithstanding, it felt good to sing. It was empowering to reclaim an essential part of himself, one that gave him such joy. He relished it. As visceral as cerebral, it was a literal rush. His mind, body, and soul, each and every part of himself engaged. Breathing life into the melody brought him more to life, too.

Indeed, though ostensibly singing the lyrics to the song, it was his own story to which Pablo gave voice. The deep well from which he drew the profound feelings expressed through the music was his own experience. Fire. Death. Silence. Relationships ended and new ones begun, including with himself. So much in so little time. It still didn't seem real, and it still wasn't over, evolving so fast he could hardly keep up.

Now an early morning motorcycle ride had led to a

nighttime stage in Granada. Nothing made sense. His heart bled sorrow, his soul breathed liberation. He was everywhere. He was nowhere. Everything and nothing. Life was unbearable pain, incomprehensible mystery, boundless love.

The popular recording of the song ended with a powerful climax. Pablo chose to keep it his own. Using less to do more, he brought his rendition full circle by returning to the intimate intensity with which he'd begun. His brazen vulnerability drawing in the audience that much more, he delivered a poignant, heartfelt conclusion.

Not a single soul present failed to take notice.

A tense silence followed, as if no one knew what to do next. It was only when a single pair of hands came together that a riotous eruption of approval ensued.

Pablo received a hero's welcome as he returned to his seat, showered with praise, patted on the back, and offered more than one free drink.

"That was incredible," said Eva, struggling to reconcile the talented performer she'd just seen onstage with the awkward, tongue-tied boy she'd met earlier.

"Thanks," said Pablo, exhausted but euphoric.

A woman he hadn't met yet, Mariloli, came up to congratulate him. Throwing her mane of long, curly hair over one shoulder and pushing up her glasses, she turned to Eva and added, "He's got to try out."

"Oh my god, you're right! I hadn't even thought of that!" Eva agreed. "You've got to try out for Gato Negro. They're having auditions next week."

"Gato Negro?" Pablo knew nothing about Granada's music scene.

"One of our most popular bands," Arturo chimed in, returning from the bar with a beer.

"It's not like they're huge or anything," Mariloli explained. "I mean, they don't have a recording contract yet. But they have put out a couple of CDs on their own, and they do have a pretty big following."

"Yeah," Arturo continued, "and even if they don't have a

contract yet, they'll definitely have one soon. Their fan base is just too big. And after the tour, they'll only be bigger."

"The tour?" asked Pablo, even more curious.

"The talk is that they're getting ready to head out, even though they haven't announced it yet. Still, that's the only reason I can think of—other than recording, obviously—for why they'd need a singer so badly."

"If they're already established, and they're probably about to go on tour, why do they need a singer at all? Don't they already have one?" Pablo wondered.

"Oh yeah," Arturo realized. "I guess you don't know the story."

"It's so sad," Eva said, as if contemplating the downfall of a beloved idol.

"Totally," Arturo agreed.

"So, what happened?" Pablo asked, dying for them to get to the point.

"Well," Eva began, "officially, all the band has said is that Joaquín's taking time off for personal reasons—whatever that's supposed to mean. But rumor has it that he can't perform anymore because he's too afraid."

"Too afraid of what?" Pablo didn't follow.

"No, that's it—just afraid." Arturo clarified. "Afraid to perform."

"You know," Mariloli interjected, "stage fright? They had to cancel their last few shows, and somehow the rumor got out that it was because Joaquín started having panic attacks every time he went onstage."

"It's not a rumor, it's true," Arturo insisted. "I heard he's totally lost it before all of their recent gigs—and that he even ran offstage in the middle of one. Apparently the only way he could go out there at all was to be drugged up on all sorts of antianxiety meds!"

"Drugs maybe, but from what I hear, it's not the prescription kind," Eva countered, unconvinced. "Your own girlfriend—who's friends with their percussionist's girlfriend's friend—told me that he's just been partying too much, and now he's got a habit that was getting in the way."

"Yeah, I know—she told me, too, but I don't buy it," retorted Arturo, unwilling to believe what he considered little more than spiteful hearsay.

"Well," said Eva, skeptically raising her eyebrows, "he definitely wasn't on the last time we saw him perform—his voice was horrible! It was so strained, like he was struggling to get through each song."

Pablo was much less concerned about the cause of the maligned singer's demise than about everything else he had just heard. Fan base? Recording contract? Tour? If they had all that going for them, the band couldn't be that bad. To the contrary, given the way his new friends were talking about them, chances were they were pretty good.

"All right you guys, I've got to take off," said Mariloli, glancing at her watch.

"What time is it, anyway?" wondered Pablo, afraid to ask.

"Almost eleven," Arturo answered.

"What! No way! How did that happen? I've got to get home!" Pablo was practically in a panic. His mom was not going to be happy.

"How do I get back to the Albaicín?"

41

The morning following his epic adventure, Pablo slept in.

He had been lucky. His mother had spent the night in Málaga, so his late-night arrival had gone unnoticed. He hadn't had to explain a thing.

When he finally woke up, his head was still full of big dreams from the day before. The novelty and excitement of his spontaneous escapade. The ease of it. Places he'd seen and people he'd met. His unexpected return to the stage.

Eva.

And something else, too.

Reaching over to the nightstand, he grabbed his wallet, pulling out the bar napkin on which Mariloli had jotted down the audition details.

Suddenly he was dreaming again.

He saw himself returning to Granada. Where the auditions would be held. Who would be there. What the band would be like. He imagined what he would sing—settling on one song, only to repeatedly think of another, better one—and how it would go. He saw himself being chosen, starting rehearsals, and embarking on an unforgettable, life-changing adventure. Magazine covers, multiplatinum recordings, and sold-out stadiums. A breakout solo career inevitably culminating in tabloid affairs, minor run-ins with the law, and a late-life tell-all where he came clean on his version of events that had defined a life in the spotlight.

His mind racing in tandem with his heart, he began thinking it through.

Could he go to Granada?

There were many daunting reasons he shouldn't even consider it, not the least being the logistical challenges of being in a band an hour and a half from home. Then there was the fact he knew almost nothing about the group, which meant he had no way of knowing if he had any chance of being chosen—never mind whether he actually wanted to be. And those were just the first few things that came to mind. If he wanted to, he could come up with countless more, paralyzing himself and deciding to forget about it.

But that was the thing: he didn't want to. The notion he might waste the time and energy coming up with a thousand reasons he shouldn't go felt foolish. Recalling one of his conversations with Victor, he was reminded that neither the opportunity nor the problems existed yet.

The only problem that mattered was the risk that, by ignoring what he felt in his heart, he might miss out on doing something worthwhile with his voice. He felt like he sometimes did when seeing a beautiful girl for the first time, mortified to approach her, yet lucidly aware that if he didn't give into his attraction, he might never see her again.

Besides, maybe going to the auditions wasn't even about being in the band. Recalling still more of Victor's advice, maybe all it was about was taking that first step. Maybe it was simply about jumping on the opportunity for no other reason than that it had presented itself and resonated so strongly, without worrying about any what-ifs, good or bad. Maybe it was about trying out for a band for the sake of trying out for a band, for the experience itself, another excuse to go to Granada and see his new friends.

He looked at the napkin, his heart filling with hope, his imagination getting still further carried away. But then, like a nun slapping his knuckles with a ruler, a rude awakening: he had overlooked a very important detail.

The auditions were on Monday. The very same day he was supposed to start his new job.

His heart sank.

Maybe it wasn't meant to be after all.

He curled back up in bed, looking for a way out—the means to somehow go both to the job and to the auditions. He didn't see any way. It was, after all, impossible to be in two places at once, particularly ones a hundred kilometers apart.

What if he asked to start on Tuesday? No, they'd never take him seriously if he couldn't even make it to work on his very first day.

What if he called in sick? He was embarrassed to even consider it, to entertain the thought of such a shamelessly transparent tactic. Besides, how did he expect not to get caught, when the site was in the village? Was there any way he could slip out of town unnoticed, while somehow keeping his absence during the entire day a secret as well? What if his mother caught wind he'd never made it to work, knowing he wasn't at home either? As Pablo knew all too well, in the village word traveled very fast and over the most improbable of paths.

The more he considered all the complexities, the more tangled the web became, each new thread a question for which he didn't have an answer. Perhaps, given that he'd decided construction was where his immediate future lay, he needed to stay the course and rule out anything that might jeopardize his success there.

And yet that didn't feel right either.

Having let the cat out of the bag, he was powerless to put it back in, flying at him with blood-curdling shrieks and claws fully drawn each time he tried. There was no denying he felt a tremendous pull toward the auditions.

Why, he wondered, increasingly frustrated, would his intuition seem to so clearly urge him to do something that was so clearly impossible?

Although it wasn't the first time he'd asked himself that

very question, it didn't make it any easier to answer it.

42

“I really feel like I’m supposed to go, but I don’t see any way I can.”

“And you’re sure you’ve got both eyes open?” Victor facetiously challenged.

When Pablo had shown up at his place, the old man had been getting ready to head down to town to run some errands. Pablo had tagged along.

Jutting out of the plain extending from the foothills to the sea, the town had a fascinating history spanning multiple civilizations, Roman, Phoenician, and Carthaginian alike. Not surprisingly, the Moors, too, had left their mark, nowhere more prominently than in the remains of the large walled fortress that crowned its promontory’s highest point, visible day and night as far as the eye could see.

Victor ran his errands in what was literally downtown, the contemporary civic center located at the foot of the whitewashed, historic neighborhood on the hill. Centered around a single-lane main street, it offered a predictable mix of offices, shops, and banks, as well as a few markets, bakeries, and bars. A stately town hall was set on a large plaza, and, facing it—ironically in the very center of the town that its massive, impenetrable stucco walls were hell-bent on keeping out—was a centuries-old convent. A self-imposed penitentiary for a pious community of culinarily gifted nuns, the only time its doors could be counted on being open was during their annual Christmas bake sale.

Strolling into the town's largest café, which, not coincidentally, was located alongside its busiest traffic circle, Pablo and Victor discovered a familiar scene reminiscent of a small-time casino: bright lights, the ubiquitous shine of chrome veneer, and three gambling machines next to the bar, each whirling and flashing in a constant state of greedy, neurotic agitation.

Although the café wasn't even a quarter full, outside was abustle. An uninterrupted flow of cars swirled around the circle like boats in a whirlpool, roaring motorcycles and buzzing scooters weaving recklessly in and out of it. A steady stream of buses rushed toward a group of stops a block away where crowds waited to be whisked up into the mountains or shuttled down to the coast.

"Very funny," retorted Pablo. "The auditions are on the same day my job starts. I really don't know what to do."

"Actually, it sounds to me like you know exactly *what* to do. The problem seems to be that you're not sure *how* to do it."

"I guess," Pablo conceded, stirring his café con leche. "But it's kind of the same thing, isn't it?"

"Oh no, I don't think so—I don't think so at all. The first step to answering any question is to define the question itself. As simple as that may sound, we often overlook it, sabotaging our endeavors from the start. No doubt, it's one of the most fundamental reasons we're often so bad at using logic. We rush to reason through something before we're clear what that something is. We're like hunters who load their guns and just start shooting, placing so much faith in their weapons that they don't bother to identify their targets. But that doesn't stop us from hitting something. And when we do, naturally we consider our hunt a success, since we didn't know what we were after in the first place!"

Victor took a sip of espresso, glancing outside before

returning to Pablo's quandary.

"All that being said, let's start with what it is you need to do."

"I need to get to the auditions. Somehow."

"So then," Victor proposed, "why don't you just go?"

"What?" Pablo wondered if the old man hadn't been following along. "Like I just got done explaining, it's not that simple."

"Why not?"

"Why not? Because . . . because—I already told you!"

"Pablo," began Victor, taking a metaphoric step back, "once you've defined the question, the next thing you do is specify the assumptions. Unless you understand every dimension of the problem with absolute certainty, you find yourself obliged to establish some premises to help you arrive at a solution. Of course, by definition you can't be sure those assumptions are valid. So, what if they're not?"

"Then," Pablo said tentatively, "I guess you have to come up with new assumptions."

"You do indeed! But what I'm specifically getting at is that if they're wrong, so is all of what follows—no matter how sound, how elegant the ensuing logic."

"OK. But what does that have to do with me?"

"Oh, just about everything, I'd say!" Victor laughed.

"What do you mean?" demanded Pablo.

"What I mean is that I'm not nearly as convinced as you that the assumptions stopping you from going to Granada are valid."

"Which ones aren't valid? I start my job Monday. That's not an assumption—it's a fact!"

"Ah yes," remarked Victor, as if reminded of an important detail that, until then, had been carelessly overlooked. "The new job."

"What about it?" wondered Pablo, still more confused.

Victor hesitated, as if unsure whether to give voice to the thought on the tip of his tongue.

"More often than not, our lives are only as complicated as

we make them. Once we stop resisting—once we truly have faith in where our intuition would lead us—everything becomes so much more simple."

Pablo's coffee cup made a jarring landing as it fell to the table, the saucer clanging noisily against the tabletop, as if it, too, shared his feelings.

"Resisting?" Pablo was both perplexed and annoyed.

"Yes, resisting," Victor maintained, barely dissimulating a smile.

"What do you mean?" Pablo asked defensively. "I know my intuition is telling me to go to Granada, and I'm trying to figure out how to get there."

"Fair enough, but tell me more about that job."

"What about it? I don't know what else to tell you . . ."

"Perhaps you could remind me how it came about," Victor suggested.

"*¡Ay, Victor!*" Pablo responded, exasperated. "You know how it happened! I needed a job, so I asked Nacho if his father needed help on the site, and he did."

"In other words, you sought it out and you made it happen?"

"Well, yeah," Pablo conceded, unable to escape the feeling that, if moments before he'd stepped into a trap, his last admission had set it off.

"And how much time did you spend looking?"

"I don't know. Not very long."

"So you solicited the job without spending much time looking for anything else. Furthermore, you did so when you didn't even actually want to be in the village at all," Victor summarized, at last cutting to the chase. "As a result, that job is now the main obstacle between you and an exciting new opportunity you feel unquestionably compelled to pursue."

Pablo felt as though the priest to whom he had just confessed had turned his words around to damn him to hell.

"I guess so," he reluctantly conceded, face-to-face with the consequences of the poor decision-making he'd exhibited ever since Barcelona fell through.

"While you might be doing your best to figure out how to get to Granada, it's your own resistance that both got you into and is preventing you from getting out of your predicament. It's not chance in either case."

Victor was right, thought Pablo. He had turned a deaf ear to his inner voice ever since becoming disillusioned with it after Barcelona and deciding that, at whatever cost, he had to set down roots again in the village. Instead of conceding it didn't feel right, he'd insisted on forcing it to work out.

"I guess I sort of got off track."

"If you want to come down to town, you don't take the road up the mountain," Victor remarked, "and you certainly can't take both at once."

Despite his malaise, Pablo let out an involuntary laugh.

"Now I just have to figure out how to get down the mountain."

"Your sights seem set in the right direction, but I'm not so sure about your continued insistence on 'figuring it out.'"

"What am I supposed to do?" asked Pablo. "Just wait for it to happen?"

"Almost," said Victor, a mischievous smile suggesting he was egging Pablo on.

"You mean I can just sit around, and I'll magically end up in Granada?"

"That would certainly make things easier. But no, that's definitely not what I'm saying," Victor replied, before clarifying. "What I'm saying, my son, is that you *let* it happen."

Pablo stopped like a deer in headlights, unclear what was coming at him, yet instinctively sensing the magnitude of its impending impact.

"And," he ventured, "how do I do that?"

"Why, you stop resisting of course!" Victor laughed, making no effort to hold back.

Pablo just looked at him, deadpan, feeling like the victim of an old, familiar joke for which he had already fallen more times than he could count.

"You're still trying to deal with it all logically!" Victor

interjected before Pablo could protest. "You're trying to get control over things you can't possibly control. So you've reached a stalemate. It's time to step into the unknown—which, after all, is just another name for possibility. Once you're not holding everything up, it will all fall into place."

A chestnut vendor had just finished setting up on the sidewalk, and the initial puffy billows of the roaster had begun to waft by the café window, absorbing Victor and Pablo alike as the smoke floated effortlessly by.

"It's really hard to believe something might work out when I can't imagine how it possibly could—even if my gut seems to be telling me it will," Pablo confessed.

"Therein lies the challenge, my friend. The good news is that your next step has been clearly laid out for you."

"Which is?"

"You have to decide you're going to Granada. That's all that really matters. Once you truly put yourself on that path, the details of how you get there will manifest themselves, and it will be made very clear how little you yourself had to go to the trouble of figuring out."

43

Walking up the road to the construction site, Pablo looked into the valley far below. The morning sun was reflecting off the reservoir as though it were filled with molten silver, the visibility picture-perfect, all the way up to the pass. If everything worked out, he'd soon be traversing it again, he told himself, encouraged by a sudden glimmer of hope.

But first he had to talk to Nacho's father.

Arriving at the site, he came across Manu, a cigarette dangling from his lip as he prepared to start up the concrete mixer.

"Hey Manu," said Pablo, "have you seen Juan Antonio?"

Before Pablo had finished the question, the engine started with an abrupt lurch and a loud roar, the revolving cylinder shaking the gravel inside like a giant rattle.

Manu shot Pablo a look that left no doubt he hadn't understood.

"Juan Antonio!"

"*¡Allí!*" Manu shouted, pointing toward the upper level of the site, a smooth concrete surface with evenly spaced clusters of rebar where support columns would soon take form.

Pablo made the brief ascent, whereupon he saw Juan Antonio. Steel-toed boots, dusty dungarees, and the tape measure clinging to his belt gave way to a button-down and unintentionally stylish frames, over which tumbled a healthy, well-kempt mane of salt-and-pepper locks. Hardworking and down-to-earth, he nonetheless exuded an air of authority. Since at the moment he was consulting with two of his men, Pablo would have to wait.

While he did, his friend's ordinarily amicable, good-natured father quickly morphed into a powerful authority figure to whom Pablo's big-time dreams were sure to amount to small-time delusions. Pablo dreaded the conversation he was about to have with him, and he could scarcely believe he was going to have it.

Once Juan Antonio's discussion began drawing to a close, Pablo made his approach. No sooner had their eyes met, than Juan Antonio was stopped by another one of his men. Although tempted to seize the last-ditch opportunity to make a run for it, Pablo held his ground, planting himself as firmly in place as if Manu had just poured concrete over his feet.

When Juan Antonio finally walked over, greetings were politely yet expediently exchanged. Pablo got straight to the point.

"It's about Monday."

"Your first day."

"Right." Pablo's throat felt as dry as if it'd been coated with dust from the site. "I was wondering . . . well, I was wondering if there was any way I could start on Tuesday instead?"

"Tuesday? Why? What's come up?" Juan Antonio was all business, a furrow etched across his brow and his eyes narrowing slightly.

Pablo felt as though Juan Antonio had essentially already said no. Still, as if possessed of a masochistic desire to hear him say it, he continued.

"I have an—I mean, I'd like to go to . . ."

"To what?" Juan Antonio patiently demanded, shooting a distracted look over Pablo's shoulder.

"An audition," Pablo blurted out, realizing his time was up.

"An audition?" Juan Antonio was more perplexed than

anything else. He'd expected a more typical, less inventive excuse like a doctor's appointment or a funeral. "For what?"

"A band," said Pablo, almost but not quite under his breath.

"You want to wait until Tuesday to start so you can try out for a band?"

"Yeah," Pablo explained. "They're having auditions Monday in Granada. I was really hoping I could go."

Juan Antonio paused for a moment, smiling to himself, satisfied the little mystery had been solved. Then, he succinctly and matter-of-factly summarized his feelings on the matter.

"Look Pablo, I think it's great if you want to try out for some band. I honestly do. I saw you sing in the festival, and you did a great job. The thing is, I've got a house to build, which means you've got a choice to make. You can prioritize your other projects—whether singing or playing soccer or chasing girls or whatever—or you can prioritize this job. You have to decide what comes first. The only reason I'm willing to train you at all right now is because the guys left me shorthanded and we're behind schedule. But now I've got some Romanians waiting for work, and I can't afford to lose another day—or even part of one. So, if you want the job, it's yours. You can show up Monday as planned. If not, you're free to do whatever else it is you'd rather do with your time. Now, if you'll excuse me, I'm being called."

And that was it.

Standing where Juan Antonio left him, unsure where to go from there, Pablo struggled to make sense of what had just happened. He felt like a fool, as though he'd gone out on a limb only to have it give under his weight, sending him falling face first to the ground.

What was he supposed to do now?

The choice seemed obvious. So obvious he wasn't sure he even had a choice to make. How could he give up the new job to go try out for a band he knew almost nothing about? How could he give up something so tangible and promising for something so rash and improbable? The very idea should have been more than enough to convince him to forget about it.

But it wasn't.

He couldn't forget about it, because he couldn't forget about the conversation he'd just had with Victor.

His confidence sagging like once-bold sails abandoned by the wind, doubt took advantage of the lull, scaling his defenses and coming at him from all sides.

Even if he didn't have to quit the job, would he be delusional to go to the auditions? Could he really have any chance of making the band, or would he just be wasting his time? Who was he to think that—out of all the people who'd be trying out—he might be chosen? Even if he were, what if he didn't like the group's music or didn't get along with the members or had to quit because Granada was too far? Then there was the most daunting, if not damning, question of all: assuming he didn't make it, what would he have accomplished, other than losing the job?

The more he thought about it, the more worked up he got, fight or flight compelling him to move on from the scene of the conversation. Like the mountain goats or golden eagles, he sought refuge in the nature reserve a short distance away.

Coming upon a small grove of iridescent young pines below a large outcrop that ensured he was out of sight and sound of the site, Pablo sat down against one of the trees. His mind was spinning, and his pulse was racing. He didn't know what to do.

Unable to resist the allure of the fresh, clear, pine-scented air, he closed his eyes and took a deep breath. His lungs expanded while his body surrendered to the reassuring touch of the soft bed of needles underfoot.

Inadvertently transported back to similar circumstances that, rather than sprightly, youthful pines, had involved a majestic old carob, he took another breath. Savoring the unimaginably sweet scent as much as he did the calming effects of the gesture, he followed it with another. And another still.

It hadn't been his intention when he sat down. When he'd been given Victor's instructions initially, he had met them with such suspicion; yet now he did his best to recall them in detail.

He made a concerted effort to let his thoughts go, over and over returning his focus to his breath.

He had only a vague sense of what he was doing. He wasn't sure he was doing it right. What he did know was that the longer he sat there—eyes closed, breath flowing, thoughts sent flying like birds through an open cage door—the more relief he felt. The doubt and confusion that had blindsided him at the site gradually subsided enough to restore some clarity. His mind quieted and his pulse slowed, giving up on a race they'd never had any hopes of winning.

Opening his eyes, he saw that yet again he'd confused the issue and obscured the truth. He'd overwhelmed himself with questions he couldn't answer. Hadn't he decided to move beyond that? Hadn't he decided that, going forward, he was going to go with what he honestly, intuitively felt compelled to do, as opposed to what reason insisted he should do?

That being the case, what was he feeling? Now that he knew going to the auditions would mean giving up his new job and the possibility of a promising future that could be his ticket out of town, did he still feel his intuition pushing him toward Granada?

What felt right, he calmly yet resolutely asked himself again. He was hesitant to even pose the question, fearing as he did what the answer might be—and require that he do.

After all, he already knew the answer. And so, like a friend he'd unfairly kept at a distance but with whom he was finally ready to reconcile, he worked up his courage until, with one last deep, resolute breath, he looked it right in the eyes.

What was true to himself was recognizing the undeniable pull toward Granada, toward wherever that road might take him. He could employ reason over and over again in attempt after attempt to blind himself to that truth, but that wouldn't change it.

It was that simple.

If it had ever been more complicated than that, it was because he had made it that way. Because he had resisted.

Taking yet another deep breath, once more bolstering his

courage, he stood up and dusted the dirt and pine needles from the back of his pants. As insane as it would sound—and, in fact, just might be—he had to tell Nacho's father he wouldn't be working at the site.

He was going to Granada.

44

Monday couldn't come fast enough. Fortunately, a few days later—right on schedule in its timeless, invariable position between Sunday and Tuesday—it did.

Waking up before his alarm went off, Pablo sprung out of bed, hardly able to contain his excitement. Carmen had already left. It wasn't long before he, too, was out the door.

Dreading her reaction, Pablo hadn't told his mom about giving up the construction job. They'd only seen each other in passing over the weekend, so it had been easy to avoid the subject. He'd have to tell her soon if he didn't want her to find out from someone else first. For now, though, his sole focus was on the auditions. His long-shot hope was that they'd go well enough for him to have something to show for quitting the job.

An hour and a half of winding country roads later, of olive and almond orchards, of tilled fields of earth, of quaint villages and lone farm houses, Pablo found himself back in Granada, looking up at the Alhambra as though no time had passed at all.

Turning his attention from the Alhambra, he went in search of another building that, though sure to have a much less spectacular past, was infinitely more important to his immediate future. Slipping into the maze of whitewashed alleys just off the plaza, he headed for the auditions.

The building in question was a cultural center housed in a sixteenth-century palace. Located a short jaunt up the hill, it was nestled among the neighborhood's densely packed dwellings on a small square of its own. The centerpiece of its stone-hewn façade was the weathered coat of arms of the nobleman who had inhabited it five hundred years earlier.

Pablo was surprised to discover so many people had already shown up. Even though the auditions weren't supposed to start for another half an hour, a line started at the building's entrance and continued up a narrow alley on the opposite side of the square.

Claiming his place at the end of the queue, he looked back toward the plaza. A wall of stone and brick rose up to the right, and to the left he saw the chipped whitewash and iron-barred windows of an apartment building.

"You made it!" came a vaguely familiar voice.

Pablo turned to see Eva's friend Mariloli bounding down the hill, hair pulled into a bushy ponytail and glasses resting on her head. She had a larger frame than Pablo recalled, appearing all the more rugged given the backpack she carried and the shoes she wore, just as suitable for mountain trails as city streets. Pablo wondered if she had, in fact, gone on a morning hike.

"Hey! What's going on!"

"I'm stopping by to say hi to a friend. He should be up front," she said, casting a glance down the line. "What about you? I'm so excited you came! How are you feeling? Are you ready?"

"It all feels like a whirlwind. But, yeah, I guess I'm ready."

"Does Eva know you're here?"

"We're having lunch."

"Great! I'll probably see you then." She shot another look toward the plaza. "All right, I've got to go find my friend. Break a leg!"

As he watched Mariloli disappear down the alley, Pablo had

to remind himself where he was. Even under normal circumstances, an hour and a half on his motorcycle was enough to confound his sense of time and space.

But these weren't normal circumstances.

It didn't matter that he was standing in the audition line. None of it seemed real. Not the ride. Not seeing Mariloli. Not being in Granada, which felt even more surreal now than the last time he had unexpectedly ended up there. It had yet to sink in. He felt like someone who had slipped out of their body and was looking down on it, an outsider observing the scene from a distance. Intellectually, he knew he was in it. Experientially, he didn't feel part of it. He had to keep reminding himself: he was doing it. He was actually trying out for the band. Any anxiety he might have felt was overshadowed by his disbelief, the improbability and novelty of the undertaking.

Pablo would spend nearly two hours in line before finding himself at the foot of the steps ceremoniously leading up to the building's entrance, the snail's pace of the auditioners going in proportionate to the painfully slow trickle of those coming out.

When one of the doors eventually opened again, he and a few others rushed inside like concertgoers storming a stage. They didn't get far, however, before their eager advance was checked by a barricade of organizers.

As he awaited his turn, Pablo looked up. The bright-blue sky was in plain sight overhead, just beyond two stories of finely crafted wooden balconies that ran along all four walls. Rather than an enclosed interior, the doors had led to an open-air patio adorned with an abundance of potted plants and a trickling stone fountain.

Once administrative details were in order, the group was led to an unremarkable hallway. More like a throwback to the 1970s than part of a treasured relic from the 1500s, it had a drop ceiling above and generic, commercial-grade tile below. Each auditioner took a seat on one of the drab plastic chairs lining the hall, and a deadly serious tension filled the air. Pablo, too, became anxious, his stomach now aflutter, aware his time had almost come.

Midway through the final audition of the preceding group, a woman who'd been collecting information at the entrance reappeared. She motioned for one of the auditioners to follow her. He would be the first to go.

Although muffled by the space that now came between them, the audition was vaguely audible in the hallway. Pablo closed his eyes in the hopes of listening more closely. It wasn't long, however, before something prompted him to open them again, something intangible yet somehow immediate.

A finger was pointed in his direction, sending a chill down his spine.

He was next.

Walking toward the door, like before going onstage at the festival, he shut himself off from everything around him. He no longer heard the faint sound of the audition, let alone the discreet whispers, stifled coughs, or nervous movements both born of and fueling the tension in the hall. His sole, undivided focus had shifted to his imminent performance.

"Go ahead!" insisted the organizer, in a tone suggesting it wasn't the first time she'd invited Pablo to step into the room. When he looked up, the door was already wide open, as if it, too, were waiting.

The woman all but shoving him inside, Pablo was jolted back to his senses.

Sitting behind two rectangular folding tables were four people. On the far left was a good-looking guy with dark wavy hair, thick-rimmed glasses, and an unassuming yet self-assured expression, appearing both intellectual and hipster in equal measure. Next came a brooding fellow with severe features, dark circles under his eyes, and a devilish goatee, his body tall and thin, his hair long and black. A petite woman followed. She had a short, dark-brown bob and her own fashionable frames, her welcoming smile highlighting prominent cheek bones and fine, delicate lips. Rounding out the group was a conservative-looking guy with close-cropped hair and a five-o'clock shadow. He wore a button-down and jeans, his handsome but otherwise unremarkable features doing little to set him apart.

With the exception of the woman, none of the members were particularly welcoming, although each gave Pablo their full attention. No doubt, after all the other auditions, it would take someone truly unique to elicit much more than that.

Pablo's only other impression concerned the alarmingly close quarters. Ironically, staring into a vast audience that filled an entire plaza allowed for a certain disconnectedness. Not only did he not have to focus on anyone in the crowd, but he found a nonconfrontational safety in its numbers. Now, face-to-face with four strangers who may as well have been on the other side of a table sharing a meal—never mind the scrutinizing lens of a camera that would be filming the entire experience—he felt like a jester preparing to perform for a small, surprisingly intimate court. It made him very uncomfortable.

Having no control over the circumstances, he did his best not to give them another thought. Instead, he said his name and the title of his first song. After taking a deep breath, he then belted out the opening line.

Already, having barely gotten started, it didn't feel right.

Maybe the long ride had dried them out? Maybe he hadn't warmed them up enough? Whatever the case, his cords were in anything but optimal form. Rather than open and lithe, ready to respond fluidly to the technical and emotional demands of the song, they felt encumbered and unresponsive, only begrudgingly submitting to what the selection asked of them. Instead of faithfully fulfilling their duty, it was as if they were only halfheartedly doing him a favor.

Pablo felt as though the floor had dropped out from under him. Tension gripped his cords like a chokehold around his neck, extending its sinister reach to the rest of his body as well. Rather than amusing jester, he feared he was about to play ridiculous fool.

Fortunately, his body had a trick up its sleeve.

As panic attacked, his nerves struck back, suffusing his body with a reflexive, do-or-die adrenaline rush, a life-saving, cord-lubricating countermeasure that carried him through the first song like a flash flood ushering the most unyielding of obstacles downstream. While his performance wasn't as perfect as he would have liked, at least an all-out disaster had been averted. It could have been much, much worse.

Once he finished, he took a moment to regroup. His heart was pounding. His body was covered in sweat. He wiped his forehead and looked up. The woman nodded as though she were also speaking on behalf of the men, none of whom said a word nor showed any reaction, good or bad. Pablo didn't know what to think.

Oh, the next one, it occurred to him, disoriented from struggling to get through the first song, coming back to his senses after nonetheless losing himself in it, and the unexpected realization it wasn't over. They wanted more.

But did he have any more to give?

Clearing his throat, he made a quick assessment of the situation. It wasn't good. Not only did his cords feel as though they'd been stripped raw, they burned like one of the countless acts of arson that send the Spanish countryside up in smoke every summer. Unfortunately, the only water in sight was a couple of the band members' own half-empty bottles.

Getting through the first number had been challenging enough. Making it through the second was going to be more daunting still.

Too late to turn back, Pablo pressed on, acutely aware that at any moment his voice could betray him.

It had happened before.

Driving down to Málaga after a serious throat infection, he knew as soon as the song came on that he shouldn't open his mouth. Yet having been denied the pleasure for over two weeks, he succumbed to temptation, giving himself over to it. At first it felt good. But as the ballad's powerful climax approached, he went too far, pleasure suddenly giving way to excruciating pain. As though someone had wrapped a string around his larynx and pulled with all their might, his voice violently constricted, the flesh on his cords curling back like shavings on a piece of wood.

It was three months before he sang another note.

Haunted by the recollection of the drive to Málaga, Pablo didn't know what to expect this time around. Now, like then, he knew he shouldn't be singing. Now, like then, he knew that if he wasn't careful, he could do real, lasting damage.

Feeling his way in the dark, he let his voice be his guide. He paid extra special attention to its limits, to how far he was going to be able to push it and where and when he was going to have to hold back.

When he felt signs of strain, he took their cue, opting for a different approach. He chose subtlety over power. He stayed in his lower register, rather than reaching into the higher one. When his voice felt good, he made the most of its strengths. He belted out soaring notes. He indulged in acrobatic flourishes. And even when it pushed him further than seemed prudent, he trusted that, too, risking it all during those brief, defining transgressions.

In the process, he stumbled upon something unexpected.

His dry, burning cords rendered his voice more raw, his delivery less refined. What hadn't occurred to him was that the vocals of the second song lent themselves to a rougher, grittier sound. By playing up rather than skirting around some of his weaknesses, he could practice a curious sort of vocal alchemy. He could spin hindrance into style. Transmuting limitation into intention, he could deftly color and texture his delivery in a way that never would have occurred to him otherwise.

And that worked.

No doubt that was why Pablo was so caught off guard when, far from the thunderous applause that he might have expected had he been onstage, his performance was received with an empty, anticlimactic silence whose implications he didn't dare venture to guess.

What felt like an eternity later, the guy with the black frames took the initiative.

"Thank you."

"Sorry?" Pablo asked, off-kilter like someone who'd woken

up during a lucid dream, their ability to distinguish between the world they'd left behind and the reality to which they'd abruptly returned momentarily compromised.

"I said thank you. That was great."

"Yeah, that was really, really nice," the woman agreed, still contemplating the performance.

"Oh," said Pablo. The good news took a second to register, contrasting as it did with the bad for which he had feared the silence was foreboding precursor. "Thanks."

A pause followed during which the band conferred among themselves. As he watched their repressed gestures, catching only occasional bits and pieces of the hushed conversation, Pablo didn't know what to think. Thankfully, it wasn't long before they wrapped up their confidential consultations.

"Could you come back at four?" the woman asked.

"Come back? For what?" Pablo was thrown.

"For the callback," she said, unable to repress a smile. "You've made it to the next round."

"Oh. The callback? Oh, OK. Sure—yeah, I can definitely come back at four." He felt like an idiot. Of course. With so many people, they couldn't decide in just one go. Just like *Operation Victory*. They had to narrow it down.

"Great. We'll see you then."

45

Pablo practically ran back to the plaza, as if he were in a rush to share his good news. In reality, he wasn't having lunch with Eva for another half an hour. Too excited to sit and wait, once he got to the café where they were meeting, he kept going.

He'd only made it to the callbacks, but he felt as if he'd already been chosen as the new singer. All the dreams he'd had while deciding whether or not to audition came rushing back. They no longer seemed foolish or delusional. Far from it, they now seemed nearly within reach.

As he flew around a corner and almost ran into a deliveryman, it hit him.

He had work to do.

First off, he had to figure out what to sing at the callbacks. His mind flooded with possibilities. Once he had made his selection, he'd have to run through it a few times. Otherwise, he needed to save his voice, resting it as much as possible until he warmed it up again immediately before the audition. In the meantime, it was imperative he start drinking water. In his excitement he'd forgotten about his throat, which was once again on fire.

When Pablo came full circle, he found Eva waiting. No sooner had they grabbed a table under the trellis than he burst out with his news.

"No way! Pablo, that's fantastic! I'm so excited for you! I knew you should try out!"

"Thanks—and thanks for letting me know about the auditions." He was beaming. "I wouldn't even be here if it weren't for you guys."

People old and young walked their dogs in the plaza, all of them united in a chorus of barks and howls when a girl flew by on a skateboard, come and gone in a flash. Along the wall where Pablo had left his bike, a dreadlocked street musician tightened the strings on his guitar, while a large group of Japanese tourists assembled near the fountain in the middle of the square.

As Pablo gave Eva the play-by-play of that morning, Mariloli showed up with her friend Andrés.

In what was as big a surprise as Pablo's news, Andrés had something of his own to share.

"I made it to the callbacks!"

Pablo sat up in his seat.

"What! You did, too? So did Pablo!" Eva exclaimed. "What are the chances you'd both get called back! That's incredible!"

The mood around the table that much more celebratory, everyone reveled in not only Pablo and Andrés's success, but the unlikely coincidence they happened to be sharing it. Spirits soared even higher when Arturo showed up with his girlfriend, Isa, prompting a whole new round of excitement.

Despite the festive, convivial atmosphere, Pablo couldn't help but feel uneasy sitting across from his competitor. Andrés was outgoing and confident. He was good-looking. Even worse, he'd been in not one but two bands. As if that weren't bad enough, he knew Gato Negro's drummer. Pablo felt like an underdog, meeting Andrés an unwelcome reality check putting a damper on his euphoria.

After two espressos—foregoing his normal café con leche to avoid the mucous-producing dairy—Pablo took leave of his friends. Being face-to-face with his competition had made the need to prepare that much more urgent.

"*¡Suerte!*" everyone called out as he headed off to find someplace to be alone.

"See you in a bit," added Andrés, with a sincere smile that nevertheless mirrored Pablo's own anxiety.

46

Pablo was exponentially more nervous about the callbacks than he had been about the auditions that morning. Now it was about much more than an exercise in going with his gut or trying out just for the experience of trying out. Now it really mattered.

Five singers had made it. Waiting his turn on the patio, Pablo staked his claim to a corner, quietly rehearsing his selection. He tried to relax, mentally and physically alike. He breathed deeply, opening his lungs and diaphragm. He loosened the muscles in his mouth. He continued drinking water.

It wasn't until the fourth time around that his name was called, his heart skipping a beat.

After a long walk down the empty corridor, it skipped another. Seeing the band members. Being in the room again. His impending performance. All of it rendered him acutely aware he was about to live a pivotal moment of truth.

The room had changed since earlier in the day. The folding tables were still there, but they'd been moved to make space for some instruments: keyboard, guitar, bass, drums. A rudimentary setup lacking the electronics, amps, and other accessories required for a gig, it was nonetheless more than enough to make some music.

"Welcome back," the woman said with a smile. "Before we get started, we should introduce ourselves. My name is Lorena and, as you probably already know, I'm the keyboardist. This is Jesús, our guitarist," she said, motioning to the guy with the goatee. "And this is Leo, our percussionist," she added, referring to the guy with glasses, who had momentarily removed them to clean a lens. "Last but not least, that's Ramón, our bassist."

"*¿Qué tal?*" said Pablo, nodding to each member as they were introduced.

"Now that you know who we are, why don't you tell us a little bit about yourself?"

"OK," Pablo found himself saying. He had been preparing himself mentally and emotionally to sing. He hadn't expected the impromptu question-and-answer session.

"I'm not really sure what to tell you . . . My name is Pablo. And I'm from a village near Vélez, where my family has a market."

"How long have you been singing?" Lorena asked. "And what about music? Who do you like—who would you say your influences are?"

"I've always sung," Pablo responded matter-of-factly, relieved to be given a more directed question. "My father sang, and I just sort of learned by listening to him I guess."

Pablo went on to mention some of the classic Flamenco musicians to whom his father had introduced him, as well as several contemporary artists, flamenco, rock, and pop alike, who were favorites.

More questions followed, about music, his other interests and, in fact, a remarkably random list of things. With each that did, Pablo was surprised to discover another waiting after it.

"We'd like to do something a little different from this morning," Lorena began, once the Q&A session came to its natural end. "We loved both pieces you did. Really. You have a great voice, and you nailed both ballads. But this time around we'd like to hear something more up-tempo, just to get a sense of your versatility—and, of course, because that's what most of our stuff is. So, we thought we'd kill two birds with one stone and have you do one of our songs—whichever one you want—while we accompanied you. And don't worry—we know you didn't expect to do this, so don't feel like it's got to be perfect. We just want to get a sense for how well we might work together."

If that morning the floor had fallen out from under him, Pablo now felt as though he were falling into the deep, dark abyss beneath it.

One of their songs? He didn't know any of their music. Not a single note. He felt like a cat who'd survived the first audition by giving up its eighth life, only to discover they now wanted his ninth as well. He didn't know what to do.

His face, which had been so flush with excitement, became the palest of whites, drained of its blood from one moment to the next. He wanted to turn and run. He had wasted their time and his. He was an impostor, and he felt like a fool. He never should have auditioned for a group he knew nothing about.

"Pablo," Lorena asked, "are you OK?"

His mind racing, he tried to come up with a way out, any way to save face. Seeing no other option, what he faced instead was the truth.

"This is really embarrassing," he confessed.

"Embarrassing?" asked Lorena.

"I don't know any of your songs. I'm really sorry. I hadn't even heard of you guys until a few days ago. My friends told me I should audition after they heard me sing karaoke."

The truth was out. He should go.

"Oh!" Lorena replied, it suddenly all making sense. "I guess . . . I guess we just assumed that everyone trying out was a fan. But . . . well, maybe that was a little presumptuous! It's cool—don't worry about it. I'm sorry to put you on the spot. Let's do this. Go ahead and give us something up-tempo—any rock or pop song you're comfortable with. After that we'll just have an informal jam session."

Pablo was almost more surprised by Lorena's response than

he had been by her request. Apparently he had another life to spare after all. Still, he couldn't help but feel she was just being nice, that in reality he'd blown it.

"La Mano de Picasso?" Jesús suggested.

"You do know La Mano de Picasso, right?" Lorena asked, afraid of making another erroneous assumption.

"Yeah, yeah, of course," Pablo was quick to respond. Just because he'd never heard of an up-and-coming band in Granada didn't mean he'd be unfamiliar with one that had attained nationwide notoriety.

Pablo chose one of their recent hits, grateful for the chance to interpret a song that required much less of him emotionally and technically than what he'd planned to sing. He had fun with it. He ventured outside the composition's safe and simple boundaries and made his own mark, his cords relaxed and responsive, his earlier troubles long forgotten.

The jam session went just as well. Lorena liked pop. Jesús had a fervent love of flamenco. Ramón's favorite genre was rock. Leo, much like Pablo, had eclectic tastes that included all of the above as well as world music, hip-hop, and soul—among others. All the same, finding songs on which everyone could agree proved easy. Not only that, but playing together was a lot of fun. So much so that Pablo nearly forgot he was at an audition, the session providing an opportunity for everyone to relax, share some laughs, and throw themselves into some spirited collaboration.

"What next?" asked Lorena, taking a drink from her water bottle.

"Maybe the next auditioner?" Leo reminded her.

"*¡Ostras!* That's right—there's another one!"

"If he's still waiting," Ramón commented with a smirk.

"Oh god! Yeah, we went a little longer than expected! You're right, we should wrap this up," she said, turning to Pablo. "So, what's your availability like?"

"My availability?" He didn't follow.

"If you were chosen, could you start rehearsing right away?"

"And is there anything that would stop you from traveling this spring?" added Leo.

"Oh. Well, ah," Pablo stuttered, taken aback by the conversation's unexpected turn. "The only thing is that my village is pretty far—like I said, I don't live in Granada, so I'd have to figure out how to get back and forth. But I did just quit my job, so traveling shouldn't be a problem. At least I don't think it would be."

"Great," said Lorena, satisfied with where Pablo's rambling response had eventually ended up. "Sounds like, if we were to choose you, the logistics wouldn't be a problem."

"Going back and forth to a village in Málaga would never work," Jesús interjected. "We have a lot of rehearsing to do in a very short amount of time."

"Definitely. He'd have to move here right away," agreed Leo.

"Good point," Lorena concurred, turning back to Pablo. "Still, as long as you're free and can get here, I'm sure we could find somebody to put you up."

"Yeah, OK," said Pablo, excited by the mere mention of a move to Granada.

"Any questions?" she asked.

From Pablo's perspective, she had overlooked the most important question of all.

"When are you going to make your decision?" he wondered.

"Oh yeah—I almost forgot! We're not sure. First we have to see the final auditioner. Then we'll talk and see whether there's someone we all agree on, or we're going to need more time to hash it out. So don't go anywhere. We'll let everyone know in a bit."

47

It was unbearable. The auditions had ended twenty minutes earlier, but there still hadn't been any word. As they paced around the patio like inmates in a prison yard, the soothing trickle of the fountain long since having become an intrusive irritation, Pablo and Andrés made a failed attempt at conversation. They were too on edge. Instead, they and the other auditioners kept to themselves. Waiting.

A small eternity later, one of the organizers came out.

"Pablo," she said.

A jolt shot through his body.

"Yeah?"

"Could you please come with me?"

Why, he wondered, as he made yet another march down the empty hall. Was this good news or bad? Was it news at all? Maybe they hadn't decided yet, and he was going to have to come back for another round of auditions. Or, perhaps he was about to be thanked for coming and shown the door. As excited as mortified, he had no idea what to expect. The walk to the audition room was even longer than the interminable wait on the patio.

"Welcome back," said Lorena. "Take a seat."

He noticed it right away. Once again, the room had

changed. Although it took him a second, he quickly realized that this time around the difference wasn't physical. It was how it felt. There was no question the atmosphere was lighter.

Lorena, who both previously and presently acted as the band's spokesperson, started things off, beginning with a lengthy critique of Pablo's auditions. Pablo hung onto his seat as tightly as he did to Lorena's every word, not moving a muscle. Everything she said was incredibly complimentary; yet she wasn't saying he had been chosen. He still wasn't sure what was happening, and it was agonizing.

Once she ran out of kudos, Lorena finally got around to broaching the subject foremost on everyone's mind.

"You obviously know that Joaquín is—or was—our lead singer, right?" she began.

"Right," said Pablo.

"Do you know why he's not singing with us now?"

Pablo hesitated, unsure whether to admit what his friends had told him.

"I heard a few different things . . ."

"I'm sure you did!" Lorena laughed. "It's amazing the rumors that get out there! And, of course, it doesn't really matter what you heard. All that matters is what actually happened and why we need a singer. Despite all the trouble it's caused, it's simple really."

Lorena paused for a drink from her water bottle, leaving Pablo hanging, a sustained drum roll rumbling in his head.

"And?" he couldn't help but ask, unable to bear the suspense.

"And," she said, setting down the bottle and picking up where she had left off, "well, like I said, it's simple: we need a singer because Joaquín has nodes."

"Nodes?"

The secret may have been out, but it was still a mystery to him.

"Yeah, nodes," Lorena repeated. "Growths on the vocal chords that can develop from oversinging. Joaquín has an amazing voice—and a very strong one at that. But from what the doctors say, he's been seriously overdoing it. So, they've ordered him to rest his voice for a few months and do some other things to see if the nodes go away on their own. If they don't, he'll have to have an operation. Then he won't be able to sing for at least a few more months after that while he recovers."

"Assuming," Jesús added, "that he does recover."

"Right," Lorena soberly acknowledged, without elaborating.

"And," deduced Pablo, "you feel like you can't wait to see if he does?"

"We don't have time," Leo interjected.

"This is one case where the rumors you might have heard are probably true," Lorena added.

"Which rumors?" Pablo suspected he knew what Lorena was about to say, but he figured it was better to let her say it.

"We're not ready to announce it yet, so we're hoping we can trust you to keep it under wraps—regardless of what happens," she began, lowering her voice, as though out of concern for any eavesdroppers.

"Of course," Pablo assured them, flattered they were ready to place any trust in him at all.

"In about three months we're going to be opening for La Mano de Picasso on the Spanish leg of their European tour," Lorena revealed, a huge smile on her face.

"No way!" Pablo exclaimed, his disbelief getting the better of him, obliterating the level-headed cool he had so convincingly exhibited until then. He didn't care—he was too excited. He may not have known anything about Gato Negro, but he definitely knew La Mano de Picasso. At least two songs from their last album had climbed to noteworthy heights on the charts. Rumor had it that their next album, which was about to be released and in support of which they were organizing their upcoming tour, was going to be an even bigger success, both critically and commercially.

"The opportunity came up before we knew about Joaquín's condition," Lorena explained. "Once he found out, we all did a lot of soul-searching. In the end, we decided—Joaquín included, before he went home to Cádiz, where he's seeing a specialist and, basically, trying not to talk—that it was in the band's best interest not to miss out on such an incredible opportunity. We just couldn't—I mean, we can't. If we don't jump on it now, we might never get another chance like this."

"So, it's sort of a strange situation," Leo concluded. "It'll be months before we can say when—or even if—Joaquín is coming back. All we know for sure is that right now we need someone to head out with us on the tour."

"And we'd like that person to be you," added Lorena.

"Right," Leo agreed, a smile acknowledging his failure to state the obvious.

Finally.

They had said it.

He was the one.

What he also was was euphoric, the bare walls that until then had felt so oppressive suddenly seeming as though they might buckle, threatened by the explosive force of his elation.

Perhaps he should have been troubled by the question mark punctuating the band's proposition. He didn't care. He was too relieved. He was too overcome with disbelief. The band wanted him to sing for them. Whether for only a few months or years to come, the opportunity truly was his for the taking.

Victor had once cautioned him to be careful what he wished for. Now, given that he found himself presented with an opportunity that wildly exceeded his expectations, it occurred to him that perhaps he hadn't allowed himself to wish for nearly enough.

"So, what do you think?" Lorena asked, as though honestly unsure how Pablo might respond, she and the others now the ones left hanging.

Pablo's reply was short and to the point.

"Even if it is just for this tour, yes. I definitely want to do it."

"Excellent!" Lorena exclaimed, lifting her water bottle high into the air, Pablo's decision coming as both relief and cause for celebration. “Here’s to our new lead singer!”

“And to Gato Negro!” Pablo added, as though it were the most natural thing in the world. In reality, the implications of what was happening hadn't even remotely begun to sink in.

“So,” asked Jesús, “can you start tomorrow?”

48

Although it covered the same exact ground, the return trip was infinitely longer than the one that morning. Pablo's overwhelming desire to be home turned it into a drawn-out marathon where unexpected delays slowed him at every turn, and any indication of the distance remaining only left him frustrated he hadn't made more progress. Neither did it help that he couldn't stop thinking about the conversation he'd have to have with his mom.

There was no way around it. Before they headed out on tour, the band had a lot to do and very little time to do it. Pablo had to start rehearsals right away. As such, he had agreed to return to Granada in two days' time, ready to go first thing Wednesday morning.

Was he insane? He just might be. After all the changes they'd gone through over the past few months, he was about to shock his mother with yet another. And it was far from a minor one. He was moving to Granada. The day after tomorrow. So he could join a band. If the opportunity hadn't been a literal dream come true, he never would have had the courage to go through with it.

But it was.

It wasn't until he traversed the pass that he regained some

piece of mind. Looking down onto the valley one thousand meters below, he let out a huge sigh of relief. He had made it, the incomparable view all the reassurance he needed; enough, even, for him to let go of the compulsive need to head straight for home. Instead, when he got to the orange grove, he flew right by it.

There was a game, and he knew Jorge and some other friends would be watching it in town. Given his big day, he could really use a beer. Besides, now that the worst of his anxiety had passed, he was bursting at the seams. He had to celebrate—even if he couldn't tell anyone why, not until he talked to his mom.

Once at the bar, Pablo found Jorge and some other friends at a table near the TV. One beer effortlessly flowed into another, each round satisfying a collective thirst that gave way to a communal hunger. A succession of *tapas* followed, plates of thinly sliced, dry-cured jamón serrano; *patatas bravas* covered in their tangy, tomatoey sauce; and *pulpo* bathing in a pool of olive oil, garlic, and lemon. *Pescaíto frito*, *calamares*, and plenty of others followed.

The match was well under way when it happened. Without warning, despite the all-consuming excitement, the two teams locked in a way-too-close-to-call tie, all Pablo's friends went quiet and looked toward the door.

Before Jorge could stop him, Pablo, too, turned to look.

He felt like he was going to be sick.

Rafa.

"Pablo," Jorge began. He wasn't sure what to say, but he felt he had to say something, do anything to shift Pablo's attention away from the door. Away from Rafa.

There was nothing Jorge could do. It was too late. Pablo and Rafa were already engaged in a tense stare-down that had the whole bar on edge, especially since half of those present were aware of their history. It was like the beginning of a barroom brawl in a Western. It could get ugly.

Pablo was furious. He was disgusted. Part of him wanted to fight; part of him wanted to take flight. He longed to pretend like none of it had ever happened, and Rafa wasn't even there.

Before the situation could escalate, Rafa conceded defeat. Diverting his gaze, he sat down with some other friends a safe distance away.

The whole bar breathing a sigh of relief, everyone returned their attention to the game.

Everyone except Pablo. His blood was boiling, his body trembling. The encounter may have been over for everyone else, but he was still very much caught up in it.

He hated seeing Rafa. He hated seeing him with an intensity he'd never experienced before. All the rage to which he hadn't given voice had shot back to the surface. The sense of betrayal. The humiliation. The grief. He felt as though he were about to break the glass he held in his hand. If he didn't do something with his feelings, they were going to do something with him.

Jorge hadn't taken his eyes off Pablo.

"Are you OK?"

Other than looking at him in acknowledgement, Pablo didn't respond.

He was not OK.

"Forget about him. You knew you were going to run into him eventually, and now you have—it's crazy it took this long. He's a jerk. Let it go. Let's just watch the game."

Should he say something? Should he throw something? A bottle or a punch? Pablo wanted to hurt Rafa the way Rafa had hurt him. He wanted him to feel even a fraction of that pain. It wasn't right, but that's what he wanted.

Unable to help himself, Pablo looked again. This time, though, he saw something he hadn't before.

Rafa had changed.

Even as he laughed with a friend, keeping up appearances, something was off. Slouched over in his chair, his hair a mess and his face unshaven, still wearing his dusty work clothes, somehow he looked defeated. Older, even. The lust for life. The irresistible charm. Perhaps it was still there, but there was less of it. He looked weary in a way that went well beyond the normal fatigue from a day on a construction site.

Pablo turned back around, perplexed.

It had never even occurred to him.

Pablo had imagined Rafa and Rosa in a constant state of bliss. So happy together. Celebrating, dreaming, planning. He had envisioned them lost in the excitement of their promising new life, the thrilling anticipation of their forthcoming bundle of joy. Showing no remorse for the past, for friends trampled along the way, they looked only ahead, upward and onward, sights set on their bright and shiny future as the happiest of families.

Rafa's tragic image shifting his perspective, Pablo suddenly saw things in an entirely different light.

Rafa didn't want to be a father any more than he did. If it were possible, he might have wanted it even less. Yet now he was trapped in the very situation Pablo had gone to such lengths to avoid. Rosa was dying to be a mother, but not half as much as he had been dying not to be a father. Not until the time came. That was why they had always used protection. Always.

Apparently Rafa hadn't taken that precaution. It was no wonder he looked weary. Never in a million years would Pablo want to be in his shoes. A baby? Now? His whole life set in stone, centered around a little bundle of responsibility for the next twenty years? At a minimum. To make matters worse, although Rafa did fine for one person, it would be tough with a family. And Rosa's day-care-center job paid only a pittance. They had jumped the gun. They weren't set up yet to be parents. They'd have to depend on their families for support. There would be blame, shame, and resentment. A nightmare.

Pablo shot Rafa another look, as if to confirm what he'd seen before, to validate what he had just come to understand.

He then took another drink of beer, the big screen little more than a blur, his mind racing.

He was right to feel what he felt. It was horrible for his friend to have gotten his ex-girlfriend pregnant, especially so soon after they had broken up, the wounds not yet healed and the potential for reconciliation far from exhausted.

But that was then, this was now. And now he got it.

He didn't want any of what Rafa had.

In a revelation as staggering as liberating, he realized something else.

That included Rosa.

He was headed to Granada, and she would be changing diapers. They were both getting what they wanted.

49

It wasn't until well into the night that Pablo zigzagged back up the mountain.

His earlier anxiety about going home long forgotten, his mind was awash with thoughts, questions, and dreams stemming from his big day. Again and again he revisited everything that had happened. Again and again he imagined where his new adventure might take him.

Consequently, he was caught that much more off guard when, walking his bike up to the house so the sound of the engine wouldn't ricochet off the alleys, he noticed a light on in the foyer.

His mother never forgot to turn the lights off. Ever. If there was one on, it could only mean one thing: she had waited up.

Why?

Taking the utmost care to open the patio gate as quietly as he could, refusing to relinquish his hold on the slight sliver of hope that maybe—just this one time—turning off the light had in fact slipped his mother's mind, Pablo walked his bike inside. He leaned it up against the wall and gently closed the gate behind him. Whereas ordinarily he would have put the bike into the garage, this time he left it out.

Hoping for the best, yet fearing the worst, with an unsteady hand he inserted the key into the front door, opening it just as quietly as he had the gate. As though the house itself were awake, he immediately sensed his mother's presence.

And she wasn't asleep.

The upstairs hall light switched on, confirming his fears.

She didn't say a word, her severe expression and crossed arms saying it all. Her features sharpened into a petrified accusation as she stared at him from the top of the stairway, she looked like a raptor preparing to swoop down upon its defenseless prey.

"*¡Mamá!*" he said, feigning surprise, "You're still up?"

She said nothing, responding only with a sardonic raise of the eyebrows, her appearance becoming more hawkish still.

It was even worse than expected.

"I was watching the game, and . . ."

"I don't care where you were tonight," she interrupted. "I'm much more interested in knowing where you were today."

There was no way. He knew she'd find out eventually. But already? The very same day? It seemed like a bad joke.

Hesitating for a moment, he quickly conceded there was no way out.

"Granada."

"Granada? What were you doing in Granada!" she demanded, her tone leaving no doubt he had succeeded in exceeding her expectations.

"I was . . ." He hesitated again, anticipating her reaction.

"You were what!"

"I was auditioning for a band."

"What!" she cried, baffled. "Weren't you supposed to be at work? I saw your friend Pepe's mother's friend Esperanza today, and she asked why you had quit your job at the construction site. Imagine my surprise when I found out that my son, who I thought was at his first day of work, wasn't at work at all—and hadn't even bothered to tell me!"

As feared—and was more the rule than the exception—word had traveled very fast and over the most unlikely of paths.

"I know Mamá, I know . . . I'm sorry," Pablo began before being cut off, his mother having plenty more to say.

"Don't start with apologies now *hijo mío.* You should have thought about that before you lied to me. But what I want to know before we go any further is whether or not I understand correctly. You gave up your job to go to these auditions, *¿verdad?*"

"*Sí,*" Pablo answered plainly.

"Are you kidding me? What were you thinking! Juan Antonio was nice enough to find a place for you, and before you even start you say 'no, thanks' and run off to audition for some band?"

Pablo couldn't recall ever seeing his mother this angry—at least not with him. All he could do was hear her out.

"What were you doing auditioning for a band?" she asked rhetorically. Her bewilderment only increasing the longer her diatribe went on, she finally gave voice to all the questions that had built up over the eternal few hours she'd waited for Pablo to come home. "And, if for whatever reason it was so important that you couldn't possibly miss it, couldn't you have talked to Juan Antonio, instead of quitting altogether—just like that!"

"But Mamá, I tried," Pablo pleaded, before being cut off yet again.

"You tried?" his mother mocked indignantly, as though unable to conceive of what Pablo's vague response might have actually meant, despite having no intention of finding out. "Well, what you're going to try to do first thing tomorrow morning is try to get your job back!"

"But Mamá!" Pablo interjected, a wave of horror washing over him, "I can't!"

"We'll see about that! And if not, then you're coming back to the store—with or without José there, we'll find something for you to do!"

"Mamá, you won't even let me explain!" Pablo protested, exasperated from not being able to tell his side of the story, to share the amazing news that would prove it had all been worth it.

"No Pablo, I won't. If you had something to explain, you should have done it before you quit your job and ran off to some auditions for some band in Granada! I, however, have something to explain to you. We have been through enough these past few months. Do you understand me? When Barcelona didn't work out, I didn't say anything to make you take some sort of rash decision—the construction job was your idea. But now you've let it go, and I've had it. So, I'm giving you two options, and that's it: you either get back to the construction site before they hammer another nail, or you're going to the warehouse before your cousin opens another box of new stock! Those are your choices, so figure out what you want to do, because tomorrow—one place or the other—you've got a job to do!"

Despite the objections and explanations to which he was dying to give voice, Pablo again bit down hard on his tongue. Even if he had dared to say anything, his words would have fallen on deaf ears. No sooner had she brought her ultimatum-laden tirade to a close than, in a flurry of swirling robes, his mother had stormed down the hall to her room, the conversation coming to its definitive close with a thunderous slam of the door.

Only then, in the aftermath of the nightmarish exchange, did Pablo find himself in a silence akin to what he had hoped to find upon returning home. But this silence was different. This silence offered him no peace, fully aware as he was that it was merely the calm before the real storm.

He wasn't looking forward to morning.

50

Pablo wasn't sure he'd even slept. His mind was spinning every bit as much as when he had gone to bed, obsessed with the same subject.

He could hear his mom downstairs. He could smell she was up to something. And, despite the hour, it had nothing to do with morning coffee.

Dreading each and every fateful step, he made a deliberate, disciplined effort not to resist what had to be done, heading down to the kitchen.

Amidst the pungent smells of onions and garlic, the telltale sounds of a knife on a cutting board and oil frying in a skillet, he found his mother in the middle of a culinary massacre. Next to the wooden block on which she was performing a host of gastronomic procedures, Pablo saw a bowl of blood-red tomatoes that had recently been skinned, drops of their juice splattered all over the countertop. Gleaming utensils were strewn about in disarray, each lying in wait, vying for their chance to cut, slice, or shred a succession of ingredients being sacrificed into a large pot on the stovetop. The fiery concoction bubbled menacingly, coagulated grease on its surface betraying the presence of flesh stewing in its depths, while blistering steam spewed out of it in regular, smoky billows.

"*Buenos días*," Pablo said, once he had gotten up the courage to say anything at all.

"*¡Ay, hijo!*" Carmen responded with a start, losing her grip on the knife, which fell to the floor in a dangerous flash of metal.

"Are you trying to give me a heart attack or what!" she exclaimed half-jokingly, leaning against the counter to catch her breath, before bending down to pick up the knife.

"Sorry!"

Notwithstanding the fact he'd nearly scared her to death, from her tone and expression Pablo could tell she was still angry from the night before.

"Am I to assume from your slow start that you're not going back to the site?" she asked, resuming her chopping.

At least he didn't have to figure out how to broach the subject—the door to it had just been thrown wide open. Now all he had to do was take a deep breath and step inside.

"The band chose me as their new singer," he blurted out, cutting to the chase.

"What?" asked Carmen, pausing once more from her chopping, every bit as abruptly as when he'd surprised her a moment before.

"The band chose me," he repeated, seizing what was sure to be only the briefest of opportunities to tell his side of the story. "They're going on tour with La Mano de Picasso. It's a really big deal. I have to go to Granada as soon as possible to start rehearsals."

His mother set down the knife, wiping her hands on her apron and momentarily neglecting the onion waiting on the cutting board, a head in a guillotine temporarily spared the fateful fall of the blade. Instead, she turned her full attention to her son, who seemed intent on keeping her life in a constant state of turmoil.

"Are you telling me you're moving to Granada?" she asked, her determination to get to the truth trumping any signs of the emotional reaction fast taking form beneath the surface. Like the scalding, acidic heat building at the bottom of the pot, it threatened to erupt high into the air at any moment.

"Yes. They chose me out of a whole bunch of other people," Pablo replied with as much enthusiasm as he could muster. "It's a really big deal. La Mano de Picasso is really famous, and Gato Negro is probably going to get a recording contract after the tour!"

His mother had no interest in the details, let alone in sharing even a modicum of the joy to which the opportunity had given rise. As though they were engaged in a barbarous struggle to outdo one another, what she was about to say would catch Pablo even more off guard than his news had caught her.

"If you do this," she began, after a long, excruciating silence during which Pablo felt like a murder-trial defendant awaiting a life-or-death verdict, "you're giving up the store. You can't have it both ways my son, and I'm tired of you taking it for granted."

"Giving up the store? Why! You were OK with Barcelona!" he rushed to remind her.

"Barcelona was different! We talked about Barcelona! You didn't spring Barcelona on me out of the blue, telling me you were up and leaving the next day! And you had a real job, and you were going to be with your cousin, not some group of musicians you don't even know but have suddenly decided to run all over the country with!"

"But Mamá!" Pablo cried, desperate to explain—how extraordinary it was he'd been chosen, why it truly was a once-in-a-lifetime opportunity, and all the other reasons there was no way he could possibly pass it up.

"Out!" she commanded authoritatively, the word and her gesture all the reminder he needed as to who was in charge, before she turned her back to him and picked up the knife, ostensibly carrying on as though they had never even had the conversation. Pablo, however, could do no such thing, reeling as he was like someone who had just come upon a bloodied corpse.

Rushing to the garage, he jumped onto his motorcycle and took to the road, as though hoping to distance himself from the chaos fast closing in on him. But it was too late for that. It had already penetrated deep inside, his thoughts and feelings running amok.

He didn't know what to think, and he didn't know what to do. While it came as no surprise his mother wouldn't be happy about him running off, never would he have expected it to come to this: losing the store. As he had just discovered, however, joining the band entailed putting much more at stake than he had ever imagined.

The very notion struck deep at his core. He loved the store, and he loved it even now, in the very present in which he hoped to relegate it to a cherished past and an indeterminate future. He wanted to leave it behind for a while—maybe even a long while, in fact—but he had assumed it was something he could always count on. Being completely and irremediably cut off from it felt like having a limb severed, like losing an intrinsic part of himself.

The scenery flew by, twist after turn, rise after fall. Isolated white houses hid behind olives, almonds, and carobs. A neighboring village came and went in the blink of an eye. Grazing goats debated whether to cross the road, and a dog slept on the side of it.

His mother was right. He had taken the store for granted. Ironic, given that for months it had been in shambles. He had taken that for granted, too, assuming it would just rise from the ashes, without him doing anything beyond the bare minimum asked of him. Meanwhile his mother had been almost single-handedly overseeing every detail of the reconstruction.

Just like she said, he wanted it both ways. For now, he didn't want anything to do with it. Yet when he was ready to return, he expected the store to be waiting for him with open arms.

But he couldn't have it both ways.

Reliving fond memories, he thought about his favorite customers, whose habits and peculiarities he'd become intimately familiar with over the years. He recalled the first time that he got to operate the cash register, when he was just a little boy, and, much later on, the first time he was allowed to manage the store by himself. He remembered when he and his dad broke up the fight between the two drunk British guys, spending hours trapped inside after a freak snow storm, and making out in the back room with Rosa.

He thought about the pride he felt being part of a village institution. Losing the store, it occurred to him, would be like losing hereditary privilege.

But what about the privilege of traveling across the country for the very first time, doing what he most loved? What about performing for adoring crowds, visiting exciting new places, and meeting fascinating people? What about embarking on the adventure of a lifetime?

Until it was over, that is. The old singer back at the helm, Pablo would be back in the village—right where he started. Except this time he'd be shut out of the store for good.

Even so, could he allow himself to be shut out of the chance to tour with La Mano de Picasso? He still couldn't even believe it was his for the taking. The reality had yet to sink in. So much was happening so fast. It still seemed too good to be true.

It was agonizing to contemplate losing the store. It was torturous to consider giving up the opportunity with the band. Nevertheless, there was more to his hesitation.

He'd never gone head-to-head with his mom. They'd had their inevitable mother-son spats, but he'd never defied her outright. After all they'd been through since the fire, could he now?

He honestly wasn't sure.

51

Pablo didn't sleep at all that night.

Somewhere in his wanderings, like a rock flying up at his helmet, it had hit him.

His mother wasn't playing fair. She was selfishly taking the store hostage and trying to sequester him there, to shelve his dreams as if they were merchandise that could be boxed up, put away, and forgotten in the storeroom.

It had shocked him. It had frightened him. But ultimately it was just another dramatic, daunting what-if, one he couldn't let come between him and the incredible opportunity. The threat of losing the store did nothing to change the calling he felt to the band, the certainty it was what he was meant to do, his next step. All that had changed was that he now had to face that leaving meant letting go of the store in much more definitive terms than he had ever imagined.

But, as difficult as it was, he would face it.

And it wouldn't stop him.

He would be leaving for Granada in the early hours of the morning, before his mother woke up. He hated the thought of it, and he wished there were another way. But he didn't see one. She had made it clear: there would be no discussion. So, having had two altercations with her in as many days, he had decided to avoid a third.

Well into the vague, dreamy interval where morning and night intermingle like the waters of the Atlantic and the Mediterranean in the Strait, each losing themselves in the other, Pablo prepared for his departure.

His first concern was packing—and it was far from a trivial one. Rather than the mundane challenges of preparing for a few days away—deciding whether to take two or three pairs of underwear, making sure he didn't forget his deodorant or toothpaste—in a matter of hours he had to figure out everything he'd need for the foreseeable future. He'd then have to fit it all into a single backpack. Somehow.

As challenging as that would be, infinitely more difficult was what to say to his mother. Leaving under the cover of darkness did not mean leaving in utter silence, after all. He loved his mom, and it killed him to have to run off without saying good-bye. At the very least, he wanted her to understand why.

His wastebasket overflowing with wadded up, aborted drafts, the final result was a heartfelt letter explaining why the opportunity was too amazing to pass up. He told her he was sorry to go the way he was, that he hoped she could forgive him, and that he loved her very much. It wasn't perfect, but in the end the letter expressed all the things he hadn't been given a chance to say the night before—and wouldn't be around to say in the morning.

After additional doubt-and-debate-ridden packing and unpacking and packing again, his bag stuffed with as many belongings as he had hastily determined he couldn't live without, the time came to go.

He hoisted his backpack over his shoulder, turned off the light, and opened the door. His heart pounding, he made his way downstairs. Every drop of blood seemed to have surged to his head, pulsating in his neck and temples and ears. His breath was short and shallow, as though he were afraid it, too, might give him away. He felt every bit as guilty as if he were committing some sort of crime, and he longed to pull it off without being caught in the act.

Everything a blur, soon he was rushing his motorcycle up to the village's main street—despite what his haste might suggest, more conflicted with every step he took. Not only what he was doing, but the fact he was actually doing it became that much more overwhelming. Its ramifications became that much more onerous, like unseen tethers exerting a greater and greater pull home. Yet an unwavering conviction he was doing what was true to himself had been set into motion, taking on its own unstoppable momentum.

At his wits' end, Pablo found himself alone in the middle of the village, not far from the main square. Neither another soul, nor a single sound. The buildings as dormant as the people inside them, blinds drawn, curtains pulled, lights out. Not a cat rummaging in the dumpsters or a bat fluttering in the sky, the barking of a dog or the hum of a distant car. Even the mountaintop, covered in its own blanket of clouds far overhead, had retired for the night.

The surreal quietude notwithstanding, Pablo felt a palpable presence. It was like whenever he walked into an impossibly still forest. Inevitably, he knew the silence wasn't natural. He knew that rather than an absence of life, it was a surefire sign he was surrounded by it, birds, squirrels, and lizards all holding their breath while they waited for him to be on his way.

It was like that now. He couldn't escape the feeling he was being observed, that the village itself had him under its watchful eye.

But then, with one final look, it turned and let him go.

Before he could be on his way, however, there was one more thing he had to do; there was someone he had to see. If it weren't for him, after all, Pablo wouldn't be going anywhere.

52

Once at the familiar bend in the road, Pablo left his bike behind and descended on foot through the olive trees. If only for the night, each gleaming leaf seemed to have ensnared its own silvery piece of moonlight, like one of the carnivorous plants high atop the cliffs might trap a luminescent fly. He suspected Victor was a morning person, and he hoped that—despite the early hour—he might just find that his friend was already up.

What he found instead was that time had forgotten the house at dusk, and the dawn had yet to take notice of it. He would have to wait until the sun had risen and coaxed Victor into doing the same.

Pablo walked back up to the road. The eastern sky had already begun to take on faint, telltale hues heralding the dawn.

It wouldn't be long.

Rather than sit around and wait, he got back onto his motorcycle. A few bone-chilling twists and turns later, he came to the picnic area where the boundary of the nature reserve dipped all the way down to the road. It was as though he had intended to end up there all along.

The only sound the trickle of a spring, Pablo easily found the trailhead on the edge of the cushion of pine needles that made up the picnic-area floor. Heading toward the trail hundreds of meters above, he climbed beyond the tree canopy and into the open mountainside. He had no idea how long it would be until he next walked the beloved trails, and he had suddenly realized he needed to take leave of them in much the same way he needed to say good-bye to Victor. The reserve had been as much a refuge for him as for the flora and fauna it protected, and he felt no small attachment to it.

Even during the day, the climb was tough, the slope steep and the trail an unstable mix of rocks and sand. Nonetheless, as though the concentration the ascent required were more a blessing than a curse, distracting him from his anxiety and confusion, Pablo pushed himself higher and higher. All the while, the stars overhead slowly lost their luster, like unpolished jewels whose shine fades with the otherwise imperceptible passage of time.

Eventually meeting up with the trail to the spring, he climbed atop an outcrop and sat down to catch his breath.

From his privileged vantage point, Pablo considered the undulating ridges of mountains, airborne islands piercing a thick sea rising up from the valley floor. It was as though the sun's fiery fury had reduced the earth to a smoldering bed of red-hot embers and, once night had fallen, some mischievous deity had sent down a deluge of cool water that had vaporized instantly, suspended there until the sun burned it off the next morning.

Despite the breathtaking beauty, the absolute peace and quiet, Pablo's heart and mind were subsumed in a state of anarchy. He felt as though everything were spinning, as if sitting at such heights had brought on a sense of vertigo totally uncharacteristic of someone who had spent his entire life on a mountain. Everything felt out of control, as the ramifications of the path upon which he was about to embark—had, in fact, already embarked upon setting foot outside his mother's house—made the brutal, unexpectedly clear-cut transition from abstraction to reality.

His mind jumping from one thought to another as

capriciously as the mountain goats from rock to rock, time and time again he saw his mother enter the kitchen. Her mind clouded by groggy morning thoughts like dew on a windowpane, she'd need to wipe them away with a cup of fresh brew. Before putting on the coffee, however, she'd notice the letter on the table. From that moment on, everything would change.

She would have no need of coffee that morning, the dark, acidic combination of rage and anguish jolting her to painful lucidity, her body trembling with an intensity far exceeding the comparatively benign effects of too much caffeine.

Then, once more, he thought of the store.

He was losing it.

No, he had already lost it. He had turned his back on the one thing that had always been at the center of his world, cutting himself loose from his main anchor, from that which rooted him firmly in place on the one hand, yet held him back from his dreams on the other.

Then there was the village itself, his friends and family. And, key among them, Victor.

What was he going to do without Victor? Victor, to whom he owed so much and upon whom he had grown so dependent. Victor had been so instrumental in getting him on the road to Granada it was almost as though Pablo had assumed he'd be coming along for the ride. But that wasn't going to happen. Thinking about it now, a chill that had nothing to do with the cold shot down Pablo's spine.

The cumulative effect of everything he had just considered undermining his confidence, Pablo had second thoughts.

Perhaps his mother hadn't woken up yet, let alone made it to the kitchen, let alone discovered the note. Maybe there was still time. Maybe, as though none of it had ever happened, as though he hadn't made a definitive break in time and space, an irreparable rupture between his old life and the new one taking form, he could rush home, grab the letter, and run upstairs, tearing it into a thousand pieces.

Having almost worked himself up to the point of believing

that not only was it possible, but it might even be advisable, as he stood up to go—whether back home or to Victor's, it wasn't entirely clear—a blinding ray of light sliced through his field of vision.

It was too late.

The letter, he was sure, was moments away from being opened by its recipient.

Like the first domino being tipped over in a long line of them, a complicated chain of events, of actions and reactions, of inadvertent causes and unforeseeable effects, had been set into motion. Each one would redefine the course of Pablo's life from that moment on. There was no longer any way to stop what he had intentionally started.

Pablo felt impotent, both perpetrator and victim, nothing he could do to go back, not home, not on his decision, not to the life that had been his. Yet at the same time and for the very same reasons, he felt an exhilarating sense of liberation. There were no longer any decisions to be made. What was done was done. In his ostensible powerlessness, an improbable and empowering freedom.

The only decision that mattered now was the one he had made the night before. In reality, it was the first domino, his mother picking up the letter just one more down the line. As such, his path forward was now clear. The sun now up, Victor hopefully was, too.

Pablo had to tell him good-bye.

53

Victor's property was still considerably darker than the ridge where Pablo had waited. Fortunately, emanating from its center was a bright light, a beacon shining like a defiant, welcoming hand outstretched into the darkness.

He was up.

Setting his bike in its usual place a short distance from the terrace, Pablo's heart began to race with anticipation; anticipation tempered only by the anxiety he felt making such an unanticipated appearance.

Even given the circumstances, showing up unannounced felt intrusive, as though he were crossing a boundary he wasn't sure he had the right to cross. It was only when he heard a cupboard close, followed by the familiar matinal sound of porcelain clanging on a countertop, that his hand came down upon the door without hesitation.

What followed was the abrupt cessation of any signs of life inside. For a split second, Pablo again wondered if he hadn't made a mistake stopping by so early without warning; but, his determination to see his friend before he left held him firmly in place. Victor would understand.

Footsteps came from behind the door, followed by more silence, an unspoken question posed from the other side.

"Victor!" said Pablo in an urgent, hushed voice. "It's me—it's Pablo!"

The sounds of locks turning and bolts sliding came by way of reply, the door opening to reveal Victor against a backdrop of bright light, blinding Pablo much like the rising sun had not long before. Wearing a white robe and slippers, his hair a tousled sea of silvery waves, and his beard, too, uncharacteristically unkempt, the old man looked like a wizard interrupted from his spells. His bright-blue eyes were alert and inquisitive as they considered the unexpected visitor.

"Pablo!" he exclaimed, pausing just long enough to make sense of what he saw before him. "Is everything OK?"

"I'm leaving, Victor. I'm really doing it!" was all Pablo could say, overcome by an upwelling of emotion, as though giving voice to it had caused the reality to sink in that much deeper. "I'm going to Granada!"

And then, too choked up to say more, "I came to say good-bye!"

Victor put his arm around his young friend's shoulder and ushered him into the house. Coffee was already brewing in the stainless-steel cafetera on Victor's stove, and it wasn't long before a cup of it found its way into Pablo's grateful hands.

Comforted by Victor's presence, the warmth of his kitchen, and the rich, familiar aroma, Pablo regained his composure. Once he had, he explained everything that had led to his surprise, crack-of-dawn appearance on the old man's doorstep.

"I can't believe I'm doing it," he rounded out his anxious ramble, both hands wrapped around his cup, clutching it even, the warmth it gave off almost as satisfying as the coffee itself. "I really can't. Being in the band and moving to Granada, it still feels right—I have to do it, and I really want to do it. But losing the store makes me wonder if I'm doing the right thing. I mean, how do I know it's all going to be worth it in the end?"

"You don't," Victor remarked with no hesitation. "If you did, it wouldn't be a risk, right? You can't know what will happen, let alone how you'll feel about it, until you go through with it. What you do know is that you feel overwhelmingly compelled to find out, which is why you have to go. Going is the right thing. What follows doesn't matter at this point."

"But what about the store?" Pablo asked.

"Rarely is it possible to make a major change without some pain and sacrifice. No doubt, it's one of the main reasons people are so averse to change in the first place."

"But she doesn't even need me right now," Pablo protested wearily. "I still don't see why I have to lose it if I go."

"Because that's not the point. You know full well she was just trying to do anything in her power to keep you from running off to Granada."

Victor paused for a drink of his coffee.

"The bigger point is that you can't create a new life while clinging to the one you want to leave behind. You can't be in two places at once, neither literally nor metaphorically. So when you start moving away from one and toward another, things get left behind—and you don't always have control over what those things are. As Einstein said, 'I must be willing to give up what I am, in order to become what I will be.'"

A long silence followed, broken only by the creaking of the coffee pot. The metal expanded and contracted as it slowly cooled off, not unlike Pablo nervously shifting about in his chair as he struggled to confront the inevitable, which was now taking form before his very eyes, just outside the kitchen window.

"I have to go," he said, his reluctance to be seen on his way out of town finally outweighing his hesitancy to do what he had to do.

"Yes, my friend, you do," Victor replied, with a knowing smile.

Pablo stood up, and Victor followed suit. Outside they discovered the morning had lost the bitter chill of earlier. It was cool, fresh, and fragrant, the pine and jasmine, the rosemary and other herbs, the very earth itself having stirred back to life while they'd been inside. The birds, too, had been roused from their slumber, providing a lively soundtrack to the new day.

"Thanks Victor," Pablo said, lowering his head out of both humility and sadness.

"Not at all, my friend, not at all," Victor replied, placing his hand on Pablo's shoulder. "Just go with your gut and follow your heart—and send me news from time to time!"

Pablo said nothing, raising his head to reveal the tears he'd begun to shed, and giving his friend an embrace that dispensed altogether with the need for words.

ABOUT THE AUTHOR

A longtime resident of San Francisco, Matthew Félix has also lived in Spain, France, and Turkey. He has published three collections of short stories about his experiences living and traveling in those countries, as well as elsewhere in the Mediterranean. *A Voice Beyond Reason* is his first novel.

matthewfelix.com

Made in the USA
San Bernardino, CA
15 November 2016